Robert Muchamore worked as a private investigator before starting to write a story for his nephew, who couldn't find anything to read. Since then, over twelve million copies of his books have been sold worldwide, and he has won numerous awards for his writing, including the Red House Children's Book Award.

Robert lives in London, supports Arsenal football club and loves modern art and watching people fall down holes.

For more information on Robert and his work, visit **www.muchamore.com**, where you can sign up to receive updates on exclusive competitions, giveaways and news.

BY ROBERT MUCHAMORE

The CHERUB series:

The Rock War series:

The Henderson's Boys series:

Start reading with *The Escape*

GUARDIAN ANGEL
Robert Muchamore

Hodder
Children's
Books

HODDER CHILDREN'S BOOKS

First published in Great Britain in 2012 by Hodder Children's Books
This paperback editioin first published in 2013
This edition published in 2018 by Hodder and Stoughton

15

Text copyright © Robert Muchamore, 2012

A CIP catalogue record for this book is available from the British Library.

ISBN 978 0 340 99922 6

Typeset in Goudy by Avon DataSet Ltd, Bidford-on-Avon, Warwickshire

Printed and bound in Great Britain by Clays Ltd, Elcograf S.p.A.

The paper and board used in this book
are made from wood from responsible sources.

MIX
Paper from
responsible sources
FSC® C104740

Hodder Children's Books
An imprint of
Hachette Children's Group
Part of Hodder and Stoughton
Carmelite House
50 Victoria Embankment
London EC4Y 0DZ

An Hachette UK Company
www.hachette.co.uk

www.hachettechildrens.co.uk

WHAT IS CHERUB?

CHERUB is a branch of British Intelligence. Its agents are aged between ten and seventeen years. Cherubs are mainly orphans who have been taken out of care homes and trained to work undercover. They live on CHERUB campus, a secret facility hidden in the English countryside.

WHAT USE ARE KIDS?

Quite a lot. Nobody realises kids do undercover missions, which means they can get away with all kinds of stuff that adults can't.

WHO ARE THEY?

About three hundred kids live on CHERUB campus. Key qualities for CHERUB recruits include high levels of intelligence and physical endurance, along with the ability to work under stress and think for oneself.

Cherubs are usually recruited between the ages of six and twelve and are allowed to work undercover from age ten, provided they can pass a gruelling hundred-day training programme.

Twelve-year-olds RYAN SHARMA and FU NING are our heroes. Ryan is regarded as a promising new CHERUB agent, although he was kicked off his first big mission in disgrace. Chinese born Ning is a more recent recruit who is nearing the end of basic training.

CHERUB STAFF

With large grounds, specialist training facilities and a combined role as a boarding school and intelligence operation, CHERUB actually has more staff than pupils. They range from cooks and gardeners, to teachers, training instructors, technical staff and mission specialists. CHERUB is run by its chairwoman, ZARA ASKER.

CHERUB T-SHIRTS

Cherubs are ranked according to the colour of the T-shirts they wear on campus. ORANGE is for visitors. RED is for kids who live on CHERUB campus but are too young to qualify as agents. BLUE is for kids undergoing CHERUB's tough one-hundred-day basic training regime. A GREY T-shirt means you're qualified for missions. NAVY is a reward for outstanding performance on a single mission. The BLACK T-shirt is the ultimate recognition for outstanding achievement over a number of missions, while the WHITE T-shirt is worn by retired CHERUB agents and some staff.

1. SHORTBREAD

12 March 2012

Twelve kids had started basic training back in December, but four quitters, two cracked bones, a badly sprained ankle, a chest infection and an asthma attack meant only three were left as the sun came up on the course's hundredth and final day.

Instructors Kazakov and Speaks had spent the night in the cabin of a dilapidated trawler, playing cards and sipping whisky while their captain navigated choppy waters off Scotland's west coast.

Daybreak had a rugged beauty: golden sky, islands shrouded in mist and the little boat struggling against the sea. But the three trainees appreciated none of this because they'd spent the night out on deck, pelted by sea spray in temperatures close to freezing.

The closest thing the trio had to shelter was a mound

of fishing gear. They'd dug in under buoys and rope and huddled together, hooking their limbs around slimy netting so that big waves didn't pitch them across the deck.

Ten-year-old Leon Sharma had the warm spot in the middle, propped against his twin Daniel with his face nestling the broad back of twelve-year-old Fu Ning. Leon had one eye open and there was enough light for him to see the angry red mosquito bites on Ning's neck, and her pale blue training shirt stained with grass, blood and rust-coloured Australian dirt.

Before basic training Leon wouldn't have been able to sleep on a wooden deck with freezing Atlantic water sloshing about, but the instructors kept trainees in a near-permanent state of exhaustion and his body had conditioned itself to take whatever sleep was on offer.

But pain had woken him up before the others. He'd lost his footing and crashed into a bush on a speed march the previous day. A thorn had driven beneath his thumbnail, splicing it down the middle and leaving a throbbing, bloody mess at the tip of his right thumb.

It was the newest and most painful of two dozen cuts, scabs and blisters on Leon's body, but an even greater torment came from a growling stomach. The fall meant he'd missed his target time for the march and Instructor Speaks had thrown his dinner on the fire as punishment.

Tantalisingly, Leon had food within reach. Trainees weren't supposed to carry food, but Leon knew Ning had a secret stash of biscuits in her pack. He'd seen her swipe them from the hostess's trolley on their plane back from Australia a few days earlier.

Ning had hooked the straps of her backpack around her ankles to stop it getting washed away. As a mini-wave swept the deck and sploshed through the mound of ropes, Leon reached towards the zip on Ning's pack.

It was a risky move: Ning was two years older and a champion boxer who could easily batter Leon if he pissed her off. Despite the throb of the trawler's propeller shaft and the sounds of wind and water, the click of each zip tooth felt like a gun going off.

Once he had an opening big enough for his hand, Leon felt blindly inside Ning's pack. He burrowed past underwear, which had been hand-washed but packed before fully dry. Grains of sand stuck to his arm as he went deeper, feeling the smooth handle of Ning's hunting knife, then at the very bottom pairs of shortcake biscuits in plastic wrapping.

As Leon pulled up shortbread, his palm touched a larger packet. It was rectangular, with the biscuits sitting in a plastic tray and a spongy feel when he pushed down. It *had* to be Jaffa Cakes.

Saliva flushed Leon's mouth as he anticipated the tang of orange and chocolate melting against his tongue. As a small wave washed over the deck, he pulled out the little package and ripped it open with his teeth. Leon hadn't eaten in eighteen hours and stifled a satisfied groan as he crammed a spongy biscuit into his mouth whole.

Soooo good!

He practically inhaled the second, but as the third Jaffa Cake neared Leon's mouth a hand touched his shoulder, making him jump.

'You just gonna scoff them all yourself?' Leon's twin, Daniel, asked quietly.

Leon turned to face his brother and spoke in a whisper. 'You got dinner last night. I'm *starving*.'

'I'll tell Ning,' Daniel threatened, as he aimed his pointing finger at her back. 'She'll crack you like an egg.'

Leon knew his brother wouldn't really grass, but this knowledge also reminded him of his bond with his twin. He pulled the biscuit apart and gave Daniel the bigger half.

As Daniel made a quiet-but-appreciative *mmm*, the sliding door at the rear of the trawler's cabin opened with a crash.

'Wipe your top lip,' Leon said anxiously, as he chewed fast and flicked chocolate flakes off his shirt. 'If he sees us eating we're dead.'

As Leon zipped Ning's pack and swallowed the evidence of his crime, Instructor Speaks stepped on to the lilting deck. Everything about Speaks said *hard man*, from the wraparound sunglasses and shaved black head, to the mirror-shined size-fourteen combat boots on his feet.

'Sleep well, maggots?' Speaks boomed, cracking a smile as he woke Ning with a dig in the ribs. 'On your feet. Line up at the double.'

Sleepy eyes blurred as Ning disentangled herself from the fishing gear, and both shoulders burned where her pack had rubbed them raw on the previous afternoon's speed march. When Speaks closed up, Ning expected a shove for being slow, but his arm delved past her into the rope mound and swooped on the wrapper from a pack of Jaffa Cakes.

Speaks held it up for inspection, jaw agape in mock horror. Ning realised one of the twins must have swiped it from her pack and glanced back to scowl at them.

'Well, well!' Speaks said, as the three trainees attempted to stand in line on the swaying deck. 'A *serious* breach of the rules. Mr Kazakov, come look at this.'

Kazakov was in his mid-fifties, but the grey-haired Ukrainian instructor looked as fit as he'd been thirty years earlier when he'd fought for Russian Special Forces in Afghanistan. He was already on his way outside when Speaks called and he came on deck holding a mesh sack filled with fluorescent life vests.

'Who ate these Jaffa Cakes?' Speaks shouted. 'Fess up now and I won't be too hard on you.'

Ning was anxious: if the instructors started an investigation and searched her pack they'd find the other biscuits she'd nabbed on the plane.

'It's just litter, sir,' Leon said. 'It probably blew on deck while the boat was docked.'

But it was a poor lie and Speaks instantly noticed chocolate stains where Leon's front teeth met his gums. The giant instructor squished Leon's cheeks between thumb and forefinger and yanked him out of line.

'If there's one thing I can't stand it's liars,' Speaks roared, as he gave Leon a shake, then grabbed his bad thumb and squeezed hard. 'Still snivelling over that pathetic little graze?'

Leon winced with pain as the scab over his broken thumbnail split and blood trickled down his hand.

'How dare you lie to me!' Speaks hissed. 'Just because it's the last day of training, don't think I'll take it easy on your bony arse. Get your kit bag over here. Let's see what other contraband you've got.'

Leon had teary eyes and drips of blood pelting the deck as he walked back to the rope mound and grabbed his pack.

While the instructors concentrated on Leon, Ning yawned and took in her surroundings. The trawler was idling into a natural harbour, with near-vertical cliffs rising out of the mist a couple of hundred metres away.

Kazakov pointed towards land and began a lecture as Speaks ripped open Leon's pack and threw all his stuff out over the sodden deck.

'It's now just before seven a.m. and basic training ends at midnight,' Kazakov began. 'Somewhere on that island you'll find three grey CHERUB T-shirts. If you find a T-shirt and put it on, you can congratulate yourselves on passing basic training. Give us a call on your radio and we'll come and pick you up. But if anyone's not wearing a shirt by midnight, I'll see you back on campus in three weeks' time and you'll start training again from day one. Questions?'

Daniel raised his hand. 'Sir, are our T-shirts all together, or hidden separately?'

Kazakov considered the question as he reached into

the sack and handed Ning a life vest.

'Figure it out,' he said eventually.

Once her life vest was zipped up, Ning went down on one knee and began pulling a waterproof rubber cover over her backpack. While she did this Leon began gathering up his gear, which was washing around the deck. But as he bent forward to take his water bottle Instructor Speaks grabbed a handful of his shorts and lifted him into the air with one muscular arm.

'Jaffa Cake-eating mummy's boy,' Speaks yelled, as Leon dangled centimetres from his face. 'I want you out of my sight, so you can make do without your kit.'

With that, Speaks took two huge strides to the stern of the trawler and lobbed Leon over the side.

'Happy swimming,' Speaks shouted, as he threw a life vest after the trainee. 'You might need this as well!'

Kazakov glared at the other two trainees as Leon made a big splash. 'Off you go then,' he ordered. 'That water's not getting any warmer.'

2. KEBABS

Ethan Kitsell had spent the first twelve years of his life in California. Home was an eight-million-dollar beachfront house, living with a mother who owned a computer security company and drove a Ferrari. He was a self-confessed geek, whose hobbies were chess and robot building.

But that life had been built on a lie. Ethan's mother wasn't Gillian Kitsell. Her real name was Galenka Aramov, daughter of Irena Aramov who ran a billion-dollar criminal network headquartered in the landlocked Central Asian republic of Kyrgyzstan.

The Aramov Clan ran sixty cargo planes that moved stuff normal airlines wouldn't touch: drugs, weapons, fakes, criminals, mercenaries and illegal immigrants. Ethan had only found this out five months earlier, when two assassins broke into his California home and executed his mother.

They'd wanted Ethan dead too, but he'd survived because the killers mistakenly killed his best friend instead. When Grandma Irena found out what had happened, she'd kidnapped Ethan from under the noses of the US authorities and smuggled him back to Kyrgyzstan.

The good news was that whoever wanted Ethan Aramov dead would be unlikely to touch him on his clan's home turf. The bad news was that Ethan hated everything about Kyrgyzstan. He often found himself thinking that a bullet through the back of the head would have been better than getting stuck in a place that felt like hell.

It was a mild spring afternoon and kids were piling out of the depressing three-storey block of Upper School Eleven (US11). Bishkek was Kyrgyzstan's capital and the wealthiest part of the country, but Ethan still found himself in classrooms with mildewed walls and ragged classmates who'd cast hungry eyes when he unpacked his lunch.

Two things kept Ethan from completely losing the will to live and one of them quickened her pace to catch up with him. After a gentle tap on the back, the girl spoke to him in Russian.

'How was your day?' Natalka asked.

She was only a month older than Ethan, although a quirk in the calendar meant she was in the year above him at school. She was a little shorter than he was, but while Ethan was stick thin she had an athletic build, pretty face and curves in all the places that boys like to find them.

'My day was shit,' Ethan told her.

'We had the same day,' Natalka said, as her freckled face cracked a smile. 'I'm *dying* for a smoke.'

They were passing a group of older lads and one spoke loudly. 'Why hang out with that loser, Natalka?'

'Just cos he's an Aramov,' another boy added.

Natalka gave the lads an up-yours gesture. 'Ignore the pricks,' she told Ethan, as they kept walking.

Being related to the super-rich Aramov Clan was a huge deal, especially in a place where some kids weren't even getting enough to eat, but Ethan's status wasn't the basis of his friendship with Natalka. They'd clicked as soon as they'd met and Natalka's *I hate everything* attitude meshed nicely with Ethan's state of depression.

'I had to sit next to Kadyr all afternoon,' Ethan moaned. 'Bad enough that he stinks of BO, but he sits with his hand down the back of his tracksuit scratching himself, then he borrows my calculator without asking.'

'Eww!' Natalka said, as she fished a cigarette packet out of her jeans. 'Bloody poor people. Screw charity. Gimme a machine gun and I'll shoot the smelly bastards.'

'Exactly,' Ethan said, laughing but only half sure that Natalka was joking. 'I couldn't even touch that thing after poo-fingers was all over the keys. I just left it there.'

'You still trying to persuade your grandma to send you abroad?'

'Trying,' Ethan said. 'But she's got this thing about

me *not living in a protected bubble*, and having to *learn my own people's culture*. Whatever the hell that means . . .'

'It's mostly slaughtering goats and kidnapping brides around here,' Natalka said, as she took a puff on her cigarette before offering it to Ethan. 'You want?'

Ethan took a long drag on Natalka's cigarette. The nicotine gave him a nice buzz as he looked up at the sky and spoke dreamily. 'Right now I'd give *anything* for a big greasy burrito, a movie at the multiplex and a big Apple Store spend-up on my mom's credit card.'

'I'm with you,' Natalka said, as Ethan took another long drag. 'When you take me to America we'll go crazy spending all the Aramov money you inherited from your mum! And give my ciggie back. I've only got two left and you're smoking the whole bastard thing.'

'Nobody smokes in America,' Ethan said, laughing as he risked a cheeky final puff before giving the cigarette back. 'They're even worried that breathing *other* people's smoke will give them cancer.'

Natalka laughed. 'Everyone here drinks themselves to death long before they're old enough to worry about cancer.'

By now they'd reached a main road a couple of hundred metres from the school, where the *Kremlin Bus* was waiting for them.

The Kremlin was the nickname given to a large, mostly residential, building at the edge of the airbase from which the Aramov Clan ran their operations. The locals had named it after the Russian president's Moscow fortress because the Aramovs and most of the pilots and mechanics who lived there were Russian or Ukrainian, rather than native Kyrgyz.

Most Kremlin residents were men working away from home. But some had school-age kids, including Natalka's mum who was a tough-as-boots Ukrainian-born cargo pilot.

All Kremlin kids made the half-hour drive into Bishkek to attend US11 where lessons were taught in Russian, rather than one of the rural schools where lessons were in Kyrgyz.

The little Kremlin kids got out of school twenty minutes before the older ones, and were already bouncing around the bus, bored off their heads. The twenty-four-seater was a quarter of a century old and was actually a crude Soviet design that wasn't so much a bus as a truck with a corrugated aluminium hut welded on the back.

The driver was Alex Aramov, the sixteen-year-old son of Ethan's uncle Leonid. He stood by the doorway with his nineteen-year-old brother Boris, both of them swigging bottles of Dutch beer.

Ethan had nothing in common with his two cousins, who'd both abandoned education at fifteen and now dedicated their lives to pumping weights on the massive outdoor stack behind the Kremlin, riding horses, chasing girls and generally using the Aramov name to act like big shots.

Once his empty beer had been smashed on the dirt road, Alex got behind the wheel. His driving style was about what you'd expect from a drunken teenager, and like everyone in Bishkek he drove with one hand on the steering wheel and one hovering over the horn, giving a blast every time he got near a junction, a sharp corner, or a fit woman.

The bus was only half full so Ethan and Natalka each got double seats and sat sideways with their trainers on the bench and their heads resting against the window. They didn't bother talking, because it was too much effort competing with horn blasts, five little kids crawling under the seats throwing pistachio shells and the glassy-eyed stoner daughter of a Belarusian mechanic who had some kind of heavy beat coming out of her iPod.

'Get me out of this zoo,' Natalka groaned.

Ethan nodded in agreement as his teenaged cousin drove a corner way too fast. As Bishkek's shabby low-rise streets passed by Ethan noticed that Natalka had undone two buttons on her plaid shirt, giving him a top-notch view down her cleavage.

'Hey,' a boy said, in English.

For an instant Ethan thought he'd been caught staring, but it was his little cousin Andre. It was hard to believe that this angel-faced ten-year-old was the son of Leonid Aramov, and brother of thuggish Alex and Boris.

'Put your feet down,' Andre said, as he squished on to the seat beside Ethan. 'I want to practise my English on you.'

Andre had a certain charm which enabled him to be bossy without you really minding.

'I'm kinda beat,' Ethan said. 'Maybe later, in my room?'

Natalka liked teasing younger kids and shouted in Andre's ear, 'Give me your cigarettes.'

'I'm not dumb enough to smoke,' Andre said indignantly. 'It's bad for your health and it makes you smell like an old sock.'

'Are you saying I smell?' Natalka growled, as she bunched her fist. 'Gimme your ciggies or I'll bash you.'

Andre gave Natalka a pitying look to show that he wasn't intimidated and spoke to Ethan in English. 'I read a joke and I don't understand.'

'Go on then,' Ethan said wearily.

'What's the Internet's favourite animal?' Andre asked.

'Dunno,' Ethan said.

'The lynx,' Andre said. 'Do you get it?'

Ethan smiled. 'It's a pun; you know when a word has two meanings? A lynx – L Y N X – is a type of wild cat. Links – L I N K S – are what you click when you're on the Internet.'

'Right,' Andre said, nodding keenly. 'I've got another one.'

Before Andre could continue the bus jerked violently and driver Alex threw everyone forward by slamming the brake pedal. Natalka came off worst because she'd been sitting sideways and Andre made no attempt to hide his amusement as she sprawled over the appallingly filthy floor in front of her seat.

'What now?' Natalka asked, glaring at Andre as they came to a squealing halt. 'Did we hit something?'

'I wouldn't be surprised, the way my brother drives,' Andre said.

Ethan turned to look out of the window. They'd left the built-up part of Bishkek and reached the start of the desolate mountain track that led up to the Kremlin. This stretch of potholed road was also used by trucks taking cargo from China to Russia, and a few locals scraped a living selling food and drink off roadside stands.

One of these sellers worked from a pitch twenty metres behind where they'd stopped. He sold spicy lamb kebabs cooked on a barbecue made out of an old oil drum. Natalka had made Ethan try them once and he'd found the kebabs delicious once he'd got over the fact that they were prepared by an elderly bloke who had an entire ecosystem growing under each nicotine-stained fingernail.

Within seconds of stopping, Alex and Boris had jumped off the bus and steamed towards the kebab seller. Boris inflated his beefy chest and shouted in Kyrgyz, a language he wasn't fluent in, while Ethan hardly understood a word.

'What's his problem?' Ethan asked.

Nobody answered because the kids were all piling towards the back of the bus to get a better view. There were more shouts in Kyrgyz and the old man looked scared as the muscular teens closed him down.

Alex threw a brutal punch, emphasising the blow with a shout of, 'Ker-pow!'

When the old man hit the ground, Alex doubled him up by putting his trainer on his stomach and walking over him. Meantime, Boris launched a kick at the hot oil drum, spewing sparks and coals across the roadside.

The kebab seller groaned as Alex ground his hand under his heel.

'Satisfied now, you old buzzard?' Alex shouted, as he beamed with sadistic pleasure.

Boris had grabbed a set of metal cooking tongs and used them to pick up a lump of hot charcoal. As Boris closed on the old man, the kids on the bus winced or looked away.

Ethan turned towards Andre and shouted accusingly, 'Why are they beating him?'

'How should I know?' Andre shouted back. 'You think I'm responsible for those nuts, just because they're my brothers?'

'We're Aramov,' Alex shouted in Russian as he stomped again. 'Nobody messes with Aramov.'

Boris pushed the smoking coal up to the old man's cheek, close enough to singe white facial hairs.

'We see you again and you're dead,' Boris hissed. 'No more warnings. Get out of town.'

3. GREY

Ning was strong, but she wasn't a great swimmer. By the time she came out of the freezing water and staggered breathlessly up the shingle beach the twins had already stripped off and were towelling their cropped hair and pulling on dry clothes.

Leon looked wary as Ning crunched towards him. 'I should have asked,' he said, holding his hands up and half expecting a slap.

'Whatever,' Ning said, as she dumped her pack and started pulling off the dripping life vest.

She was angry, not so much because she begrudged Leon a Jaffa Cake but because going down her pack was an invasion of privacy. But she let it go because she might need the twins' help later on.

Ning had a change of clothes, but the instructors hadn't given her time to take off her boots before diving in, so she'd be squelching on cold, wet feet for the rest of the day.

'Split up or stay together?' Leon asked, as he looked about thoughtfully. 'The island doesn't seem very big.'

'I reckon we can cover the whole place in an hour or so,' Daniel said. 'They'll have to go easy on us. Nine trainees failed already and they've got to get *some* new recruits out of this course!'

'I'm not sure that's how it works,' Ning said. 'The passing standard is fixed. You either make it or you don't.'

But while Daniel and Ning debated, Leon was walking across the beach towards something he'd eyed sticking out of the reeds.

Leon called excitedly, 'Stop yapping and get over here, losers.'

As Ning zipped a dry hoodie and hurried up the beach, Leon cautiously stepped into the reeds, studying a battered metal trunk designed for carrying ammunition.

'Watch it,' Daniel warned. 'It might be booby-trapped.'

Ning had learned that lesson on the third day of training, when she'd run eagerly towards her target only to snag a trap and spend the next two and a half hours swaying from a net in the branches of a tree.

'I'm not *that* dumb,' Leon said. 'Find me a stick or something.'

The case's lid had a locking clasp, but there was no padlock fitted. Daniel found a nice long chunk of driftwood and held it out towards his brother.

'I found the box,' Leon said, as he backed away from the stick. 'You open it.'

'I'll toss you for it,' Daniel said. 'Except I haven't got a coin.'

Ning sighed and snatched the stick. 'Grow up,' she grunted.

Kids in basic training quickly realise that instructors aren't out to actually kill them, so as Ning hooked the metre-long stick under the rim of the metal box's lid, she was more wary than afraid: a swarm of angry bugs, an electric shock or the flash of a stun grenade were possible, but it wasn't like she was about to get her legs blown off.

Leon and Daniel shielded their eyes as Ning lifted the lid and kept the maximum possible distance between the box and herself.

The hollow clank of the hinged lid was an anticlimax. The box seemed full, with the top layer of contents wrapped in a red-and-white-checked tablecloth. Ning peeled the cloth away, revealing a continental-style spread of boiled eggs, cheese, sliced meats and a vacuum flask filled with hot tea.

'Take it out carefully, you never know,' Daniel warned.

But Leon's growling stomach made him brave and he dived in and started cramming slices of salami down his neck.

'Oh man, I *need* this!' he said, grinning wildly.

Ning was more interested in getting warm and began unscrewing the hot flask. They could see bottles of mineral water and something wrapped in brown paper directly below.

'All right to nab the last boiled egg?' Leon asked keenly, with both cheeks bulging. 'I've got a good feeling about today. And I think you're right, Daniel. They *can't* run basic training for three and a half months and end up without a single qualified agent.'

'Famous last words if I ever heard them,' Ning said, as she rolled a salami slice around a stick of cheese and pushed it into her mouth. 'One of you grab the cloth. I wanna see what's underneath.'

Leon took the cloth and dabbed up cheese crumbs with his fingertip, while Ning lifted the water bottles out of the box and then began cautiously unwrapping the brown paper package.

'T-shirts,' Ning gasped, as she saw the grey fabric and the unmistakable outline of a CHERUB logo inside a rectangular glass box.

The twins zoomed in so fast that they almost cracked heads.

'Is it all three shirts?' Leon asked anxiously.

Making one shirt easy to find so that the trainees fought over it was *exactly* the kind of trick the instructors would pull. Breakfast had warmed their spirits, but a horrible tension came over the trio the instant Leon queried the number of shirts.

'If you get your giant heads out of my light I might be able to tell you,' Ning said angrily.

But the twins wouldn't back off: Ning was stronger than them and if she got her hands on a shirt first they wouldn't be able to stop her putting it on.

'Drawing lots is the only fair way to do it,' Daniel suggested.

'I'm injured,' Leon pointed out.

'Only your bloody finger!' Daniel scoffed. 'Besides, whoever gets the shirt can still help the other trainees.'

'Shut up, both of you,' Ning said. She was getting frustrated because it was dark inside the box and the brown paper was held in place with thick parcel tape which was a bugger to rip.

When she finally snapped it and tore the paper away, Ning immediately noticed the number of shirts inside the glass box.

'It's all three of 'em,' she said. 'But this is *too* easy.'

When Ning tilted the glass box on its side to unsnag the wrapping trapped beneath, she was shocked by how heavy it was. Then she noticed that the shirts hadn't moved when she'd tilted it.

'This thing's solid,' Ning said. 'Back out.'

As the boys backed away from the trunk, Ning grasped the glass-encased T-shirts. It took all her strength to lift it out of the trunk, then it slipped from Ning's grasp and hit the shingles with a big crunch.

'*Christ* that weighs a ton,' Ning moaned.

'We need something thick and heavy to smash it open,' Daniel said.

'How about your head?' Leon suggested.

'You funny man,' Daniel said, as he picked up the biggest rock he could see. 'Mind your eyes. This might end up with glass flying everywhere.'

Daniel raised the rock above his head and thrust it down against the middle of the glass slab. There was a hollow chinking sound and another when he made a second attempt. But Ning was disappointed when she crouched down and inspected the glass.

'Not even a scratch,' she said.

'Maybe try breaking bits off from the edge rather than smashing the whole thing in the middle,' Leon suggested.

'Worth a try,' Daniel agreed.

Daniel yelped with pain as he bashed the rock against the edge of the glass slab. The rock had shattered on impact and the sharp edge had cut his palm open.

'Shit!' Daniel yelled, as he staggered backwards clutching a bloody hand. 'Stupid poxy bloody rock.'

'Leon, make him a bandage out of the tablecloth,' Ning suggested.

'It's not that bad,' Daniel said, as he rubbed his bloody hand against the sleeve of his fleece. 'Just stings like hell.'

'So what now?' Leon asked. 'Make a fire and see if it melts?'

'Perhaps,' Ning said thoughtfully, 'but I doubt it'll be that easy. There's going to be something on this island that enables us to break that glass. We've got to scout around and try to find it.'

'I hate Kazakov and Speaks,' Leon said, shaking his head as he kicked up a storm of little pebbles. 'I bet those two dicks are warm, and dry, and laughing their arses off right now.'

4. KREMLIN

The ideal spot for an airfield is a large flat area, with run-off areas for bad landings and nothing too tall nearby so that aircraft can take off gently and even glide back to the runway if they suffer an engine failure on take-off.

The Aramov Clan's base was the exact opposite of this. The cramped facility had hangars, fuel tanks and the stripped-out hulks of Soviet military aircraft close to the runway and it was set in the base of a valley. On approach and take-off, pilots had to bank sharply and fly through a three-hundred-metre-wide channel, and if they got their heading wrong the plane would smash into the side of a mountain.

But the old Soviet Union Air Force had built an airbase in this location for a reason: radar waves can't see through mountains and spy satellites have a tough time penetrating the dense cloud that forms around mountain peaks.

In the 1970s and '80s, Soviet bombers and spy planes could take off and land here without America or China seeing what they were up to. Thirty years later, this run-down ex-military airfield made the perfect base for a smuggling operation.

The Kremlin building itself was a typical Soviet-era monstrosity. Six storeys of prefabricated concrete situated half a kilometre from the airfield, but still close enough that the biggest of the Aramov Clan's cargo planes would set the bronze hammer and sickle on the roof rattling when they took off.

Two guards armed with Kalashnikovs held the lobby doors open as the kids came off the Kremlin bus. Getting to the lifts meant a walk over threadbare orange carpet tiles and on through a bar, where the only life at this time of day came from flashing lights on a line of fruit machines.

'You wanna come up to my room later?' Ethan asked Natalka. 'I've got all them movies I bought at Dordoi Bazaar on Saturday.'

Natalka didn't exactly look thrilled at the prospect. 'I'll see,' she said weakly.

Ethan was disappointed, but tried not to let it show.

Natalka shared a room with her mum on the first floor, so she took the stairs. The Aramovs all lived up top on the sixth floor and Ethan quickened his pace when he saw that cousin Andre was holding the lift for him.

'Thanks,' Ethan said, as he stepped into a narrow car with one bulb out of three working and a missing service panel at the back so that you could stick your arm out into the lift shaft.

'That Natalka's a cow,' Andre said. 'And she'll never go out with you. She only likes older guys.'

'We're mates,' Ethan said irritably. 'And who says I fancy her?'

The lift doors had half closed, but jammed until Andre gave them an almighty boot. 'This lift is so crap!'

'Like everything else around here,' Ethan said.

The doors almost closed at the second attempt, but a trainer wedged itself in the gap and Boris and Alex muscled their way in, each holding another bottle of beer.

'Look who it is!' Alex said drunkenly. 'My geek baby brother and even geekier Yank cousin.'

Boris laughed. 'Probably going up to their room to snog each other.'

'Show us how you do it,' Alex said noisily, as the lift started going up. Then more aggressively as he faced Ethan off, 'Go on.'

'Show what?' Ethan asked, trying to hide his fear.

'Kiss your boyfriend,' Alex explained, as he grabbed Ethan behind the neck and shoved him towards Andre.

'I'm not gay,' Andre protested, as he squirmed into a corner behind Boris. 'Get off him.'

'Or what?' Alex repeated.

'I'll tell Grandma that you beat up the old kebab

seller,' Andre blurted. 'Why'd you do that anyway? He was all right.'

Boris solved the mystery. 'We bought kebabs off him this morning. Gave him twenty som, but he only gave me change from ten.'

'Called us *thieving little liars*, didn't he, Boris?' Alex added, as he got fed up with the kissing thing and let Ethan go. 'Bet he's sorry he said that right now.'

'Gonna be in pain for days from that beating,' Boris said, taking a cheerful slug of his beer. 'He's lucky I didn't burn him up.'

By this time the lift had stopped. The door jammed again but Alex strong-armed it the rest of the way.

'Later, geeks!' Alex said when they were all out in the sixth-floor hallway.

Before heading off, Boris gave Ethan a shove into the wall. It wasn't that hard, but Ethan caught his elbow on a radiator and winced with pain.

'Your brothers are mental,' Ethan said, shaking his head warily. 'Stone-cold psychos.'

Andre was concerned because Ethan seemed to be in more pain than a shove against the wall should have merited. 'Is it where you got run over?'

Ethan nodded. 'My arm's OK most of the time now, but not when some tit-head smashes into you.'

'I can't believe what they did to the old man,' Andre said. 'I wish I could help him.'

'He'll be in hiding,' Ethan said.

'I'm gonna see how Grandma is,' Andre said. 'You coming?'

Ethan found his cancer-riddled grandmother depressing, but the only other thing he had to do was go back to his room and sulk, so he tagged along behind Andre.

The sixth floor had originally been officers' quarters and was mostly divided up into small rooms with kitchenettes and bathrooms with terrible plumbing.

The Aramovs had more money than taste and the corridor floor was decked out in leaf-green shag pile carpet, with a mixture of gaudy abstract paintings and photos of Aramov family members shaking hands with politicians, celebs and minor royals. Pride of place went to a picture of Irena Aramov shaking hands with a US general, after she'd landed a lucrative contract for her planes to deliver cargo for the US Army in Iraq.

The Aramovs also had enemies, so the skylights and windows had huge mortar-proof grilles. There were armour-plated doors that could be closed in the event of an attack, and an emergency escape chute leading to a nuclear bunker in the basement.

Ethan's grandma Irena was the boss of the Aramov Clan and had knocked a couple of walls down to give herself a decent living space, with a long balcony that overlooked the airfield. The boys found her propped on a white leather sofa, surrounded by her collection of coloured glass vases and a huge LCD screen showing a Chinese soap opera with the sound turned off.

Irena's exact age was a mystery to everyone but herself, but she'd been suffering with lung cancer for more than two years and looked extremely frail. She had a drip in her arm and an oxygen cylinder at her side, but the woman who'd turned the Aramov Clan from a small-time regional smuggling operation into one of the world's richest criminal empires still had her wits about her. She even refused pain medication because it weakened her grip on reality.

'My boys!' Irena said, lighting up as soon as she saw her two youngest grandsons. Then she shouted for her long-suffering Chinese nurse. 'Yang, bring milk and chocolate biscuits. The good ones from Dubai.

'So how are you? How was school?'

'School's school,' Andre said, giving a shrug. 'You look better. It's good to see you're out of bed today.'

Irena smiled as the boys each sunk into a wallowy leather armchair and the nurse set a plate of chocolate biscuits on the table between them.

'I feel like mud,' Irena said. 'But it's good of you to flatter me, Andre. If only your father weren't so quarrelsome.'

'Were you arguing again?' Andre asked.

Irena slapped the leather cushion beside her. 'Leonid may well become boss of our clan when I'm gone, but I'm not dead yet.'

Andre smiled and shook his head. 'I bet you won't be dead for a long time, either.'

'All this flattery!' Irena said. 'You must be after something, Andre.'

Andre had grown up with his grandmother and bantered effortlessly with her, but Ethan had only met her when he'd arrived in Bishkek four months earlier.

He found being around the old girl awkward and concentrated on scoffing chocolate biscuits until he felt he'd stayed long enough to leave without seeming rude.

'I've got a few bits of homework to crack on with,' Ethan lied, as he stood up. 'Thanks for the biscuits, Grandma.'

'Always good to see you, Ethan,' Irena said fondly. 'You're still not really happy here, are you?'

Ethan couldn't bring himself to tell his sick grandmother that he thought her domain was the biggest crap-hole on the face of the earth, so he shrugged, then mumbled, 'It's very different to what I'm used to.'

Irena raised one eyebrow. 'Certainly not California, is it?' she said, stifling a laugh because it would have reduced her to a coughing fit. 'Your mother got out of here as soon as she was old enough, and I don't think the Kremlin is what she'd have wanted for you. I've had some papers put in your room. Take a look through and tell me what you think.'

5. GLASS

The three trainees split up. Ning stayed on the beach and built a fire from a mix of dry reeds and driftwood. She used the metal ammunition box in the hope that it would reflect heat, making the fire hotter and giving a better chance of melting the glass around the T-shirts.

Daniel and Leon went on reconnaissance, each taking one side of the island. They hoped to find something that would help them smash the glass, or maybe even a more accessible T-shirt or three. But they were back within half an hour and neither twin looked ecstatic.

'No good?' Ning asked.

Leon shook his head. 'Had a rummage. Island's maybe five hundred metres by eight hundred. Mostly stubby trees and undergrowth, couple of small caves that didn't amount to anything. The only thing I found was a few rusty bolts, and lots of spent ammunition cartridges.'

Daniel told a similar story. 'The only thing I found was an old turret with a couple of rusty old cannons inside. Must have been used to fend off invaders in the olden days.'

Ning nodded thoughtfully, before explaining what she'd been doing on the beach.

'The fire is set to burn in the metal box. But if the glass starts melting the flames could burn the T-shirts, so we'll need to be able to pull it out quickly.'

The twins nodded to indicate they were following before Ning continued.

'So I've tied a rope around the box, and I've got some big bits of driftwood. So if the experiment works and the glass starts to melt in the heat, we tug the rope to tip the box over, then we can sweep the glass slab out of the flames with the sticks. I've also filled my rubber backpack cover with sea water so we can douse it.'

'But if you stop the glass melting we won't be able to get to the T-shirts,' Leon said.

The twins loved an opportunity to outsmart one another and Daniel jumped in and answered on Ning's behalf.

'She's experimenting, dummy,' Daniel said. 'If we find out that the glass melts, we can build a frame or something and melt it a bit at a time.'

Leon bristled. 'What temperature does glass melt at?' he asked.

'I think glass melts in a fire,' Ning said. 'At least I've

seen them doing glass blowing on TV. But normal glass shatters when you smash a rock against it as well.'

'Only one way to find out,' Daniel said warily.

'It had *better* melt,' Leon said. 'Cos there's bugger all else on this island.'

Ning had already heaved the glass-encased T-shirts into the steel box. She had a magnesium-block firelighter which she used to spark some kindling and she then used this to ignite a length of driftwood. When she dropped the burning torch into the box the dry reeds erupted in a fog of damp smoke.

'Your kindling's too wet,' Daniel said anxiously. 'It's gonna fizzle.'

But Ning fanned the sparks and soon bigger flames began erupting beneath the damp smoke. As the fire took hold, she squinted as she leaned into the stinging smoke, tossing on more reeds and bits of driftwood.

'Is it melting?' Leon asked, once the fire had really started to roar.

'Can't see much,' Ning answered.

Daniel grabbed one of the big pieces of driftwood and gave the glass a poke. 'Still feels solid.'

Over the next quarter-hour, Ning and the twins fed the flames and occasionally jabbed the glass slab.

'Shit!' Daniel shouted, as he gave the glass its umpteenth nudge. 'We're wasting our time.'

Ning gave the flames a couple more minutes before reaching the same conclusion. With Leon's help she tugged the now badly singed rope to pull the box on to its side. Daniel created a blast of steam as he drenched the embers in seawater from Ning's rubber pouch.

When they'd pushed the slab away and given it time to cool, the three trainees squatted around it, while Leon scraped off a layer of soot with the blade of his hunting knife.

'It's not even melted a tiny bit at the edges,' Leon said. 'It looks like we're gonna have to find some way to smash it.'

Ning stared thoughtfully at the sky. The early cloud had burnt off and although there was a strong breeze coming off the sea it was turning into a decent spring day.

She turned to Leon. 'Did you go up close to the cliffs?'

Leon's mind had already been down this path. He skipped the question and took Ning straight to his conclusion. 'The cliffs go about fifteen metres high in the tallest spots, but they're over water so the slab will splash down and get washed away.'

'Did you see any cliffs that overlooked a beach?'

Leon nodded. 'But the biggest drop was only eight metres.'

'Well there *has* to be a solution and we've got until midnight to find it,' Ning said dejectedly.

Daniel jumped in to correct her as he glanced at his watch. 'We're way up north. It's eleven a.m. now and it'll be dark by half-three, four o'clock at the latest.'

Leon nodded solemnly. 'We won't be able to do much by torchlight.'

'What about the cannon?' Ning asked.

'I think it was out of order,' Leon said. 'Shortage of explosives.'

Ning wasn't in the mood for sarcasm and tutted. 'But was there a big metal piece? Something heavy that we could carry between the three of us?'

'Probably,' Leon agreed.

'OK,' Ning said. 'The slab's not gonna break just by dropping it off a low cliff. But what if we put the slab at the bottom of the cliff and drop something *really* heavy on to it?'

Daniel nodded. 'Could work. Especially if you put something under the slab.'

'I don't get you,' Ning said.

'Like a hammer and chisel,' Daniel explained. 'The thing we drop acts like the hammer. The chisel is a rock or a piece of metal that we lay under the slab.'

Ning still didn't get it, but Leon did. 'Like a car windscreen,' Leon explained. 'If you bang into it it doesn't break, but if you give one spot a sharp punch the whole windscreen shatters.'

'Oh, I see,' Ning said, feeling a bit dim. 'That does make sense.'

'One obvious problem, though,' Daniel said, as he pointed across the island. 'The cannon is on that side of the island. The cliffs are waaaaay over there.'

Ning smiled. 'About as far apart as you can get. And I bet that's *exactly* how the instructors planned it.'

*

As noon approached for the three trainees in Scotland, the clock in Ethan's room at the Kremlin clicked over to 6 p.m.

The space had once been the quarters of a Soviet

Air Force colonel. Its mini kitchen and bathroom had been refurbished shortly before Ethan arrived in Kyrgyzstan, but while it was clean and all the furniture and fittings were new, the tiny barred windows, sagging ceiling and vile odours rising out of all the plugholes were a constant reminder that he was far from California.

But hope lay inside the board-backed envelope Grandma Irena had sent over. Ethan had been through the contents twice and excitedly started for a third time when he got to the end. The first item was a letter addressed to Irena from a Mr Douglas Miles, who described himself as an *education consultant*.

Accompanying the letter were brochures for English language boarding schools, three in Dubai and one in Bahrain. The glossy pages were full of smiling, uniformed kids, sitting at computers, or standing in front of Bunsen burners dressed in lab coats and safety goggles.

The brochures presented an idealised version of school life, along with lots of puff about *startling academic achievement* and *admission to Ivy League universities* while *encouraging strong morals and building the skill-set required by the leaders of tomorrow*.

Ethan wasn't naive enough to believe the hype: the burly kid running with the rugby ball was exactly the type who'd slam a geek like him into the changing room wall, all of the headmasters looked like smarmy dicks and those cute girls playing soccer wouldn't be part of *his* social circle.

But although starting boarding school might be

stressful, Ethan didn't see how it could be any worse than living next to a runway and going to a school where classmates rocked up with horse manure on their boots.

He was reading about *an ethos of charity and lifelong friendship* in one of the brochures when someone knocked on the door. He feared Andre wanting to play stupid Wii games or practise his English, but Natalka's voice came through the door.

'Hey,' Ethan said, grinning harder than he should have. 'I thought you were busy.'

Natalka shrugged as she came in, accompanied by the whiff of cigarettes. 'Got kinda bored, so I thought *why not find some skinny kid and blow his mind with two hours of wild sex?*'

'You're too late,' Ethan laughed as he opened up a cabinet on the wall and pulled out the stack of pirate DVDs he'd bought at Dordoi Bazaar two days earlier. 'I just had a couple of gorgeous blondes over and I'm all tapped out.'

'Got any cigarettes?' Natalka asked, as she picked one of the school brochures off Ethan's bed.

'You can get ciggies from the vending machine in the lobby,' Ethan said.

'You can get ciggies from the vending machine in the lobby, *if you have money to pay for them*,' Natalka answered, as she opened up a fold-out brochure. 'These kids all look *disturbingly* well behaved. They must put tranquillisers in their water supply.'

'It's just a brochure,' Ethan said defensively.

'So what made Irena change her mind?'

Ethan shrugged. 'Maybe she just got sick of me whining. All I know is, I'm gonna get myself out of this bunghole as fast as I can.'

*

The trainees' boots twisted in gravel as their bodies strained. The cast-iron cannon barrel made a grating sound as it moved from a position against a crumbling brick wall. It must have been in the spot for years, because the roots of weeds and moss had grown around it.

'Step backwards,' Ning gasped, all the tendons in her arms on show as she held up the fat end of the barrel, with Daniel in the middle and Leon at the muzzle.

While the three trainees were pleased to have pulled the cannon free, the same couldn't be said for a large house spider who'd been living inside it. It crept out of the muzzle and one long black leg tickled the back of Leon's hand.

'AAARGH Jesus!'

As Leon sprang backwards, the weight of the cannon became too much for Daniel and Ning. The cast-iron tube tilted, then hit the gravel path with a clang, grazing fingers and narrowly missing toes.

'What are you doing?' Ning screamed, glowering at Leon.

'Why'd you let go?' Daniel added furiously.

'It was massive,' Leon said, as he pointed at the ground. 'Bloody tarantula or something. I thought it was gonna bite me.'

Daniel and Ning both inspected the spider, which

had decided that the best survival policy was to crawl into a tuft of grass and stay still.

'It's a house spider,' Ning said.

'You're such a dick face!' Daniel said, as he launched his boot at his twin's arse. 'That almost broke my toes.'

The kick wasn't hard, but there was a nice fleshy slap as boot connected with buttock.

'I can't help being scared of spiders,' Leon shouted bitterly. 'And next time you kick me, I'll kick back harder.'

Ning pressed the grass tuft under the tip of her boot, and twisted to kill the spider.

'Now you don't have to worry about it,' she said. 'Get back in place. This'll be hard enough without you two acting like prats.'

6. ANGEL

There were two things that kept Ethan sane. Natalka was one, Ryan Brasker was the other. Ethan had first met Ryan in California a couple of months before his mum was murdered, a short period during which Ryan had twice saved his life.

The first time, Ethan had been knocked down by a car and swallowed his tongue. Ryan cleared his airway, saving him from suffocation. Weeks later when assassins killed his mother, Ryan helped Ethan escape through a tiny window before the killers got to him.

Ethan felt that he owed Ryan and jokingly called him his Guardian Angel. Now the two boys maintained a secret online friendship, but there was a *lot* that Ethan didn't know about Ryan Brasker.

For starters, he was really Ryan Sharma – thirteen-year-old brother of Leon and Daniel and a qualified

CHERUB agent. Ryan had been sent to California the previous autumn. His mission was to befriend Ethan and find out as much as he could about Ethan's mother and her links with the Aramov Clan.

Secondly, Ryan was no guardian angel. His plan to befriend Ethan had involved turning a gang of bullies against him. The theory was that Ryan would step in and save Ethan's butt, after which they'd become mates. But the plan went awry when the bullies chased Ethan into the path of a moving car.

When Irena Aramov arranged for Ethan to be snatched away from California child protection after his mother's murder there was no plausible way for CHERUB agent Ryan to follow Ethan to Kyrgyzstan, but Ryan had maintained his friendship with Ethan in the virtual world, staying in touch by Hotmail and Facebook, playing online chess and speaking on Skype.

This relationship between a CHERUB agent and the grandson to the head of a major criminal network gave British and American intelligence a valuable window into Aramov Clan operations. But it was tough to maintain because Irena Aramov had told Ethan to cut off all contact with anyone he'd known in California, and a lack of fast Internet and mobile phone coverage in the remote valley around the Kremlin made this ban relatively easy to enforce.

The pilots and staff who worked for the Aramovs had access to a couple of public computers on a slow Internet connection, but these terminals were in the Kremlin's ground-floor lobby and their usage was monitored by Aramov security teams. More usefully, Ethan had discovered three private computers on the sixth floor which were used for Aramov Clan business and linked up to a reasonably fast satellite-based Internet connection.

One computer was in the quarters of Ethan's uncle, Josef Aramov. Irena's oldest son was a man of limited intelligence who was basically a glorified caretaker around the Kremlin. But Josef kept his rooms locked and Ethan had never got within two metres of his computer.

The second computer was in Leonid Aramov's rooms. Ethan's friendship with Leonid's son Andre meant he could get near, but Uncle Leonid wasn't the kind of man you wanted to piss off, especially as Ethan suspected that he was behind the killing of his mother.

Luckily for Ethan, the third computer belonged to his grandma Irena and was easy to access. Irena was rarely awake after 8 p.m. Once the old lady went to bed her nurse, Yang, would gulp several glasses of wine and sit watching Chinese TV with the volume up so loud that she never heard Ethan walking along the hallway and cutting into her boss's unlocked office.

A couple of hours watching *Pineapple Express* with Natalka and the prospect of moving to a school in Dubai or Bahrain put Ethan in a better-than-usual mood as he jogged furtively along the sixth-floor hallway on socked feet.

Irena's computer was an aged Windows box, surrounded by overstuffed paper trays and yellow books:

Internet for Dummies, *Windows for Dummies*, *Excel for Dummies*. The machine had a network password, but Irena had her login scrawled on a strawberry-scented notelet taped to the bottom of the monitor.

Ethan had always been more comfortable with virtual worlds than in the real one and felt a sense of longing as Windows 98 booted up. Having a mouse in his hand and clicking on the 'e' to open Internet Explorer felt good, but this was illicit activity and he thought how great it would be to have a laptop in his room so that he could spend hours watching YouTube clips, downloading music and playing online games like when he'd lived in California.

Ethan logged into MSN under his American name, Ethan Kitsell. He only had seven names in his contact book and two of those – former best friend Yannis and his mother – were dead. Of the surviving five, four were kids Ethan had met at chess tournaments and the last was Ryan Brasker, who was showing as online.

Ethan opened a chat window. He typed fast but Ryan got in first.

Ryan – UR on late tonight.
Ethan – Watched a movie with Natalka. BIG NEWS!
Ryan – She let you feel her titties? ☺
Ethan – Better! My gran got me school brochures. I might FINALLY be getting out of here, at least for term time.
Ryan – Sweet!!!!!
Ethan – I'll send your chess move through

tomorrow. Can't chat long tonight. Wanna look at the websites for those schools.

Ryan – Remember what you asked about hacking Uncle Leonid's computer?

Ethan – 4 sure.

Ryan – I did some surfing like U asked, hacking sites & stuff. I've downloaded a little app that hijacks a computer.

Ethan – Does it work?

Ryan – Seems to. I tested it on Amy's computer.

Ethan – If you got any naked pictures of your sister, send 'em on over ☺

Ryan – PERVO! All you do is load the app on a USB stick and plug it into the PC. The program loads up in the background when the computer gets turned on. Couple of days later you pull the stick out and it's logged everything that's been typed and copied any files that have been opened.

Ethan – Trouble is Leonid and my two older cousins are SCARY bastard steroid heads.

Ryan – FFS! I spent hours online finding this out for you & now UR too chicken!

Ethan – Gotta be careful. I'm 75% sure Leonid killed my mum and wants me dead too.

Ryan – Why RU so sure?

Ethan – Can't prove Jack shit, but he's the kind of guy who'd kill his own sister. My mum got murdered a month after Grandma asked her to get involved in clan business, and Leonid wanted to run the show.

Ryan – At some point U have 2 man up.

Ethan – Easy 4U 2B brave with your butt safe in California. People who cross Leonid Aramov die SLOW painful deaths.

Ryan – So you do nothing? THE GUY PROBABLY KILLED YOUR MOTHER and will come after you again once your gran dies and can't protect you.

Ethan – Tell me something I don't know. Just not sure what hacking Leonid's computer proves? It's not like he's gonna have 'Tuesday, kill sister and nephew' written in his Google calendar.

Ryan – Who knows what you'll find? Maybe passwords or payment details. INFORMATION IS POWER! Hacking Leonid's computer could put U1 step ahead of anything he's up to.

Ethan – *BIG SIGH* UR right, I have to try SOMETHING. Uncle Josef's no good and my mum's dead. I'm the only barrier to Leonid and his boys taking over the Aramov business and inheriting Grandma's entire fortune when she dies.

Ryan – U seen Grandma?

Ethan – After school today. The cancer is supposed to be incurable but she's clinging on. If anything she's stronger than when I arrived here a few months back. I don't think she'll be dying anytime soon.

Ryan – Anything else U want me to look into? If U can get hold of a small USB stick, that program I found will do the rest 4U.

Ethan – I'm scared, but I can't sit back and wait for

Leonid to come after me. I can buy a USB stick in the bazaar. If I can prove to Grandma that Leonid killed my mom, she'll protect me.

Ryan - UR A CLEVER BASTARD WITH COMPUTERS. I KNOW U CAN PULL THIS OFF!!!!!!

Ethan - Better go. Wanna look at these school websites and can't sit in this office all night.

Ryan - I'll upload the hacking programs to an FTP* site and send you a link. Speak tomorrow!

Ethan - Thanks. Good to know my guardian angel is STILL looking out for me ☺

ETHAN KITSELL has logged off

RYAN BRASKER has logged off

*

The trainees got the cannon across the island with a mixture of rolling, dragging and carrying. It wasn't warm, but by the time they'd reached the cliff edge Ning had sweat streaking down her face and palms scraped raw by the rusty surface of the cannon.

Daniel threw the glass slab over the edge of the shallow cliff, much to the distress of several large gulls. Then he scrambled down after it, reaching a narrow strip of shale beach with hands and clothes streaked white with bird lime.

'You OK?' Ning shouted from the cliff top, eight metres up.

'Tide's coming in,' Daniel shouted back. 'We need to get on with this.'

---

* FTP – File Transfer Protocol.

Daniel pulled a shard of metal they'd found near the cannon from his pack. He wedged it pointing upwards between two rocks, then balanced the glass slab so that its centre leaned on the metal. By the time he'd done this, the biggest waves were getting close to his heels.

'We're only gonna get one shot at this,' Daniel shouted up. 'Tide's close and there's no way we can haul the cannon back up the cliff without ropes.'

Ning nodded from up top. 'Help us line up.'

As Ning and Leon grabbed either end of the cannon, Daniel stepped back until the sea was near the brim of his waterproof boots.

'You're close,' Daniel shouted. 'Maybe a quarter-step to the left.'

As Ning and Leon adjusted their position, Daniel stared at the glass slab. He'd just lived the hundred toughest days of his life and didn't think he could go through it all over again. Either the falling cannon smashed the glass and released the T-shirts, or his CHERUB career was over.

'I think you're OK!' Daniel shouted.

The cannon was too heavy for Ning and Leon to hang about. They both groaned as they threw it. As it fell, Daniel had an alarming feeling that it might bounce off the cliff face and flatten him so he took some quick backwards steps along the shoreline.

As the cannon landed, Daniel trod awkwardly on to a rock and lost balance. He splashed down in water less than ten centimetres deep, but within a second a breaking wave had completely engulfed him.

Daniel's head snapped backwards as freezing Atlantic water poured down his neck. His whole body shuddered from the cold, but his mind stayed focused on the glass-encased T-shirts. He quickly found his feet and began wading towards them.

'Bull's-eye!' Leon shouted, as he looked anxiously down over the cliff face. 'What's it like down there?'

Ning was too anxious to wait for Daniel's prognosis and was scrambling down a gently sloped section of the cliffs, pebbles tumbling as she shuffled ungraciously on her bum.

The cannon had hit the glass slab with enough force to knock a huge lump off one of the boulders on which it had been set. The slab itself had slid down into surrounding pebbles, but when Daniel brushed them away he felt like he'd been kicked in the guts.

'Nothing,' Daniel gasped, as he inspected the slab.

'Well?' Leon shouted from up top.

As Daniel stepped backwards shaking his head, Ning arrived and checked out the slab for herself.

'There's not even a tiny scratch,' she shouted, as she went down on one knee. 'I can't believe it. How are we supposed to break this thing?'

'Maybe this is a red herring,' Daniel said, as he peeled his wet T-shirt over his head to wring out. 'If this is unbreakable there *must* be another set of T-shirts hidden somewhere on the island.'

'Where?' Ning asked. 'It's not like we haven't looked.'

Daniel glanced at his watch. 'It'll start getting dark in an hour. We can't get the cannon back up the cliff, but we can take the slab in case we think of something else.'

'There has to be a way to do this,' Ning said, as she cupped her hands around her head. 'We can't fail now, we've got to *think*!'

7. SCHOOL

The three trainees spent the remaining daylight hunting for more T-shirts, or a tool which would enable them to smash the glass slab. But they got nowhere and by 11.20 p.m. Ning, Daniel and Leon had given up. They sat around a fire close to the spot where they'd landed, staring at the stars and feeling sorry for themselves.

'I just *know* the solution is gonna be something simple,' Ning said, as she warmed her hands close to the flames. 'We'll kick ourselves *so* hard.'

'At least it's over,' Leon said. 'Get back to campus tomorrow. Proper hot shower, clean clothes, big greasy breakfast.'

'And all our mates taking the piss because we failed training,' Daniel added sourly.

Leon's stomach rumbled as he sifted small pebbles between his fingers. 'Even if we worked out what we were supposed to do now, it's probably too late to get it done.'

'Maybe the instructors forgot something,' Ning said. 'I mean, some piece of equipment we were supposed to have, because I just can't think of a way to do this.'

As Ning spoke, Daniel heard a buzzing sound in his pocket. He dived into his shorts and pulled out a matchbox-sized walkie-talkie.

'We've been expecting your call all day,' Instructor Speaks said cheerfully. 'Wearing those grey T-shirts yet?'

'No, sir,' Leon told the walkie-talkie miserably.

'Ask him for a clue or something,' Daniel whispered. 'Can't do any harm at this stage.'

Speaks' crackly voice came over the intercom. 'I didn't copy that, trainee.'

'It was nothing, sir,' Leon said. 'Just Daniel asking for a clue.'

Mr Speaks gave one of his most evil laughs, and the trainees were pretty sure they could hear Mr Kazakov chortling in the background too.

'A clue,' Speaks said incredulously. 'How about I tell you what the glass is made of?'

'I guess that could help,' Leon said.

'It's bullet-proof glass,' Speaks explained. 'The kind you'd fit in the window of a presidential limousine. It's designed to withstand three thousand degrees heat, or a direct hit from an artillery shell travelling at supersonic speed. Your chances of breaking it with anything on that island were nil.'

Leon gasped. 'So there's some other hidden T-shirts on the island somewhere?'

'Nope,' Speaks said.

Leon sounded irritated. 'So how are we supposed to get our grey T-shirts?'

'Trouble is, twelve trainees started basic training and with only three left we couldn't really have any more dropping out on the last day. But rather than tell you you'd passed, we thought we'd make you suffer until the last moment.'

'So this was impossible?' Leon said, as Ning and Daniel joined him in staring incredulously at the walkie-talkie. 'Does this mean we get our shirts?'

'Mr Kazakov and I are about to get in a motorboat and come across from the next island. I've got some chicken and rice in a hot box, a few cold Cokes and three grey CHERUB T-shirts. I reckon you'll be wearing them before midnight. Speaks out.'

'This better not be some twisted joke,' Ning said, as Leon put the radio back in his pocket. 'If it is, I *swear* to God I'll castrate one of those instructors.'

*

One of the few good things about being at the Kremlin – at least if your surname was Aramov – was the catering. Ethan set his alarm for 7.20 on school days and ten minutes later a woman would knock and bring in a tray of whatever he'd ordered from the basement kitchen before going to sleep the night before.

It had taken the chef a while to master American-style pancakes with bacon, but now that they'd had decent maple syrup flown in from Canada it was as good as anything Ethan had been served in a flash hotel.

But once Ethan's stomach was satisfied there was only the prospect of a grim Tuesday of school and another evening of movies or video games. When Ethan got to the school bus he was pissed off to find Natalka talking to Vladimir, the sixteen-year-old son of an aircraft mechanic.

Very few boys stayed at school beyond the age of fifteen and Vlad was no exception. He was using the bus to hitch a ride into Bishkek and he seemed to be trying to persuade Natalka to bunk off and spend the day in town with him. The dude had all the personality of a brick wall, but Natalka dug his muscular body and wavy blond hair and was flirting like mad.

'Total slut,' Andre said as he came up to Ethan. 'Didn't I say that just yesterday?'

Ethan tutted and looked irritated, but Andre spoke again before he thought of a response.

'My dad wants to see you.'

Ethan gulped. Leonid Aramov didn't summon people for tea and biscuits, or a nice chat.

'What for?'

'Don't ask me. I just heard him telling Boris not to let you on the school bus.'

'Did he sound angry?' Ethan asked.

Andre smirked. 'My dad always sounds angry.'

Ethan grew more anxious when his nineteen-year-old cousin Boris came bounding out of the Kremlin lobby and gave the bus keys to Vlad.

'You know the route?' Boris barked.

As Vlad settled in the driving seat and the other kids started boarding the bus, Boris took Ethan by his upper arm and gave him a yank.

'Your uncle wants to see you at the stable.'

Ethan had assumed Leonid would want to see him in his sixth-floor office. Trekking out to the Aramovs' stables made matters more sinister. The only positive thing was that it seemed unlikely that his uncle would try anything underhand after it had been announced that he wanted to see him at the stables in front of a dozen witnesses.

The stables were a kilometre's walk across rocky ground.

'You know why your dad wants to see me?' Ethan asked, as he struggled to keep pace with his much larger cousin.

'Just shut your face and do what you're told,' Boris snapped back.

There was a steep downwards slope on the final approach to the stables. The ground was slippery and when Ethan hesitated, Boris gave him an almighty shove accompanied by an enthusiastic shout of, 'DOOSH!'

Ethan crashed forward, sprawling out and smashing his elbow on a wooden post. Boris closed in and threw a kick, but as Ethan flinched Boris pulled the blow.

'How can a skinny tit like you be related to me?' Boris shouted, getting his head right in Ethan's face as he yanked him to his feet. 'I've plucked chickens that are tougher than you.'

Ethan shuddered as his cousin walked close behind him. The stable block was in an L-shape, running along two sides of a muddy paddock. Most of the horses kept here were used by Aramov security men who patrolled the surrounding hillsides looking for thieves, spies and covert surveillance devices.

Leonid Aramov's stable office had a big stone fireplace and hunting trophies mounted on the wall behind his desk. He wasn't as pumped as his two sons, but Leonid's eyes were mean little slits and he fitted the Russian gangster stereotype nicely with a tight leather jacket and three days' stubble.

'My little nephew,' Leonid said. 'How are you settling in?'

'I'm getting by,' Ethan said, feeling uncomfortable with Boris towering behind and the thought that the man at the desk had almost certainly ordered his mother's death.

Leonid went into his desk drawer. He pulled out a small stack of papers and beckoned Ethan closer.

'SatCom Internet bill,' Leonid explained, waggling papers in the air as Boris shoved Ethan closer to the desk. 'Our bill has been four or five hundred US dollars a month since forever. But you arrive and suddenly, we get bills for sixteen hundred, eighteen hundred dollars.'

Ethan pretended to be mystified. 'I don't have a computer. I'm not even allowed to use the Internet.'

'Cut the shit,' Leonid boomed, as he made an angry stab with his pointing finger. 'Only family can get on the sixth floor and use computers on the satellite link.'

'There's loads of staff on our floor,' Ethan said.

'Whoever it is uses a proxy and wipes their history every time they log off, so we can't tell what they've been looking at,' Leonid said. 'Do you think your grandma's nurse could manage that? Or that one of the other staff would suddenly start doing it as a kid who happens to know an awful lot about computers arrives on our floor?'

Boris growled in Ethan's ear. 'Confess or I'll pulp you.'

'OK, I admit it,' Ethan said. 'My mum left me money. So what if I surfed a few sites? I'll *pay* for your satellite bandwidth.'

Leonid rose up from his desk and thumped the table. 'I don't like that smart mouth. You were *told* not to communicate with anyone from your past life. The CIA and FBI will be monitoring all your online accounts. The clan still has major business interests in the United States and after your mother's death and your disappearance the authorities there are over us like a rash. You start spouting your mouth off about something you shouldn't and you could screw that up.'

'You think I'm an idiot?' Ethan snapped back. 'I'm not a baby. You think I didn't keep secrets when I lived with my mum in California?'

Ethan heard an almighty crack as Boris smacked him around the back of the head. 'You dare talk back to my father?'

As Ethan stumbled, Leonid walked around the desk to face him off.

'There's a natural order to things,' Leonid explained.

'I'm at the top, you're at the bottom. If I can't trust you when you're living two rooms away, I sure can't trust you to keep your trap shut when you're off at some poncy school in Dubai.'

To drive the argument home Leonid twisted Ethan's ear.

'You can't stop me from going to boarding school,' Ethan said, his voice getting higher as his uncle cranked up the pain. 'You're not the boss of the clan. It's up to Irena.'

'I ought to smash your fingers for this defiance,' Leonid shouted. 'You'd better learn to respect me, because your grandma won't be around for much longer, and then . . .'

'Then what?' Ethan shouted, as Leonid tailed off. 'Maybe I'll get murdered, like my mom did?'

Leonid laughed and snapped his fingers. 'If I wanted you killed, I could kill you like that.'

'If that was true I doubt I'd be standing here,' Ethan scoffed. 'Irena has eyes and ears all over the Kremlin. You might act like the big man, but you can't take a shit without your mommy knowing all about it.'

Leonid cracked a knuckle, then laughed incredulously. 'What makes you so sure that I killed your mother?'

Ethan shrugged. 'It would make a *lot* of sense.'

'You have no idea what you're talking about and you'd best be careful who you go spouting your theories to,' Leonid said. 'Besides, I'm not here to debate with a child. Just stay away from the computers or there will be deep trouble.'

Ethan shook his head contemptuously as he turned towards the office door. This insolence popped Leonid's fuse and within seconds Ethan found himself face down against the desktop, with Leonid's thumb jammed painfully between his shoulder blades.

Leonid looked at Boris as Ethan squirmed. 'Get the cosh.'

'Piss off,' Ethan spat.

Ethan couldn't look around far enough to see Boris taking a half-metre-long rubber cosh out of a filing cabinet, but he felt Leonid ripping his jeans and boxers down to his knees in a single violent stroke.

'Noooo!' Ethan moaned, as Leonid enthusiastically swung the cosh against his bare arse.

The pain was extraordinary and the humiliation compounded by Boris howling with laughter and pulling an Android phone out of a pocket.

'Say cheese!' Boris whooped, as he snapped a picture. 'I wonder what Natalka will say when she sees this.'

Fortunately Leonid only gave his nephew three strokes before turning Ethan on to his back and eyeballing him.

'Mouth shut, fingers off computers,' Leonid ordered. 'And no school for the rest of this month. You can come out here to the stables and shovel horse shit.'

'I'll tell Irena,' Ethan said. 'She's my guardian, not you.'

'You don't know my mother so well,' Leonid laughed. 'Go *right* ahead. Tell her you've been using her computer when she ordered you not to, but don't be surprised if one of her security guards gives you a *lot* worse than three strokes on the arse.'

Ethan wasn't sure if Leonid was bluffing as he meekly pulled his trousers back over his stinging arse, but he'd heard that Irena could be ruthless with family members who pissed her off and he'd already pushed Leonid as far as he dared.

Leonid smiled. 'Right, Boris, go introduce our little California girl to the stable hands. And tell 'em that if I catch Ethan slacking, I'll blame them and dock them half a day's pay.'

8. RYAN

CHERUB campus always looked immaculate, not least because there were plenty of kids on punishment duty sweeping paths, pulling weeds and mowing several hundred acres of lawn. On this sunny March day it looked especially picturesque because the sun had come out and the Japanese cherry trees lining the central path from the education block to the training compound were in full blossom.

'Spring pisses me off,' Amy Collins said, rubbing her nose before exploding into a sneezing fit. 'Stupid pollen.'

The stunning twenty-four-year-old was strolling alongside Ryan Sharma. She was a former CHERUB agent who now worked for TFU (Transnational Facilitator Unit), a branch of the American intelligence service that was targeting the Aramov Clan. She'd also played the role of Ryan's older sister on his mission in California.

'So you were chatting on MSN with Ethan last night?' Amy asked.

Ryan nodded. 'I've uploaded a hijack program and some other hacking tools to an FTP site.'

'Will Ethan have the guts to install it?'

Ryan shrugged. 'Fifty-fifty, I'd guess. He asked about you. Or more specifically, I told him I'd hacked my sister's computer and he asked if I'd found any naked pictures of you.'

'Dirty boy,' Amy laughed. 'It'll be a pity if he does get sent to school in Dubai. There's a much better chance that he'll feed us accurate information while he's inside the Kremlin.'

Ryan nodded thoughtfully. 'Can you stop him getting admitted to a school in Dubai?'

'There are ways of manipulating things so that a kid gets put in a certain class, or doesn't get into one particular school, but even if we could get Ethan locked out of *every* English language boarding school in the Middle East it would seem highly suspicious.'

'I don't mind really,' Ryan said. 'After all Ethan's been through in the last year the poor bastard deserves a break.'

'And how about you?' Amy asked. 'Still feeling frustrated?'

'A bit,' Ryan confessed. 'I know being Ethan's *virtual friend* means I'm technically on a mission, but I'd really like to get stuck into something meatier.'

Amy nodded. 'Kicking some arse off campus.'

'Exactly,' Ryan said. 'Although they've sent me on a couple of one-day things which have been fun. I shouldn't really tell you but this is hilarious. Last month me and Alfie got sent to this estate in Liverpool—'

'No,' Amy said firmly, raising her hands. 'I don't want to hear it, no matter how funny it is. There are good security reasons why agents shouldn't talk about their missions.'

Ryan looked hurt.

'You're lucky I work for TFU. A CHERUB staff member would be dishing out punishment laps for breaching security.'

'All right, sorry I spoke,' Ryan said, then cheekily, 'So have you got any naked pictures I can send Ethan to prove that the hacking program works?'

Before Amy could answer, the pair jumped out of their skins as a high-pitched shout of 'Banzai!' came from the branches above Ryan's head.

The shouter leapt from a tree fork and clamped himself to Ryan's back. Ryan staggered forwards, but his assailant was too little to knock him completely off balance.

'Bloody hell, Theo!' Ryan yelled, clutching his chest as his seven-year-old brother let go and hit the path with a gravelly crunch.

Theo had dressed up for the ambush, wearing a blue martial arts suit over his red CHERUB shirt and with the towelling belt from a bathrobe knotted around his head.

'That was so cool!' Theo giggled, as he pointed at Ryan. 'I bet you've got skidmarks!'

Theo was a cute kid, with the same dark hair and olive complexion as Ryan, but Ryan had always been slim, whereas Theo was stockier.

Theo lunged playfully, going head first into Ryan's belly.

'Stop acting up,' Ryan said. He always tried to sound parental, but Theo never took any notice.

A more effective technique was to lift Theo up, tickle him briefly under the ribcage and dump him on the verge of the path with a boot heel pinning him gently to the grass.

'You big bully!' Theo protested, only half serious. 'You wait till I'm grown up.'

'If I let you up, will you be sensible?' Ryan asked.

'Kiss my butt!' Theo said.

Ryan wriggled two fingers, indicating that he was going to tickle Theo again.

'OK, I'll be good,' Theo shrieked, as he curled up.

'This is Amy,' Ryan said, as he offered Theo a hand.

Theo spoke in an absurd robotic voice. 'Hello Amy. It is very, very, nice to meet you.'

'I see the family resemblance,' Amy said.

'I don't look like *him*,' Theo said, shaking his head. 'I'm beautiful. He looks worse than he smells.'

'Theo's showing off because he thinks you're cute,' Ryan explained, as he put an arm around Theo's neck and mock-strangled him.

'Shut your face!' Theo said. 'You love Amy, not me!'

'Why aren't you in lessons, anyway?' Ryan asked.

'Going to meet Leon and Daniel coming out of training. Same as you, dumbo.'

Ryan laughed. 'You can't stand the twins.'

Theo smiled. 'Gets me out of maths. And the twins are OK, except when they gang up on me.'

Amy laughed as they walked on, with Theo acting like a madman, launching himself into bushes and pretending to strangle himself with the towelling belt.

'Your brother's *adorable*,' Amy said quietly.

Ryan raised an eyebrow. 'In small doses. But see if you still feel that way after he's been jumping on your bed for three hours.'

Theo sprinted the last hundred metres to the gates of the training compound, but the exertion was wasted because the instructors were keeping CHERUB's three newest grey shirts back while they gave the training area a final scrub and tidied all their kit away ready for the next batch of trainees.

'Fart heads!' Theo shouted, when Leon and Daniel finally emerged from the training dorm and started walking towards the gate with Ning a few steps behind. The trio had all showered and dressed in neatly ironed combat trousers, with brand new boots to go with hard-earned grey T-shirts.

The trainees had been allowed to keep one ripped, stained and unwashed blue training shirt as a memento of their hundred days and Leon immediately draped his over Theo's head. Theo thought this was funny and pretended he was blind as he hugged his two older brothers.

Ryan didn't often feel proud of his brothers, but a tear welled up as the quartet hugged. He thought about how his dead mum would have liked to see them all mucking about together in the sunshine.

'Can't believe only three trainees made it and you dweebs are two of 'em,' Ryan said.

Daniel eyed Theo as they broke apart. 'Two and a bit years, Theo. You'd better be scared!'

'I'm not scared of basic training,' Theo replied.

A couple of metres away, Amy was hugging Ning and congratulating her, but Ning looked disappointed.

'It got so that half the kids on campus were skiving off every time basic training finished,' Ryan explained. 'So now only relatives are allowed out of lessons. You'll see Grace and Chloe and everyone at lunchtime.'

'Cool,' Ning said.

'And now we get to do the fun bit,' Ryan said, as he pulled three keys from his trouser pocket and gave them a jangle. 'Time to check out your new bedrooms.'

*

'Ethan, are you in there, mate?'

Usually Ethan liked nothing more than hearing Natalka's voice on the other side of his door, but he hadn't put any clothes over his burning arse after taking a shower and he didn't have time to hide the fact he'd been crying.

'I'm sick,' Ethan answered weakly. 'Probably contagious, so it's better if you stay away.'

'I saw Boris drag you off,' Natalka said, as she put her

head around the door. 'What did Leonid do to you?'

Ethan sniffed. 'Leave me alone.'

The lights were off, but there was enough twilight creeping through the barred windows for Natalka to glimpse pubes as Ethan hurriedly yanked his duvet over his midriff.

'Why does it smell of horse shit in here?' Natalka asked.

'Go away,' Ethan sniffed. 'There's nothing you can do.'

But Natalka ignored the plea and sat beside Ethan on the bed.

'Did Leonid beat you?' Natalka asked.

'Massive rubber cosh on my arse,' Ethan said. 'I've got mega bruises, and I spent all day working at the stables. They're giving me all the dirtiest jobs and I can't go back to school until the end of the month.'

'Sounds rough,' Natalka said. 'Why's he pissed off with you?'

'They found out I've been using the Internet.'

'What, when we go to the web café in the bazaar?'

'No, here. On Irena's computer. I'm not supposed to go online in case the Americans are tracking me or something. And I might not be allowed to go off to school in Dubai now either.'

'Shit!' Natalka said. 'Did you try speaking to Irena?'

'Leonid got to her first. She's really mad at me. I had to go to her room and she yelled at me. Said I was lucky to only get three whacks with the cosh and that it was time I acted like a man instead of a spoilt brat.'

'Is there anything I can do?' Natalka asked. 'Bruise cream or something?'

'I hate it so much here,' Ethan said. 'I might as well be dead.'

'Now you *do* sound like a spoilt brat,' Natalka said, her voice becoming firmer.

Ethan sobbed loudly. 'Just go away.'

'Make me,' Natalka said.

Ethan scowled. 'What? Now *you're* gonna torment me like everyone else?'

Natalka grunted. 'Jesus, Ethan! Your mum's dead, your grandma's dying and Leonid's a bastard. You've every right to be pissed off, but you've got to fight it. I've got no sympathy if you curl up and sniffle.'

Ethan snorted. 'If I step out of line again, Leonid and his boys will squish me like a bug.'

Natalka stood up. 'I came up here to see if you were OK and maybe help you out. But I can't help someone who's given up, so I might as well go down to the bar. With any luck Vlad will try getting me drunk.'

Ethan managed a slight smile. 'How can you even be near that guy? He's such a dum-dum.'

'He's my big blond bimbo,' Natalka explained.

Ethan looked slightly more cheerful as he reached into a bedside drawer unit and pulled out six one-thousand-som notes.

'Well how about you bunk school and go to the bazaar with your bimbo?' Ethan asked. 'I'll need you to buy me a USB stick. That should be plenty to buy a sixteen- or thirty-two-gigabyte one. Get the biggest capacity in the smallest-sized key you can find. Then I need you to go in one of the web cafés and download a file for me.'

Natalka looked uncertain. 'Why do you need a memory stick? You haven't even got a computer.'

'The less you know the better,' Ethan said. 'But you said you wanted to help me out, and you can keep the change. Use it to smoke yourself to death, or buy condoms to shag bimbo boy. Get the super-safe ones, you wouldn't want any nasty accidents with that ape.'

Natalka was happy that Ethan had bucked up, but she didn't regard this as a licence to be cheeky.

'You're going the right way about getting a smack in the chops,' she warned. 'But I'll see what I can do.'

9. LOCK

Every new grey shirt gets a week off to recover from basic training. Ning's first two days passed in a blur of meals, bubble baths and long naps, but as the week went on and her energy returned she found herself getting bored.

Everyone apart from Leon and Daniel was either in training or lessons all day and she'd spent more than enough hours with the ten-year-old twins during training. But things livened up with a sixth-floor corridor party on Friday night and on Saturday she joined a coachload of cherubs who got up early for a day trip to London.

'I don't care what you get up to, as long as it's legal,' CHERUB's chief handler Meryl Spencer yelled sternly, as the thirty-two-seat coach stood in a bus lane at the side of London's St Pancras Station. 'But you always stay in groups of two or more and you're back here to get on the coach at six o'clock sharp. Unless you have a good excuse, you'll lose one pound of pocket money for every minute you're late. Is that *crystal* clear?'

'Yes, miss,' the kids droned, apart from a couple who made chicken noises and one who went *moo*.

Meryl was a former Olympic sprinter but she still struggled to get out of the way quickly enough as the driver opened the coach's hydraulic main door and the kids charged into the street.

A bunch of little kids were being taken to the London Eye, others were going to Leicester Square for a movie or to the Oxford Street shops, but Ning had accumulated three months' pocket money while she'd been in training and as her tastes veered towards the punkish her two mates Chloe and Grace reckoned she'd enjoy lightening her wallet in Camden Lock Market.

Chloe was a slender blonde twelve-year-old who most of the younger agents on campus regarded as a bit of a bombshell. Grace was a full head shorter, with freckles and long frizzy hair. The pair had been best mates since coming to CHERUB as red shirts and had taken Ning under their wing as soon as she'd arrived on campus.

When the trio got on the underground heading north to Camden, they were surprised to see Ryan and his two best mates, mischievous Max and burly half-French Alfie, charge into the carriage behind them as the doors closed.

'All right, slags!' Max said cheerfully, beating Grace to the last free seat and flipping her off as the train moved away.

'Where are you turds going?' Grace asked.

'Camden Market, same as,' Max explained.

Ning liked Ryan and had no problem with his two best mates, but Grace and Chloe groaned.

'You're not hanging around with us,' Chloe said.

'We're looking at clothes for Ning,' Grace added, hoping to put them off.

'I've never been to Camden before,' Alfie explained, with his heavy French accent. 'I'm told it's the place to buy leather jackets. You know any good shops?'

'A few,' Chloe said reluctantly. 'I suppose I can show you.'

'But only if you take us in Starbucks and buy us both frappuccinos,' Grace said.

Camden was only two stops and as Starbucks was deep inside the market the three boys and three girls wandered along, stopping in shops and diverting into narrow alleyways lined with stalls.

Although Grace and Chloe had assumed the boys would get on their nerves, they all had a decent time. Ryan and Max bought T-shirts. Alfie tried on six leather jackets but couldn't decide what he wanted, while Ning bought some black canvas plimsolls, smellies in Body Shop and a bunch of rock music and film posters to enliven the bare walls in her new room.

By the time they reached the canal-side Starbucks in the centre of the market it was past noon. The streets were so busy that bodies were spilling off the kerb into the road. The queue for Starbucks was out the door and into the street, so they diverted into another alleyway lined with ethnic food stalls.

Ning was impressed by a stall selling Chinese food – the kind that you get in China rather than the perverted version normally available in Chinese takeaways. She'd been away from China for more than six months and found herself excitedly babbling to the stall's husband and wife owners in Mandarin, before encouraging anxious friends to try the alien mixture of noodles, seafood and deep-fried buns.

Max was a picky eater and went for hot dog and chips from an adjoining van, but Ryan, Alfie, Chloe and Grace all took Ning's advice on what was good and good-naturedly sampled bits of each other's lunch while shuffling through the crowd trying to find a place to sit.

'You must eat prawns,' Chloe said, as she waved a battered prawn speared on a chopstick in Max's face.

'Away, away!' Max protested. 'All foreign muck makes me puke.'

Chloe snorted. 'That's rich, slagging off our food while eating a hot dog made from cow's eyeballs and sheep gonads.'

Ning joined the joke and waggled a piece of fish. 'Try the eel, Max. It's delicious.'

As they laughed, Ryan noticed a bunch of people sitting with their legs hanging over the edge of the canal that gave the market its name.

'Let's sit over there,' he said. 'I can't do chopsticks standing up.'

It was still only March so the canal-side concrete chilled their bums, but it was dry and the steaming foil trays made the cold tolerable. Max and Alfie both had cans of Coke and ripped off huge belches.

Once Ryan was seated with legs hanging over the canal side and his foil dish tucked between his knees, he pulled a BlackBerry from his hoodie and entered a four-digit pin. This pin took him into a hidden duplicate of the phone's operating system that was set up exclusively for his Ryan Brasker persona.

'You're always staring at that phone,' Chloe noted. 'Is some hot babe not returning her calls?'

'Sensible if she isn't,' Grace added.

Ryan and Grace had paired off six months earlier. It had ended with a massive row that involved flying macaroni cheese, and relations had been awkward ever since.

'You'd better be quiet,' Alfie said, his voice packed with mock seriousness. 'That's Ryan's *mission*.'

Max laughed as Ryan logged into his *Ryan Brasker* Facebook page and checked to see if there was any sign of activity from Ethan. He'd heard nothing in four days and was beginning to worry.

'It's his virtual mission,' Alfie explained. 'While real men like me go out in the real world and bust some heads, Ryan's got his *special* BlackBerry and his *virtual* mission.'

Ryan was irritated because Alfie and Max were always teasing him about this. Fortunately Chloe shot Alfie down as Ryan logged in to see if Ethan had tried to contact him on MSN.

'So you're a real man?' Chloe scoffed. 'Because to be frank, Alfie, I've seen your equipment in the showers after training and I didn't realise that real men had wobbly bellies and penises the size of Jelly Beans.'

Max was now laughing so hard that he almost dropped his chips into the canal.

'Who cares what *you* think,' Alfie said, his tone making it clear that he cared a great deal. 'All I know is, I'm a year younger than everyone here except Ning, but I've been on three decent missions already and I *will* be promoted to navy shirt before any of you.'

'I'll bet you one Jelly Bean,' Grace said, as she gulped down a can of Dr Pepper. 'And if you don't have a Jelly Bean when I get my navy shirt before you, you can substitute your penis.'

Max laughed. 'So, Grace, you're saying you *want* Alfie's penis?'

'Already spoken for,' Alfie said. 'Doris would kill me if I cheated on her.'

Ryan was ignoring the banter, but Ning had noticed his concerned expression and asked if everything was OK.

'Not really,' Ryan said, as he put the phone back in his pocket. 'But don't worry about it. We're here to have fun today.'

As Ryan said this, Grace did a huge belch right in Max's ear. Alfie topped her with a belch of his own, as Chloe made an *EWW* sound.

'You're animals,' Ryan said. 'So immature.'

Then he erupted into a burp so loud that an elderly passer-by shook her head and muttered, 'Disgusting,' under her breath.

'Disgusting,' Grace said, mocking the old woman's voice as she gave Ryan a gentle poke.

The laughter came to an abrupt halt as a group of four big skinheads – two in Man Utd shirts – came down the steps towards the canal. They'd all strolled out of a pub holding on to their pints and as they reached the canal side one drained his beer and lobbed his glass into the canal.

The splash wasn't big, but it got the leg of Chloe's jeans and the face of a toddler walking the canal-side path with his dad.

'Careful,' Chloe tutted.

The skinhead ignored Chloe, but the father of the little boy had turned instinctively and angrily towards the men who'd threatened his child. He backed off when he saw four dudes who were all bigger than him, but not before the one who'd thrown his glass in the canal reared up.

'What are you looking at?' the skinhead roared, slurring his words drunkenly. 'You want me to smash your head in?'

The little boy grabbed his dad's leg and looked like he was about to cry, while the dad kept a nervous silence.

'You deaf *and* stupid?' the skinhead asked, before turning back to his three mates. 'Look at this skinny brat shitting himself.'

There were loads of people around, but they all walked by acting like nothing was wrong while a few others sitting by the canal were standing up and moving away.

'Bet he's an Arsenal fan,' the youngest of the four skinheads quipped. 'No bottle.'

Grace was the shortest of the six kids, but she stood up quickly and poked the skinhead who'd thrown the glass in the back.

'Grace, stay out of it,' Chloe whispered anxiously.

'You're *well* impressive, aren't you?' Grace said loudly. 'Picking on someone half your size, with three mates backing you up.'

The skinhead turned towards Grace and gave a dismissive sweep of his hand. 'Piss off and mind your own.'

As Grace heard this, the five other cherubs formed a semicircle behind her.

'Arsenal are the greatest team in the world, you bald-headed shit,' Alfie spat, piling his accent on thick. 'Of course, this is because they are managed by a Frenchman.'

Now the skinhead looked pissed off. He turned and shouted, 'You brats wanna swim in the canal?'

The father used the distraction to snatch his toddler and back away, but the other three skinheads penned him in and one shoved him precariously close to the canal's edge.

'I'm warning you,' Grace said, eyeballing the huge man standing in front of her.

As the skinhead laughed, Ryan looked around hoping to see one of the cops he'd spotted in the crowded market earlier on. One of the other skinheads spat beer over the man as the little boy started to bawl.

The man and boy were now centimetres from the

canal's edge and Grace decided she had to act before they ended up in the filthy water. The problem was, while CHERUB training had made her into a black belt in Karate with expertise in the deadlier elements of several other fighting techniques, there's a limit to what you can achieve at close range against an opponent three times your weight.

But Grace did have a mini sachet of sweet chilli sauce in her coat pocket and as the skinhead stooped to make another snide remark she ripped it open and squirted the contents at his face.

An eyeful of hot chilli made the skinhead stumble back. Grace followed up with a hard shove and the instant Ning saw that the skinhead was off balance she waded in with an almighty sideways shove that sent him crashing into the canal.

The speed with which this happened made the other three skinheads lose concentration just long enough for Ryan, Max and Alfie to circle behind them. Alfie was biggest and attacked first, picking up the toddler's folded pushchair and ramming it hard into the middle bloke's guts. Max went for the guy closest to the canal, dishing out a pivoting head kick that crumpled him backwards into a metal bollard and knocked him cold.

The passing crowds now stopped ignoring things and seemed to think they were witnessing a piece of bizarre street theatre. As the dude on the far end tried getting his arm around Alfie's neck, Ryan smashed him in the temple with his palm, then bashed his jaw with his knee as he went down.

The father and toddler stumbled through the tangle of cherubs as one of the skinheads threw his glass. It sailed past Grace before shattering on the footpath.

Chloe was the only cherub who'd not got involved in the action. 'Let's get out of here,' she shouted, as Max and Alfie delivered final blows to one skinhead and Ning stomped the fingertips of the guy trying to pull himself out of the water.

As Chloe turned back to grab everyone's backpacks and shopping bags she saw three cops running down some canal-side steps towards them.

'Oh *now* they turn up,' Ryan sneered.

Ryan felt that they'd done the right thing morally, but he wasn't sure that the cops would see it that way and doubted that senior staff on CHERUB campus would be happy when they found out that five agents had been arrested for scrapping with a bunch of skinheads in a crowded street market.

'Don't forget my new shoes,' Ning shouted to Chloe, as the lead cop jumped the last four stairs and the six CHERUB agents began sprinting away.

10. ACHES

'How's your arse?' Natalka asked.

It was the same scene as a few nights earlier: Natalka coming around the door of Ethan's room as he lay on his bed feeling sorry for himself.

'Arse isn't bad, but everywhere else hurts now,' Ethan moaned. 'Five hours shovelling rotted-down horse shit into potato sacks. Then I had to load 'em all up on to a truck to be sold at the bazaar. My whole body aches and if I dare to stop work the stable workers go crazy because Leonid told 'em he'll dock their pay if he sees me slacking.'

'Will this cheer you up?' Natalka asked, as she pulled a USB memory stick out of her pocket. 'I got to Dordoi Bazaar this afternoon.'

It was still in its packaging, but the blister pack had been ripped open.

'Thirty-two GB, nice and small, and black so it'll be hard to spot,' Ethan said, straining his aching back as he sat up.

But when he reached out to grab it, Natalka swept the key out of reach.

'When you said you were using Irena's computer I thought you meant to play games, maybe a little porno or a chat with your Facebook chums. But I did a Google on the file I downloaded from the FTP site. It's a suite of tools designed to hijack a computer.'

Ethan tried to sound unruffled. 'I told you already, the less you know the better.'

Natalka stepped closer and put on a slightly menacing expression. 'I kinda thought about that, but you know what? That's not gonna wash when you get caught, and you confess that I was involved.'

'I'd never grass you up,' Ethan said.

'Not willingly, but how about when one of Leonid's heavies gets the pliers out and starts yanking out fingernails?'

Ethan had never told Natalka that he suspected Leonid had murdered his mother.

'It's better that you don't know,' he repeated, as he struggled to think of a stronger argument.

Natalka pushed the memory stick back into her jeans. 'If that's all you've got, you can't have this,' she said firmly.

'Natalka,' Ethan said, sighing with desperation. 'You took my money. We had a deal.'

'Let me know when you change your mind,' Natalka

said, as she turned towards the door. 'I'm not giving you this until I know that you're not going to use it to try something that might get me into shit.'

Ethan buried his head in his hands. 'Fine,' he said angrily.

Ethan found Natalka quite mercenary – turning up when she wanted cigarettes or money and then giving him the cold shoulder whenever she had something better going on. He liked her a lot, but wasn't certain that he could trust her.

'It's going into Leonid's computer,' he said reluctantly. 'The program hijacks the computer. Logs every keystroke, takes regular screenshots and saves every file that's opened in unencrypted form.'

'Who uploaded the program to the FTP site?'

'My mate Ryan from back in California. I've only had limited access to the net, so he's been helping me out by doing searches. Trying to learn about hacking and stuff.'

'You trust this Ryan kid?'

Ethan nodded. 'He's some kid at my school from before my mum died. He saved my life when I got hit by a car. And I make sure we use picture messaging or Skype sometimes, so I know it's really him, not some goon from the CIA who ripped off his MSN account.'

'You should still be careful,' Natalka said. 'Especially if he's in America.'

Ethan shrugged. 'It's not like I've got queues of friends lining up to help me out, Natalka. Maybe I'm only ninety-nine per cent sure that Ryan is trustworthy, but I'm a hundred per cent sure that Leonid wants to take the clan over unopposed. I think he killed my mom and tried to kill me back in California.'

'But he's two rooms away,' Natalka said. 'If he wants you dead it wouldn't be hard.'

'He has to do it subtly,' Ethan explained. 'If my grandma worked out that Leonid killed my mom, she'd kick him out of the clan. So she's shielding me now, but I'll be shit out of luck when she finally keels over.'

'So how does hacking Leonid's computer help?'

'I'm not sure exactly what it will give us,' Ethan said. 'But information is power. Maybe I can find something I can use to blackmail him. Maybe I can stitch him up. There's even an outside chance that I'll find evidence that I can show to Grandma to prove that he killed my mom.'

'Irena's not stupid,' Natalka said. 'She must have her suspicions that Leonid killed your mum. Plenty of other people in the Kremlin reckon he was behind it.'

Ethan was surprised by this. 'Really?'

'For sure,' Natalka said. 'Quite a few of the pilots my mum knows have said as much.'

'I hardly know anyone in the Kremlin,' Ethan said. 'I'm out of the loop on all the gossip.'

Natalka nodded. 'Plus you're Aramov, so they'll avoid talking in front of you in case it gets back to Leonid.'

'I think my grandma's got a blind spot. Leonid's her golden boy, or something. She covers up for a lot of his crazy shit, and even though they fight all the time, I've noticed that Leonid nearly always gets his way.'

Natalka nodded. 'Like a lot of parents: she thinks the

sun shines out of her kid's arse.'

Ethan smiled fondly. 'My mom used to argue with my PE teachers on parents' night. She used to say they never gave me a chance. She could never accept that I'm totally uncoordinated and crap at sports.'

'Speaking of school,' Natalka said, 'how's the Dubai thing going?'

Ethan shrugged. 'Nothing's for sure and Grandma's still annoyed that I was sneaking in to use her PC, but hopefully it's on again – once I've served my time at the stables.'

'Cool,' Natalka nodded, as she threw the USB memory stick at Ethan. 'There you go,' she said. 'So what's your plan for getting it in the back of Leonid's computer?'

*

The six CHERUB agents belted along the canal footpath with three cops in hot pursuit. The fattest cop didn't keep up after the first couple of hundred metres, but the other two were an athletic black dude and a big-arsed woman who moved way faster than you'd have thought possible.

The crowds thinned out as they moved away from the market and Max led the way as the narrow canal-side path skimmed beneath their feet.

'Split up,' Chloe yelled, as she passed a couple of the heavier shopping bags over to Ning.

The cherubs had all been taught that cops have radios and will send more officers in a car to intercept you if you're daft enough to run in a straight line.

Max and Alfie took the first escape route, jumping up to grab an iron road bridge crossing the canal, then swinging their bodies over the riveted beams. Chloe and Ning made an easier exit a hundred metres further along, running up an embankment and into an alleyway beside a bus depot.

This left Ryan and Grace on the canal path. Ryan had moved a good twenty metres ahead of Grace, who was the smallest and slowest. As he rounded a short corner he had the horrible realisation that the footpath only ran on for a couple of hundred metres.

The only way out was up a grass embankment and over a graffitied brick wall. The wall's top had been cemented with glass shards to stop people climbing into the recycling depot on the other side.

'Screw it,' Grace said breathlessly, as she stopped running and spun around, seeking options.

They couldn't see any cops, but they could hear boots on the canal path less than a hundred metres away.

'I'll give you a boost,' Ryan said.

He went down on one knee and Grace hopped on to his shoulders as he stood up. Ryan was banking on Grace giving him an arm up, but she jumped straight down the other side.

'Hey!' Ryan shouted.

'What?' Grace asked. 'Can't you reach the top of the wall?'

By this time the big black cop was in sight. Ryan made a desperate jump at the wall, but his fingertips didn't get within thirty centimetres of the top and there was nothing around that he could use as a step.

'Get your hands where I can see 'em,' the cop shouted.

Ryan looked about. He'd been kicked off his first mission in disgrace. Attacking a cop might get him kicked out of CHERUB for good, so he decided the best option was to jump into the canal and swim.

'I'm warning you,' the cop shouted, as Ryan hesitated.

As the cop ripped something off his belt, Ryan sprinted down the embankment, preparing to jump in. The water was going to be cold and filthy, but he was a strong swimmer and it was his best shot at not getting caught.

Two steps from the water, Ryan felt an enormous jolt as the cop fired a Taser barb into his thigh. He fell sideways with his body sprawled across the footpath, legs twitching and his head hanging over the water. At the same moment a police siren whooped in a street not too far away.

'I warned you,' the cop shouted, as he strode purposefully towards Ryan's shuddering body.

Ryan was face down, so he didn't see what happened next, but he did hear an almighty crash, followed by a splash as the cop hit the water.

When Grace jumped off the wall, she'd found herself balanced on a mound of old kitchen appliances. As the cop pulled his Taser, she'd grabbed a sturdy metal-sided toaster, clambered to the highest point of the mound and used a two-handed overhead throw to lob it at the policeman's head.

Ryan's leg muscles twitched from the Taser blast, but

he'd been zapped several times in training and knew that the effects would only be temporary as he pulled the metal barb out through his jeans.

'You OK?' Grace shouted anxiously, as she balanced on the mound, leaning over the wall. 'I've got a fridge door you can use as a step up.'

As the cop pulled himself furiously out of the water, there was no sign of his female colleague, who must have broken off to chase Chloe and Ning. Ryan hobbled up the embankment and by the time he reached the wall Grace had grabbed a fridge door and lobbed it over the wall.

'Just you wait!' the cop roared.

As the cop came up on to the embankment, dripping filthy canal water and crippled by the weight of soggy body armour and cop equipment, Ryan used the fridge door as a makeshift step, positioning his hand carefully to avoid the jutting glass atop the wall as he swung over into a crunching mound of discarded inkjet printers, food mixers and LCD screens.

'Nice move with the toaster,' he told Grace, smiling warily as they scrambled down the unstable mound looking for a quick way out of the recycling yard. 'But if we get caught after you whacked a cop we are in *so* much trouble.'

11. HORMONES

'Hellloooooo!' Tamara Aramov said. 'Good to see you, Ethan, and it's Natasha, isn't it?'

'Natalka,' Natalka corrected, as she eyed the petite smiling woman who was Andre's mother and had been Leonid Aramov's second wife.

While Leonid was still legally married to a third wife, who'd returned to live in China, his second wife Tamara had never left the Kremlin. She remained close to Leonid, more for Andre's sake than out of any lingering affection for her thuggish ex-husband.

'Leonid says excellent things about your mother,' Tamara told Natalka. 'One of his best pilots.'

As Natalka found herself hunting for something to say, Andre came out of the living-room wearing pyjama bottoms and a Mighty Ducks hockey shirt.

'Oh, hi,' he said, marginally surprised by Ethan, who

he invited regularly but who rarely visited, but utterly shocked to see Natalka. 'What do you guys want?'

'Bored,' Natalka admitted, as she came through the door of Leonid's apartment. 'Ethan said you had a heap of Wii games.'

Andre's face lit up, but then he looked awkwardly at his mum. 'We were kind of watching a movie.'

'*The Jungle Book*,' Tamara added. 'His favourite!'

Andre was ten, but often seemed younger. 'Mum!' he said, embarrassed. 'It's *not* my favourite.'

Normally Natalka would have ripped into Andre, but they needed to get into Leonid's room so she shrugged and said, 'Cool movie. Baloo cracks me up.'

'Why don't you all come in?' Tamara said. 'I can make some hot chocolate. If you want to play games we can finish our movie another time.'

They walked down a short hallway, past Leonid Aramov's living-room and into the titchy space that Andre had as a bedroom. It was slightly wider than his single bed. The end wall was stacked with shelves of video games and there was an obscenely large telly screwed to the wall.

'I'm getting rid of this,' Andre said, embarrassed again as he flung a Ben 10 duvet cover off his bed.

'Probably best, before you start having chicks over,' Natalka said, unable to resist teasing. 'So where are the gorillas?'

'Boris and Alex went out with my dad,' Andre explained. 'Partying with some new Chinese girls.'

Natalka shuddered. These 'new' girls were part of a

regular trade bussed in from the rural provinces of western China. They'd spend a few days in a dormitory close to the airfield, before being flown off to Europe or America with false passports.

Most had left China with the promise of well-paid factory jobs, but would end up being forced into prostitution. And while Andre was remarkably innocent, Ethan and Natalka knew that his older brothers' idea of a party with vulnerable young girls wouldn't be the kind that involved cake and candles.

'So they won't be back for a while,' Ethan said. 'Have you got that boxing game? The mad one where you're all in those kind of wheelchair things and you get power ups and end up with massive boxing gloves?'

'Wii Sports,' Andre said. 'It's really old. I've got *way* better games than that.'

'Pick something where I don't have to remember what eight different buttons do,' Natalka said, instinctively knowing that being a hot girl in the company of two younger boys gave her the right to be bossy.

'I need a piss before we start,' Ethan said.

As Ethan headed back into the hall, Natalka stood in the doorway and kept watch. Leonid Aramov might have been a billionaire, but his apartment was still just four sets of officers' quarters knocked into one, and he was certainly no aficionado of interior design, with junk from skis to cigar boxes piled in every available space.

'What you looking at?' Andre asked Natalka, as the Wii gobbled a silver disk.

'Just seeing how your mum's getting along with the hot chocolate,' she lied. 'She might need a hand carrying the mugs.'

'She'll be fine,' Andre said.

Ethan cut into Leonid Aramov's office, which was actually a dead section of hallway created when some walls got knocked down. If anyone saw him, he'd claim to have got confused and gone the wrong way.

The computer was a chunky old Toshiba laptop, but it had a printer and stuff wired up and the build-up of dust on the desk around it indicated that the machine never moved off its spot. Ethan reached quickly around the back of the machine, where he was relieved to find a pair of empty USB ports.

He jolted at a flash of light, but he'd only nudged the mouse, making a screensaver pop up.

'Done,' he whispered to Natalka, when he got back into Andre's room. 'So what game are we gonna play?'

*

It was a Saturday, so the recycling depot was busy with cars dropping off junk. Getting on to the street involved a brisk walk past a couple of council workers in orange high-vis jackets and a young mum unloading the rear of a people carrier while two brats squawked in the back.

Ryan and Grace jogged until they were certain the soggy cop had given up. But there were sure to be other cops looking for them, so Ryan was delighted by the orange for-hire light of a black London taxi and put his arm out to hail it.

The driver pulled over but looked wary. 'Where are you kids going?'

'I've got dosh,' Ryan said, pulling a twenty out of his pocket and waving it.

'We've been out, but we've forgotten our keys,' Grace explained. 'We've got to go to my mum's office.'

'And where's that?' the driver asked.

'The one that's shaped like a gherkin,' Grace said, coming out with the only London office block she could think of. 'It's dead famous, do you know it?'

'Thirty St Mary Axe,' the driver said. 'In you hop.'

Ryan and Grace took a few seconds catching their breath in the back seat as the taxi pulled away, then exchanged relieved smiles.

'That was kinda cool with the chilli sauce,' Ryan said. 'I'm glad you stood up to those dicks.'

'Cheers,' Grace said. 'But I'm not sure that's how the campus staff will see things if they find out.'

Ryan nodded warily. 'If *any* of us get busted, it'll take Meryl about four seconds to work out who else was involved. You try calling Chloe. I'll get Max.'

Ryan pulled his phone out, but instead of doing the same, Grace kept smiling at him.

'What?' Ryan asked. 'Did I say something stupid?'

'I shredded the sole of my shoe on the glass on top of that wall,' Grace said, as she lifted her leg off the floor of the taxi.

But as Ryan leaned forwards to look, Grace gave him a peck on the cheek.

'You're all red and sweaty, but you're cute,' she

said, machine-gunning the words like she was scared to say them.

Ryan looked stunned, but before he could respond his phone rang and the screen flashed *Ning Calling*.

'Are you guys OK?' Ning asked.

'Bit of a close shave but we've grabbed a taxi,' Ryan explained. 'How about you?'

'Back in the market, blending into a crowd. We saw Max and Alfie too, but we split cos there's less chance of being recognised.'

Chloe spoke in the background. 'We should probably stay apart for the rest of the day, just to be on the safe side.'

'Chloe says—'

Ryan interrupted. 'I heard her. I guess I'll stay with Grace then. See you back at the bus this evening. And I'd try putting some more distance between yourselves and the canal.'

'That's what we're doing,' Ning said. 'We decided that Camden Town tube's too obvious, but once we're away from the market we're getting on the first bus we can find.'

Ryan gasped with relief as he pressed *end call* on his phone.

'So it's you and me with six hours to kill,' Grace said, smiling sweetly as she shifted across the bench towards Ryan. 'What do you fancy doing?'

Grace had proved to be extremely clingy and a bit of a lunatic during their previous brief relationship, but even though Ryan knew he was opening himself up to a world of neediness and flying macaroni, Grace had a cute face and nice legs. Also her boobs were bigger than they'd been six months earlier and Ryan liked the idea of getting a feel.

'We could go for a coffee or something,' Ryan said, trying to sound mature when he was actually completely flustered. 'Then maybe somewhere quiet like a park. We can talk, or whatever . . .'

'I can think of some things we can do in a park,' Grace said, as she put her hand on Ryan's jeans and studied the dot of blood where the Taser barb had snagged him.

12. SCHOOLS

28 March (11 days later)
It was quarter to eleven on a Wednesday night and every surface in Ryan's bedroom was covered with torn-out magazine articles, hastily scribbled notes and web printouts, plus tape, glue and scissors.

Alfie was crawling around the floor in a grubby Karate suit, cutting out a picture of bashed-up cars floating down an overflowing river. As he glued it to a big sheet of paper with 'Freak Weather' written at the top in marker pen, Ryan came through the door holding a plastic A3 folio case.

'I got Grace and Chloe's project!' Ryan said excitedly.

Like Alfie, Ryan was in Karate kit and the lads stood over the end of Ryan's bed to study the folio's contents.

'Finally something useful out of you getting off with Grace.'

Ryan looked anxious. 'She's on that late night training thing. So I swiped it and she'll *murder* me if she knows we're copying her stuff, so let's not hang about.'

Ryan opened the folio's plastic catch and was simultaneously awed and irritated by the girls' weather project. The first page was a carefully drawn cartoon of a hurricane with dustbins, stick-men and stick-dogs getting blown around in the vortex.

'They're such swots,' Alfie complained. 'Our project's gonna look so crap compared to this.'

Ryan shrugged. 'Who gives a damn about humanities? Let's just glue some shit on, rip off a couple of the girls' articles and try getting to bed before midnight. I don't care what mark we get as long as there's a bunch of pages we can hand in to old cock face tomorrow morning.'

'I've got fitness training first thing and we're supposed to be going to the cinema tomorrow night,' Alfie groaned. 'I will be shattered.'

'You'll have to try catching up on your sleep during lessons,' Ryan joked.

Ryan had left his door slightly ajar and twenty-two-year-old Beatha Johannsson leaned into the room. The sturdy brunette was a former CHERUB agent, whose career ended at age fourteen when a mission led to her face being all over the national news. She couldn't work undercover after that, but after a forced exile in Switzerland and university in Canada she'd recently returned to campus to work as a carer.

'Why aren't you two in bed?' Beatha asked, stepping in and then hurriedly wrapping an arm over her nose. 'Jesus, it *reeks* in here. Open the windows, then take showers!'

'We've *got* to finish this project,' Ryan explained, as he dragged a pillow over the girls' project to hide his intention to copy.

Beatha crouched down and looked at some of the sheets that Ryan and Alfie had put together with Pritt Stick and poor scissor skills.

'This looks really shoddy,' she said. 'Why'd you leave it until the last minute?'

Ryan shrugged. 'Forgot . . . Kinda.'

'Well you're not gonna get it done tonight, anyway,' Beatha said. 'Ryan, you're wanted in the meeting room downstairs.'

'Who?' he asked anxiously.

Nobody had been fingered for the canal incident, but even after nearly two weeks Ryan and his friends still feared that news would creep back to campus.

'I don't know,' Beatha said. 'I was heading up and Zara asked me to get you out of bed.'

Zara was CHERUB's chairwoman.

'Have I got to shower first?' Ryan asked.

'Sounded urgent, so I'd go straight down.'

Ryan smiled pleadingly and put his hands together in mock prayer. 'Then *please* can you get me an extension for my project. After all, I had to go on mission business.'

Beatha could be a soft touch, but she snorted as she grabbed Chloe and Grace's folio off the bed. 'You should have finished your project days ago, but I will give you a break by taking this back and not reporting you for copying. Especially as you both so kindly agreed to vacuum the entire sixth-floor hallway and stairs this Sunday morning.'

Alfie looked mystified. 'We did?'

Ryan couldn't believe Alfie was being so dense. 'She's *making* us.'

'Oh!' Alfie said, then his face sank. 'Ryan, I'll see how much of this I can get done on my own, but try and get back as soon as you can, yeah?'

'And open a goddamned window,' Beatha said, as she headed back into the hallway.

Ryan hurriedly swapped his sweaty Karate suit for a cleanish hoodie and combat trousers and pushed black-soled feet into boots before getting the lift down to the ground-floor meeting room.

As it was just him being called down, he doubted it was anything to do with the canal incident but it was still a relief to step into the conference room to find CHERUB's chairwoman Zara Asker sitting at the table with Amy Collins and a Texan CIA agent named Ted Brasker.

Ted had played the role of Ryan and Amy's dad on their California mission and Ryan cracked a big smile. Firstly because Ted was a nice guy, but mainly because his presence guaranteed this was nothing to do with the canal punch-up.

'You're sprouting!' Ted said, as the ex-US Marine locked tattooed arms around Ryan and gave his back a solid thump. 'A good couple of inches since I last saw you.'

'Doesn't smell so good, mind,' Amy added, as she wafted her hand in front of her face.

Zara laughed and pointed at the far end of the table. 'Sit up that end, what *have* you been doing?'

'I'd shower if I had time,' Ryan protested. 'Today I had fitness training and a session in the dojo, and I'm gonna get nailed by old cock fa—'

Zara looked shocked and sat bolt upright. 'Pardon me?' she snapped.

'Err . . . nailed by Mr Gilligan,' Ryan spluttered, as the colour drained out of his face. 'I have to get my humanities project finished by the morning or he'll kill me.'

Zara looked stern. 'Why do you boys *always* leave homework until the last minute?'

'You've had plenty of time for Grace, so I hear,' Amy teased.

Ted burst out laughing. 'Oh, you've got a girlfriend now. Is she a hottie?'

Ryan didn't answer, but he squirmed with embarrassment as the three adults smirked.

'I take it I'm here for *some* reason?' Ryan said irritably.

'You still haven't heard from Ethan?' Zara asked.

Ryan shook his head. 'It's been fifteen days.'

'Well there's good news and bad on that score, Ryan,' Amy said, as she slid some papers down the long meeting table. 'That's a copy of a fax intercepted by the Echelon communications monitoring network. It was sent to the Kremlin from an educational consultant named Douglas Miles.'

Ryan skimmed through the text:

Dear Mrs Aramov . . . Pleased to say that based upon his academic credentials your grandson Ethan has been accepted into DESA (Dubai English Speaking Academy) without the requirement for an entrance exam.

Although this new school has less rigorous entry requirements than its more established rivals, I am well acquainted with the senior staff there and can assure you that Ethan will receive a most excellent education . . .

Ryan checked the top of the letter and was pleased to see it had been sent on March 25th.

'That's last Friday,' Ryan said, as he cracked a smile. 'So I've still got no idea why Ethan's stopped using the Internet, but at least it looks like nothing serious has happened to him.'

Amy nodded. 'And based upon some other faxes, plus information we've intercepted from Douglas Miles' office, the plan is for Ethan to start at DESA on the first day of summer term. That's Monday April 16th. A little over two weeks from now.'

Zara took over the conversation. 'The best thing in that fax is that *the school has less rigorous entry requirements*. Our nightmare situation at CHERUB is when we have to try getting an agent into a popular or oversubscribed school. We can usually manage it, but never at two or three weeks' notice. However, as *less rigorous entry requirements* basically means that the school is desperate and takes any kids whose parents are willing to pay the fees, we're in luck.'

'Isn't it a bit of a heavy coincidence if I turn up there?' Ryan said.

'Not *you*, obviously,' Amy said, smiling at the thought. 'When Ethan arrives at DESA there are going to be two other new kids who we hope will become his new best friends. CHERUB agents of course. A boy to be his mate, and a girl who can stir up Ethan's teenage hormones. You can work closely with them.'

'But what can they find out that I don't know already?' Ryan asked.

Amy explained. 'People your age can be fickle. We have to accept the possibility that Ethan has stopped communicating with you simply because he's bored. Maybe he's made a new friend in Kyrgyzstan. Maybe he's been swept off his feet by that Natalka girl he mentions all the time in his MSN conversations.

'Secondly, it's worth sending in more agents because any information we can get about the Aramov Clan is incredibly important. Their planes supply arms that fuel wars in Africa, tons of drugs transported from growers in Afghanistan and South America to markets in Europe and America, plus counterfeit goods and hundreds of young girls to sex traffickers.'

Ted put the argument more concisely. 'If you get the Aramovs' transportation network, you cut the legs off of a dozen other crime syndicates. But the Aramovs have got powerful friends in China and Russia, and practically every senior cop, general and politician in Kyrgyzstan is in their pocket. So we *have* to tread delicately and Ethan is our only window into the top level of the Aramov organisation.'

'Ryan, you're the only person in this room who knows Ethan well,' Zara said. 'You know most of the kids your age on campus. So which boy and girl would you pick as good prospects to make friends with Ethan?'

Ryan shifted awkwardly in his chair. 'People might get upset with me if they know I didn't pick them.'

Zara nodded. 'Whatever you say will stay in this room.'

'Do they have to be experienced?' Ryan asked.

Amy answered this one. 'The mission looks standard at this stage, but you never know with these things. Your mission in California looked routine when it started, but that ended up with murders and explosions and all sorts.'

'OK,' Ryan said thoughtfully. 'Ethan's OK-looking, but he's kinda skinny and he's gonna know something's weird if a really hot girl comes on to him. I'd go with someone like Ning. I mean, she's not a dog, but she's not smoking hot either.'

Zara interrupted. 'Doesn't Ning have previous with Leonid Aramov?'

Amy nodded. 'Ning escaped from China via Kyrgyzstan. Leonid Aramov tortured Ning and killed her stepmother.'

'But Ethan was in California at that time, so there's no possible way that he could ever have seen Ning,' Ryan said. 'It's not like Leonid Aramov is gonna be turning up at DESA for parents' evenings, and I'd think Ning will be happy to get involved in any mission that might help bring down the people who killed her stepmother.'

Amy nodded in agreement. 'Ning also did well in basic training, and the way she's found friends and settled in since arriving on campus bodes well for her ability to become fast friends with Ethan.'

'Ning it is then,' Zara said, 'as long as you're certain that nobody will recognise her. And for the boy?'

'It could be my mate Max, I guess,' Ryan said. 'I know he gets in heaps of trouble, but I'm sure Ethan would get his sense of humour.'

Zara seemed less sure, leaning forward and steepling her fingers. 'I'd be very concerned about Max being able to focus on a slow-burning mission. I think he'll make a good agent in the long run, but he's yet to demonstrate that he can control his mischievous personality over a long mission.'

Ryan didn't want to slag his friend off, but Zara probably had a point and he kept quiet.

'Alfie then,' Ryan said, as he realised that he was basically rolling off the names of his best friends. 'He's actually a year younger than me and Ethan, but he's big so he can easily pass for thirteen.'

Zara was more positive about this idea and wagged her finger. 'Yes!' she said. 'And that nice French accent of his would fit in perfectly at an international school.'

'Plus Alfie plays the flute,' Ryan said. 'So even chess players and computer nerds will have something to look down on.'

'Ted and I will work on mission briefings and

backgrounds on the Aramov Clan for Alfie and Ning,' Amy said. 'I'll need you to write a report containing everything you know about Ethan, Ryan, along with any strategies you can think of for Ning and Alfie to pal up with him.'

Ryan sighed. 'I'm kinda busy,' he said. 'To get this done I'll need you to give me a pass to get out of my humanities project?'

Zara rocked back in her chair and stared into Ryan's eyes as if she was digging for some hidden truth.

'One pass on the geography project and five one-lesson passes so that you've got time to write the report properly,' Zara said, and then in a harsher tone accompanied by a wagging finger, 'but I expect you to be *working* in those hours, not mucking about.'

Ryan was happy enough with a pass and getting out of five hours' lessons, but he kept his involuntary grin under control.

'Oh and one other thing before you go up to bed,' Zara said. 'From now on you shower after *every* training session no matter how busy your schedule gets. Come in here stinking up my meeting room again and I'll *personally* take you over to vehicle maintenance and hose you off in the car wash.'

13. UNIFORM

13 April (two weeks later)

'So you're not shovelling horse manure any more?' Natalka asked.

She was in the Kremlin lobby with Ethan, awaiting a car that was supposed to take them to Dordoi Bazaar.

'Grandma's put her foot down,' Ethan explained. 'Leonid didn't want me going to school in Dubai, but she told the old fart to mind his own. I've had all the uniform delivered, bags are packed and I told Grandma that I needed to go into town for some deodorant and pens and stuff.'

Natalka went unusually quiet, staring down at her wrecked turquoise Converse.

'Ahh!' Ethan smiled. 'You're all sad. You're gonna miss me!'

He expected Natalka to tell him to piss off, or maybe

a shoulder punch, but she looked across and nodded grudgingly.

'You're the only person I can have an intelligent conversation with around here,' she said. 'But don't let that go to your head, or I'll slap you one.'

Natalka saying she'd miss Ethan gave his self-esteem a nice boost.

'Stop grinning,' Natalka said, regretting her honesty.

'Your mum's still here,' Ethan said. 'I've only met her a couple of times, but she's cool.'

Natalka tutted. 'My mum's great, but she's away flying half the time. Besides, mums and mates aren't the same thing.'

'What about Vladimir?' Ethan asked. 'Your blond bimbo.'

Natalka suddenly looked angry. 'Screw him. He's getting tight with Boris and Alex and their manners are rubbing off on him.'

'Partying with Chinese girls, I heard,' Ethan said.

Natalka tutted again and changed the subject. 'So, you got the memory key from Leonid's office?'

Ethan nodded, then patted the pocket of his jeans. 'I pulled it when I went to play Wii with Andre last night. We'll find a web café and upload it for Ryan. But it's been four weeks, so I hope he's not forgotten about me.'

'Can't you look at what's in the files yourself?'

'Not without my own computer,' Ethan said. 'And it might be risky spending hours going through Aramov stuff in a web café. The good news is, every kid has to have a laptop at my new school. And since I'll need it for homework and stuff, I don't see how Leonid can stop me from bringing it home for holidays.'

A trashed Mercedes M-class 4×4 was rolling up outside. One of the Aramovs' many Kremlin-based flunkies put a hairy arm out of the driver's-side window.

'Taking you to the bazaar, yeah?' he shouted.

The driver was stubbly and looked like he'd gone a while since his last decent wash, but he got excited when he realised he'd be driving an Aramov and made a big fuss of getting out and opening the door for Ethan, while Natalka fended for herself.

'Cigarette?' the driver asked, as he floored the accelerator and got a little squeal out of the back tyres.

'Thanks,' Natalka said, as she snatched the packet off the armrest.

*

Ning swished a changing-room curtain and looked at herself standing before a mirrored wall: grey tights, grey pleated skirt, blue and white striped blouse and a straw hat.

'I feel like *such* a twonk,' Ning said.

They were in the school uniform section of one of Dubai's biggest department stores. Alfie was in no position to criticise, because he looked almost as bad in the boys' version of DESA's uniform, but Ryan was only in Dubai to dole out Ethan-related advice and couldn't resist taking the piss.

'Don't worry,' Ryan said, as he looked on dressed in cargo shorts and a Ralph Lauren polo shirt. 'You've only got to wear those monkey suits for ten or twelve hours a day, six days a week.'

'Wool makes me itch,' Alfie said, as he rubbed his blazer. 'And who makes kids wear a get-up like this in the middle of a desert?'

Over at a glass counter, Amy Collins stood by a mound of brand new PE kit, while an Indian clerk with a dodgy wig went through drawers looking for gym shorts in Alfie's size.

'The computer says we have them,' he said, when his head bobbed up. 'But this isn't my department and I can't find them.'

Ryan looked at Alfie. 'If you don't have shorts, I bet they'll make you do PE in your underpants.'

Alfie tutted. 'Ryan, if you don't shut up I will fart on your head when we get back to the hotel.'

'I'm greased lightning,' Ryan said, adopting a boxing stance and throwing half a dozen quick punches. 'You wouldn't get that fat piggy butt of yours anywhere near me.'

'I'm starving,' Ning moaned, as she stepped back into the changing cubicle, swapping the uniform for jeans and a singlet. 'Can we get something to eat after this?'

They'd only arrived in Dubai the night before, but only Amy seemed to be suffering jet lag.

'One shopping trip with you three is more than enough to persuade me never to have kids,' Amy said wearily, as the assistant blipped over a thousand dirhams' worth of school uniform and PE kit through a barcode reader. 'It's probably easiest to get room service back at the hotel.'

'Can't we just get something quick?' Alfie asked. 'Burgers or something.'

'There's a food court,' Ning added. 'I think we've got to go back past it on the way to the hire car.'

'When I get back to my room I'm having at least three gin and tonics from the minibar,' Amy said.

'Me too,' Ryan joked.

The mall was quiet and they found themselves amidst less than a dozen diners in a food court with over two hundred tables. All the kids got McDonald's, while Amy went for the strongest coffee on Starbucks' menu and hoped the caffeine would give her a boost.

Amy looked at Ning and Alfie. 'When we get back to the hotel I *don't* want you two bouncing off the walls. Relax, have a swim or whatever. Then I want you to go back to your rooms and work. This will be your last proper chance to read through your notes on Ethan. Ryan, you be on hand to help them with any questions.'

'I had one idea,' Ning said, as she chomped a cheeseburger. 'I've tried learning chess, but based on what Ryan's shown me so far I'll never be able to play competitively against Ethan. So I was thinking that if I got friendly with Ethan I could ask him to teach me to play chess.'

Amy nodded. 'I've certainly heard worse ideas.'

Alfie tutted. 'You could have thought of that before we spent *days* reading boring-arsed books on chess strategies.'

As Alfie spoke, Ryan's BlackBerry chimed to indicate a text message.

'Now who might that be?' Alfie said, grinning.

The text was from Grace. Alfie read it over Ryan's shoulder and burst out laughing:

U scum sucking dick hole. I hate U. UR dead!

'She's gonna kick your arse,' Alfie predicted.

'What's this all about?' Amy asked.

'Grace is so possessive,' Ryan said. 'Texting me all the time, wanting to know where I'm going. I want a girlfriend to hang out with and have a bit of fun, but she was like a 24/7 job.'

'He was too chicken to break up to her face,' Alfie explained. 'So he sent her a break-up text before we got on the plane yesterday.'

Amy gasped. 'You broke up by text message! You pig; I hope she *does* kick your arse.'

Ryan looked uncomfortable. 'Last time I broke up with Grace she threw macaroni cheese at my head, trashed one of my chemistry books and poured yellow paint on my best jeans. I figured if I sent her a text, she'll have had time to calm down before I get back to campus early next week.'

'It's a shame I won't be on campus when she catches up with you,' Ning said. 'It's gonna be hilarious!'

'Grace is only little, but she's deadly with oven-hot pasta,' Alfie added.

'If the first time was such a nightmare, why go out with her again?' Amy asked.

Ryan shrugged. 'We were in the back of a taxi, chatting

away. She looked hot and it's not like heaps of other girls were throwing themselves at me . . .'

'For some strange reason,' Ning added.

'I still say you need to fake your own death,' Alfie said. 'It's your only real chance of survival.'

Ryan raised a finger. 'Alfie, why don't you go sit on my middle digit and spin?'

Amy found all this pretty funny. It also made her nostalgic because the banter between the kids reminded her of all the dramas during her own teenage years on CHERUB campus. But she didn't want her three agents having a serious falling-out, so she put her foot down before good-natured jabs could turn nasty.

'We need to forget Ryan's love life and focus on our mission,' Amy said firmly, as she glanced at her watch. 'First impressions are critical and every detail needs to be *spot* on when you meet Ethan at your new school on Monday.'

*

The centre of Bishkek was mainly home to government buildings, international hotels and communist era monuments, but for locals Dordoi Bazaar in the northern outskirts was the city's real heart.

The market stretched for more than two kilometres, with a mix of open and covered areas. Traders worked out of metal shipping containers stacked two or three high, with the ground-level container serving as a shop, and the ones above used for storage.

With over six thousand traders, most areas of the vast bazaar had become specialised. Ethan had told Grandma

Irena that he needed pens and other school stuff, so they got the driver to drop them near a cluster of traders selling stationery and gift wrap. But after a couple of quick purchases and some doubling back to ensure that Leonid wasn't having him followed, Ethan led Natalka past several hundred tightly stacked containers to an area that mainly attracted teenagers.

The containers here sold pirate music, software and DVDs, a mix of punk and Goth clothes, plus every kind of cheap Chinese-produced fake from Nike basketball boots to Nirvana hoodies and *Star Wars* light sabres.

Crowds of older teens hung out in web cafés, where network gaming was more popular than web surfing. The day was mild, but the heat from tightly wedged computers in poorly ventilated containers pushed the temperature way up and the clammy teenage patrons gave them a distinctly locker-roomish aroma.

Ethan picked one of the slightly less crowded containers and paid for an hour's Internet. Natalka scowled at the gamer boys who eyed her up as they squeezed past lines of cheap office chairs and sat together in front of a glowing LED screen in the farthest corner of the container. A big electric fan swung from side to side, but it only shifted funky air from one spot to another.

'I know better web cafés than this,' Natalka moaned, as beads of sweat bristled on her neck.

'But Leonid's goons would stick out around here,' Ethan explained, as he opened up his Facebook. 'Everyone's our age.'

'Oooh, he's cute,' Natalka said, as she saw Ryan's profile picture in Ethan's friend list. 'Not what I expected at all.'

'What were you expecting?' Ethan asked.

Natalka grinned. 'More of a geeky loser like you.'

'You're too kind,' Ethan said.

The Russian keyboard layout was confusing, but Ethan was soon tapping out a response to one of several *Where are you, hope you're OK* type messages from Ryan.

I've got a memory key from Leonid's computer, Ethan typed. *I'm gonna load everything up to our FTP site. Maybe you can take a look if you have time? If not, I'll look myself because I'm heading off on Sunday, starting school in Dubai on Monday. Plan is to grab a couple more USB sticks in the bazaar today. Leonid mainly works from a computer out at the stables so I want to know what he's up to out there.*

*

The Facebook, e-mail and MSN accounts for Ryan Brasker and Ethan Kitsell were monitored 24/7 through a CIA office in Dallas. Ryan's BlackBerry bleeped, and within moments he was hurrying down the corridor of his posh Dubai hotel and banging on the door of Amy's room.

'Ethan's back online,' Ryan said excitedly, as Amy opened up dressed in a white hotel robe. She was rubbing her eyes and seemed half asleep. 'He's sent me a long message and he's uploading files from Leonid's computer to the FTP site.'

'Can you log in and talk to him?' Amy asked, as she stepped back to let Ryan in.

'We're screwed on the time difference,' Ryan said. 'It's three p.m. in Bishkek. Ethan thinks I'm in California and it's two in the morning there. It's not credible for me to be online.'

Amy tapped her chin thoughtfully. 'Call Ted Brasker and let him know what's happening. I'll call the Information Management team in Dallas and make sure that the analysts start going through Ethan's upload as soon as they get it.'

'I hope this has been worth Ethan risking his neck,' Ryan said. 'Because I can't help wondering if Leonid Aramov is the kind of guy who stores his darkest secrets on a hard drive . . .'

14. HAPPY

Dubai wasn't the solution to all Ethan's problems, but he wouldn't miss the Kremlin's gloomy strip lighting and tobacco-stained walls, and he liked the idea of putting some physical distance between himself and Uncle Leonid.

Grandma Irena was doing OK for someone who'd been given six months to live more than two years earlier. When Ethan entered her cramped bedroom she was propped on pillows next to a breakfast tray, watching CNN. Her words slurred because she didn't have her top denture in.

'Take a look over there!' Irena said, aiming her wrinkled arm at a space between the wall and a bedside table. 'I don't know of these things, but I'm told it's good.'

Ethan brushed along the wall, being careful not to

knock down picture frames. He beamed as he picked up a top-of-the-line Toshiba laptop, still in its box. Alongside was a plastic bag filled with accessories: mouse, office software, neoprene case and even a stack of the latest pirate games from the bazaar.

'Awesome!' Ethan said.

'Is it a good one?' Irena asked.

Ethan nodded. 'Really good.'

'I'm letting you go to school in Dubai and have a computer because you have a right to live your own life,' Irena said. 'But you *must* be sensible with things you've heard here, and don't contact anyone you knew in the United States.'

'Of course, Grandma.'

'I know you don't feel like one of us,' Irena said. 'But never forget that you're an Aramov.'

Ethan nodded again.

'Do I deserve a hug then?' she asked.

Ethan smiled as he leaned across the bed and hugged his grandmother. Her nightdress smelled of menthol rub and her rings dug into his back, but he enjoyed the moment because it was the first time he'd ever felt an emotional bond with his grandmother.

'You're turning into a good-looking young man,' Irena said, as Ethan moved back around the bed. 'You're so like your mother, in your gestures and your voice.'

The comment made Ethan feel rueful: maybe he wasn't bad-looking, but he hated his gangly body. He almost let the mention of his mother slip by, but he was leaving soon and with Irena in poor health this might be his only chance to learn what she really thought.

'Who do you think killed my mum?' Ethan asked.

'If I knew for sure they'd already be dead,' Irena said.

'Even if it was Uncle Leonid?'

As Ethan said this, Irena shuddered and took a strange kind of double breath. A tense hand crept towards her oxygen mask, but didn't quite make it.

'Who put that idea in your head?' Irena asked harshly.

'Nobody,' Ethan said, as the sudden tension made goosebumps ripple across his back. 'But he's ambitious. Everyone says you asked my mum to come back here because you didn't want Leonid running the clan alone.'

Irena wagged a pointing finger.

'No,' she said resolutely. 'Galenka and Leonid were close. They used to play beautifully together. And Leonid has a few rough edges, but not that! A mother knows her own children and it's just not possible.'

Ethan's stomach suddenly felt horribly light. Even accounting for the fact that parents always want to see the best in their kids, how could anyone describe a raging psycho like Leonid as having *a few rough edges*?

'I suppose I'd better get cracking,' Ethan said. 'Find somewhere to pack this laptop and stuff.'

'Don't forget to call and let me know how you're doing,' Irena said.

'For sure,' Ethan said.

He moved quickly down the hallway and dropped the laptop and bag of accessories inside the door of his room. He glanced at his watch and realised that he had about eighty minutes until his flight to Dubai and one piece of unfinished business.

Placing the memory key in the laptop in Leonid's apartment hadn't been a problem, but Ethan now knew that Leonid spent more time working at the stables than the Kremlin. After checking that he'd put a USB memory stick in his pocket, Ethan took the stairs down to the ground floor, exited the Kremlin through a rear fire door and started a brisk trek along a rugged path.

Ethan hadn't exactly made friends at the stable, but he'd picked up a few lines of Kyrgyz and won favour with some of the younger stable hands by being generous with cigarettes. He got a couple of nods and hellos as he walked through the yard, but nobody cared enough to ask Ethan what he was up to as he entered the little admin shed and knocked on the door of Leonid's metal-doored office.

He wasn't expecting a reply and he didn't get one. Leonid spent his Friday nights at a casino in Bishkek, and never surfaced before noon on a Saturday. Despite the reinforcement, the door was never locked. Ethan had the USB stick out of his pocket and was down on one knee plugging it into the back of Leonid's computer within five seconds of entering the room.

There was always a chance that the key might be discovered, but judging by all the filth and dust behind the computer, even the cleaner hadn't been back there in years.

For the return walk, Ethan unthinkingly took a shortcut that brought him past the open-air weight stack behind the Kremlin. The square had originally been a Soviet Air Force training area. The wire fence now hung down in rusted curls and the basketball courts were covered in huge potholes, but the outdoor weight benches and chin-up bars were still in regular use, not least by Boris and Alex Aramov.

'Get over here,' Alex shouted.

Ethan pretended like he hadn't heard and kept walking.

'Don't make me come over there, little cousin,' Alex warned.

Ethan cursed his luck – knowing he had to turn around and face whatever his two mad cousins planned to dish out.

The scene with benches and massive weights reminded Ethan of a prison movie. Besides Alex and Boris, there was Vlad and half a dozen other seriously pumped teenagers, either bare chested or in muscle vests.

Ethan stopped walking and pointed towards the airfield. 'I've got to go,' he said warily. 'My plane's leaving in a minute.'

'Won't take off without you, will it?' Alex shouted, as he pointed at the ground in front of his trainers. 'Get here, now!'

'Look at this bandy-legged weakling,' Boris said, making all the other lads roar with approval as he loomed over Ethan from behind. 'How can this puny brat share *my* genes?'

'I doubt he's even the same species as me,' Alex said, as he wrapped Ethan in a sweaty headlock and wrenched his neck painfully. 'How much can you bench press, cousin?'

'About three kilos,' one of the hangers-on joked.

Alex dragged Ethan several metres across the concrete towards a chin-up bar.

'If you can do ten chin-ups I'll let you go,' Alex said. 'Otherwise, I'm gonna beat you hard.'

Ethan rubbed his throat as he looked at the bars. A month's manual labour at the stables had built stamina, but Ethan was still weedy and the bodybuilders cracked up as he grabbed the bars and tried pulling himself up.

'Look at his arms shaking!' Boris jeered, as the other bodybuilders laughed. 'He's not even gonna do one.'

Ethan pulled mightily and managed a single chin-up, with the rusted bar grazing his hands. On the way down he lost his grip and dropped off. Alex waded in, knocking Ethan down with a palm in the back, then planting a damp trainer across his chest.

'You look like you're gonna piss your pants,' Alex said, as Boris walked around to stand by Ethan's head.

Ethan expected blows, but instead Boris hacked up a big phlegm ball and gobbed it in his face.

'We could beat you now,' Boris explained, as he slammed a fist into his palm. 'But it's more fun if you know you've got it coming when you get back. Now get out of my face.'

Ethan was determined not to give anyone the satisfaction of seeing him cry as he limped away with Alex, Boris and the other lads laughing and making humiliating comments like *such a weed* and *I want front row tickets when he gets battered!* Ethan had put some of his best gear on for the trip to Dubai, but now he was covered in gravel and he had Boris' snot running down his face.

*

Amy Collins sat at the desk in her hotel room. The three kids – Ryan, Ning and Alfie – were perched on the end of her unmade bed.

'We've got preliminary analysis of the data Ethan uploaded from Leonid Aramov's computer,' Amy began. 'There's nothing spectacular, which is no surprise because the Aramovs haven't stayed in business this long by being careless with their secrets. But Leonid Aramov did use the computer to type letters and notes, and made a couple of small transactions through an online bank.

'Everything on the computer is encrypted, but the spy software caught screenshots and saved copies of many documents in unencrypted form. Hopefully analysis will enable us to pick up some encryption keys for the rest.'

'Keys are always good,' Alfie said. 'If he's like most of us, Leonid uses the same encryption for everything he does.'

'What type of letters were they?' Ryan asked.

'There's about two hundred scraped off the computer's hard drive, dating back to when the computer was first installed five years ago,' Amy said. 'Information Management are still working through all the data. There's some info on the Aramov Clan's secret bank accounts and names of previously unknown Aramov associates who can be investigated further.'

'Is there anything I can tell Ethan next time I talk to him?' Ryan asked.

'Stall him for now,' Amy said. 'Say you've only glanced at the data because you have a lot of homework. Ethan's about to start a new school, so he'll hopefully have other things to focus his mind on over the next few days.'

The mention of Ethan made Ning and Alfie glance towards each other, exchanging nervous smiles.

'So are today's plans finalised?' Alfie asked.

'Looks like it,' Amy said. 'Civilian aircraft have to file flight plans at least three hours before take-off. A Kyrgyz-registered plane flying under the Aramov's *Clanair* banner put in a flight plan from the Kremlin to the Emirate of Sharjah.'

'So Ethan's not flying into Dubai?' Alfie asked.

Amy shook her head. 'Dubai has a world-class international airport, with all the costs and security implications that go with it. Sharjah Airport is less than twenty kilometres down the road. It's mainly a cargo terminal, but it's also the base for a lot of tiny seat-of-the-pants airlines who fly to less glamorous spots, such as Congo, Afghanistan and Central Asia. The Aramovs are on *very* friendly terms with the authorities at Sharjah and their planes fly in and out regularly with minimal interference.

'As soon as the Aramov flight plan was filed, I filed one of my own for a small plane from Egypt. I've told DESA school that Alfie is arriving on this plane, and they'll be sending a bus to pick you up. As the planes land within ten minutes of each other, it's a near certainty that Alfie will get to ride on the school bus with Ethan.'

There was a friendly rivalry between Alfie and Ning over who could make friends with Ethan first and Alfie couldn't resist poking his tongue out at Ning.

'I'll make sure my chess set is poking out of my backpack,' Alfie said. 'We'll be best buds before we ride through the school gate.'

Ryan laughed. 'Just don't actually try playing Ethan at chess. You're still shite and he'll wipe you out in less than ten moves.'

'So that's where we're at right now,' Amy said, as she looked at Ning and rubbed her hands together. 'First mission, eh? I bet you're dead excited.'

Ning nodded. 'Kind of, but also worried that I'll screw it up!'

*

Alex and Boris made so many threats that Ethan hoped they'd have forgotten by the time he got back from Dubai, but he still had a shaky feeling as he took a quick shower and put on fresh clothes.

Andre entered as Ethan was lacing his Nike. He wheeled Ethan's biggest case towards the lift, while Ethan himself dealt with two smaller bags and his new laptop.

'You'll let me know what it's like, won't you?' Andre said eagerly, as the rattly lift took them down to the ground floor. 'I think I'd like to go to boarding school, but I'd have to ask my dad . . .'

'It might be tough for you,' Ethan said. 'I'm not saying

you're stupid or anything, but your English isn't fantastic and you'd probably be behind the other kids because US11 isn't *exactly* an elite school.'

'My dad wouldn't have it anyway,' Andre said sadly. 'I wish my life wasn't so boring.'

There was a porter from the airfield waiting in the lobby. He glanced at his watch to indicate that Ethan was late, but even the youngest members of the Aramov family commanded respect around the Kremlin, so he didn't complain.

The porter loaded the luggage into the back of a tiny truck which had originally been designed for loading bombs. Andre came along for the ride as they clattered away from the Kremlin, shuddering over gravel until reaching a much smoother taxiway at the edge of the airfield.

They had to hang back while a big Ilyushin cargo plane blasted off, then they drove through a haze of jet fumes and along the main runway towards a little Yak 40 jet.

In standard configuration the Yak could seat twenty-two, but after a quick high five and a goodbye to Cousin Andre, Ethan walked up ten steps into a cabin with just seven large armchairs and a bar fitted with crystal decanters.

The plane had been built in Russia in the early 1970s, as VIP transport for the Soviet communist party. The aircraft's yellowed interior panels and noisy air vents gave its vintage away, but the carpets seemed new and the smart leather chairs had DVD players in the armrests, along with iPod sockets and noise-cancelling headphones.

The cockpit door was open and Ethan leaned in to look at a short grey-haired pilot running through pre-flight checks with his much younger assistant.

'Just so you know I'm on board,' Ethan said warmly, as he gave a little wave. 'What's our flying time to Sharjah?'

The co-pilot tapped one of the charts on his clipboard. 'We're looking at the weather patterns. I'll let you know when I've worked it out.'

'Are we expecting any other passengers?' Ethan asked.

'Looks like he's arriving now,' the co-pilot said.

Ethan looked out the front of the cockpit and gulped as he saw Leonid Aramov lifting a small case out the back of his Mercedes.

15. DIVERSION

Alfie sat in the meet and greet area in Sharjah International Airport, with a half-drunk Coke bottle in hand and his baggage sprawled in front of him. He'd been through plenty of airports, but this was the first one where the departure board offered flights to Chebalynsk, Krasnodar, Turbat, Dushanbe and a whole bunch of other places he'd never heard of.

After waiting around for more than two hours the haggard DESA Chemistry teacher who'd been sent to pick Alfie and Ethan up had gone off, hoping to find an airport official who might know why Ethan's flight hadn't arrived.

As soon as the teacher was out of sight, Alfie pulled his iPhone and called Amy.

'Where the hell is he?' Alfie asked. 'Ethan should have been here at least two hours ago.'

Amy sounded flustered. 'We tracked the flight transponder. The aircraft left the Kremlin on time. It stuck to the filed flight plan for forty-five minutes before deviating.'

'Deviating?' Alfie asked, sounding frustrated as he glanced back to make sure that the teacher was still out of sight.

'Changing course,' Amy explained. 'It moved briefly into an air corridor used by the Russian military, then the transponder got switched off.'

'What, it disappeared from radar?'

'Not radar,' Amy explained. 'Civilian aircraft have transponders that transmit an identity signal. It makes it easy for air traffic control and other pilots to know exactly where they are. You can even download apps to track civilian aircraft movements on your mobile. I've called my head office in Dallas and they're trying to work out what has happened.'

'Could the plane have crashed?' Alfie asked. 'Or made an emergency landing?'

'That's not impossible,' Amy said. 'But we know that the Aramovs have powerful connections inside the Russian Air Force and we suspect that the aircraft deliberately diverted into Russian military airspace. I've asked the United States Air Force to try and find out where the plane went using their radar or satellite logs, but the bottom line is, Ethan Aramov won't be arriving in Sharjah any time soon.'

'So where does that leave me?' Alfie asked.

'It's possible the plane could be dropping cargo at a

Russian airport and will turn up in Sharjah a few hours late,' Amy said. 'Right now, you just have to sit and wait. Ning's already at DESA and I expect your teacher will get fed up of waiting for Ethan's flight and take you back to the school on your own.'

'This mission better not be a bust,' Alfie said. 'After I spent so many hours reading about chess.'

*

Leonid had smacked Ethan out of his seat as soon as the little jet took off from the Kremlin. He'd then stripped out his pockets, snatched his watch and left him on the floor with a swollen eye, a squash ball rammed in his mouth and no explanation.

Ethan reckoned they'd flown for about three hours as he clanked down aircraft steps with his mouth still taped and Leonid wrenching his arm behind his back. The windswept landing strip had nothing but a long-dead radar dish, a hut with the door missing and a gravel road that vanished over the horizon. A second Aramov-owned Yak 40 jet stood a couple of hundred metres away, its fuselage stained with dirt and hastily repaired bullet holes.

When they reached the bottom step, Leonid let Ethan go and the thirteen-year-old immediately pulled down the front of his jeans and boxers and moaned with relief as he started pissing in the reddish dirt.

'Should have told me if you wanted to pee,' Leonid said, as he smirked at Ethan's discomfort.

There was a man striding across the dirt from another plane. He was very large, and black-skinned in the truest sense. He wore a shabby pale blue suit and gold sunglasses.

'This your sister's boy?' he asked, shouting over the sound of idling jet engines as he shook hands with Leonid. The tone and body language indicated that the two men were close.

'Good to see you again, Kessie,' Leonid said, speaking poor English as they bumped fists. 'Are my instructions clear?'

'Clear as a bell,' Kessie said, as Ethan looked around at nothing but dirt and a couple of knobbly hills. 'I look after the boy and make sure he says the right things if his grandmother calls to ask about his school.'

'And keep him out of sight,' Leonid added. 'My mother's been in this game a long time. She has eyes and ears all over. If she finds out too soon, we're both dead men.'

'How long do you reckon?' Kessie asked.

'It'll take a while to get control of all my mother's financial assets,' Leonid said. 'The boy might make a useful bargaining chip if things go wrong, but once all the Aramov bank accounts are under my control . . .'

Leonid ended the sentence by sweeping his hand across his own throat and making a gurgling sound.

'You want a video?' Kessie asked.

Leonid looked at Ethan and smiled. 'Not that I don't trust you, but videos can be faked.'

'Lower jaw?' Kessie suggested.

Leonid nodded. 'Yeah, hack off his lower jaw and send it to Kuban at the Sharjah office. I'll wire the other half of your money as soon as we receive it.'

Ethan had been scared before, but never like this, trapped in the middle of nowhere with two guys talking about his corpse as if his death was just a formality.

'Always a pleasure doing business,' Kessie said as he grabbed Ethan by the back of his neck. 'You're not gonna give me trouble, are you, boy?'

Ethan couldn't speak with the squash ball wedging his tongue to the bottom his mouth, but he was shaking with fear and had tears welling in his eyes. Leonid gave a little salute as he started walking backwards towards his plane.

'Nice knowing you, nephew,' Leonid said. 'And when you get to heaven, tell your ma to go screw herself.'

*

As an employee of American intelligence, Amy had access to the world's best radar and satellite networks. But there was no single resource she could use to track the path of an aircraft.

While Alfie and Ning spent a first uncertain night at DESA just in case Ethan turned up, Amy and Ryan sat up studying a US Air Force radar plot of everything that had moved over Central Asia that day.

There were too many aircraft movements for it to be of any use, but an hour later an updated version came through with the tracks of planes with registered flight plans removed. After paying the hotel's night manager two nights' wages to have a printer brought up to her room, Amy printed a hard copy and Ryan highlighted a couple of dozen flight paths.

Amy overlaid the flight paths with coordinates of known airfields and sent in a request for the most up-to-date satellite images. It took less than fifteen minutes for two dozen high-resolution images to come through. Some airfields had cloud cover, some had no images at all because the spy satellite scheduled to fly over that afternoon had malfunctioned, but the odds worked in their favour.

'Here,' Ryan said, scrambling across Amy's crumpled bed and shoving a colour printout between her face and the laptop.

The image was hazy, but unmistakably showed the outlines of two Yak 40 jets parked a few hundred metres apart.

'It's a remote region of southern Russia. The nearest city is called Klsvodsk,' Ryan explained. 'The photo was taken late afternoon, which fits in perfectly with the time that the transponder dropped off Ethan's plane.'

Amy nodded. 'Has to be. You can even see a smudge of the Clanair livery on the tail. I can't see any refuelling gear or even a car in the photograph, so I'd guess that these planes just landed, switched cargo or passengers and then took off again.'

'Exactly,' Ryan said. 'How often is the area imaged?'

'Since it's Russia and close to the border with Georgia, we're probably in luck.'

The frequency with which US spy satellites photograph an area depends on how politically sensitive it is. And since Russia had invaded Georgia in 2008, Amy was able to download high-resolution images of the airstrip taken at ninety-second interludes.

The hotel Internet connection wasn't the fastest, but Amy had over twenty images which she could click through on her laptop like a flip book.

It seemed that the plane had landed and waited for twelve minutes for the second Yak to arrive. The resolution from the satellite pictures wasn't high enough to identify faces, but the sequence showed two smudges coming out of one plane, meeting a smudge from another plane, and then two smudges getting on the plane that landed first.

'I'd bet my right boob that that's Ethan being transferred to the other plane,' Amy said.

'One of Leonid Aramov's goons must have kidnapped him,' Ryan said, shaking his head sadly.

'But why transfer him to another plane?' Amy asked. 'Why not just kill him?'

'Good question,' Ryan said. 'Maybe we'll get the answer when we see where the two planes flew next.'

It only took a few moments to look at the radar traces and see that the plane that had taken Ethan from the Kremlin made a short-hop flight to another Russian airfield, then turned on a transponder identifying the aircraft as a different call sign and flew to a resort town near the Black Sea.

'Leonid Aramov has been known to gamble there,' Amy said.

'So you think it might be Leonid who boarded the plane with Ethan?' Ryan asked.

Amy shrugged. 'Maybe. If the CIA has an agent

in that area I can get them to try and find out if Leonid's around.'

'OK, let's try and track the other plane.'

Amy quickly found that an Aramov-owned Yak 40 had left Bulgaria early that morning. Ryan traced the aircraft registration and found a couple of photographs on the CIA database.

'It says it's a long-range variant,' Ryan said, as he showed Amy the photos on his laptop. 'See the bulge under the fuselage? That's extra fuel tanks.'

'Pity,' Amy said. 'It widens the area to which Ethan could have flown. And I think the pilot diddled us in the mountains.'

'You can't find it?'

Amy shook her head. 'It's mountainous between Georgia and Russia. I can track the plane south from the airfield, but once it gets into the mountains it vanishes. If it flew low enough, radar won't have picked it up and there'll be nothing in the radar logs.'

'Shit,' Ryan said as Amy zoomed out the map on her laptop screen and drew a big circle with her fingertips.

'As the Yak has the extra fuel tanks, Ethan might end up anywhere from Siberia in the north, to central Africa in the south. Europe's within reach but unlikely, or he might even have flown back towards Kyrgyzstan.'

'Is there anything we can do?' Ryan asked.

'The CIA has analysts who specialise in tracking the paths of aircraft, but it's not an exact science. I once asked them to try tracking a couple of Aramov drug-smuggling flights. It took them days to analyse the data and all they came back with was a range of twenty possible destinations.'

Ryan slumped backwards on to the edge of Amy's bed and kicked out at a floor lamp. 'We've lost Ethan,' he spluttered. 'And if Leonid kills him this is all *our* fault. We never should have let Irena's people get hold of him after his mum was murdered.'

16. FUEL

Irena Aramov built her smuggling operation by buying ex-Soviet Air Force planes on the cheap. But maintaining these old birds could be expensive and she'd shrewdly calculated that it was more profitable to skimp on maintenance, forge airworthiness documents and suffer an occasional crash than to pay top dollar for spare parts and maintenance.

Even by Aramov standards, Ethan found himself flying in a piece of junk. While the bullet holes on the outside had been patched, the interior of the small jet looked like someone had used it to film the final sequence of an action movie, with the trim shredded and bloody fingermarks on the interior panels.

A dozen seats had been ripped out to create a cargo bay. There were boxes of junk and cartridge shells that clattered about every time the plane shuddered and to make Ethan's in-flight experience absolutely perfect, he'd been handcuffed to a seat that stank of urine and whose broken plastic frame jarred his lower back.

After three hours in the air the jet made a rapid descent and a night landing at a tarmac strip lit by a ground crew holding phosphorous flares. Kessie stepped out and began a noisy conversation with men Ethan couldn't see, while a refuelling crew attached a hose under the wing.

The air blowing through the open cabin door was tropical hot and men began running up and down the steps bringing on overstuffed sports bags and big plastic tubs marked as *bovine antibiotics*, but which Ethan suspected contained something far less legal.

After this came a more gruesome cargo – and an explanation for the blood smeared over the plane's interior. First came a clear sack filled with curved Ibex horns, then uncured grey pelts from a wolf-like creature, followed by unmistakable spotted skins peeled from cheetahs. Lastly, a fresh lion pelt with gory head attached came aboard.

Even though the goods were loaded, Kessie was still out on the dirt strip, engaged in bitter haggling with a posse of men and doling out bricks of some obscure currency.

'Onwards!' Kessie told the two-man crew. He looked pleased with himself as he pulled up the door.

Each pelt was loosely wrapped in clear plastic, but the air in the small plane now had a strong gamey smell and dozens of flies whizzed about. With his hands cuffed to the armrest, Ethan had no way to flick off the bugs crawling over his neck and a huge metallic-green blowfly that was determined to drink from the corner of his eye.

Kessie found Ethan's discomfort amusing, but as the plane accelerated for take-off he whipped a can of fly-spray from the pouch in front of his seat and gave it a blast.

'You know you're in Africa when you've got flies on your face,' Kessie said, as he cracked one of his enormous white-toothed smiles.

*

They landed again after another two hours in the air and parked on an uneven strip with Kalashnikov-toting guards surrounding the plane. From what Ethan overheard, there was some kind of civil war in the area and it was better to make the last leg of the journey in daylight when the Aramov plane wouldn't be mistaken for an enemy fighter.

Ethan wondered how deep into Africa he'd travelled. Breathing was hard with the strong smell and the squash ball wedged in his mouth and he was too scared to sleep. He tried to work out where he was, but while he knew the names of most African countries he had no clue how they all fitted together on a map.

The final leg of the journey began at sunrise and lasted less than an hour. As the jet dropped below morning cloud, Ethan stared out the window at a medium-sized town with lines of copper-roofed houses radiating out of the town centre on dirt roads.

This built-up area thinned out as they made their

final approach towards a tarmac strip with proper runway lights and neat yellow markings.

The airstrip was surrounded by metal-fenced enclosures containing different species, from mundane herds of deer-like animals to more exotic beasts such as rhinos, zebras and giraffes. Besides a selection of corrugated metal barns there was a colonial-style ranch house which bristled with aerials and satellite dishes.

'How do you like my ranch?' Kessie said proudly, as he leaned across the aisle and ripped the tape from Ethan's mouth.

Ethan immediately began coughing. He'd not drunk since Leonid wedged in the squash ball more than twelve hours earlier and as Kessie helped Ethan spit it out his tongue felt like a scouring pad scratching bone-dry cheeks.

'This is mine, as far as you can see,' Kessie explained. 'You'll just be another animal in a cage.'

Ethan erupted into a coughing fit while the plane touched down, with only the tiniest jolt as wheels touched tarmac. As soon as the aircraft steps were down, Kessie stood in the doorway shouting orders to a group of young men and women who'd sprinted after the plane as it taxied.

A lad of about seventeen came aboard and undid Ethan's cuffs. His shirt was unbuttoned, exposing a powerful torso, and he wore grubby tracksuit bottoms and rubber boots with a thick coating of muck.

Ethan's thirst was desperate and he risked upsetting this new guard by swiping a half-drunk Evian bottle left on Kessie's seat.

The youth gave Ethan a hurry-up shove, but let him gulp the water. The air was nowhere near as hot as it had been at their night-time refuelling spot and as the grassland on which Kessie's animals were grazing seemed quite lush, Ethan reckoned he'd crossed the equator and had reached southern Africa.

None of Ethan's luggage had made it and the youth walked him briskly over dry paths between farm buildings. The morning air swarmed with flies, attracted by the powerful aroma of dung.

'You stay here, you stay quiet,' the youth said, speaking in stilted English as he slid a bolt across the door of a tin-roofed shed built with lines of uneven breeze blocks.

The inside was divided into six empty cages. Heavy bars and the empty gun rack near the entrance suggested that these pens had been built to hold something a lot more vicious than a skinny thirteen-year-old.

The youth slid a barred door and told Ethan to get inside. The empty enclosures had been well hosed and there was a smell of a lemony disinfectant, but there were still crusts of dried manure in the corners and in the open drainage channel that ran along one edge.

There was a big bucket to serve either as a toilet or a seat if you turned it upside down, a yellowed mattress on the floor and some cushions.

'My name's Michael,' the youth said. 'I don't want to be a bad guy, but the boss has told me to beat you if you cause trouble. I'll get you a cup and a toothbrush. One of the girls from the kitchen will bring your food. OK?'

'Fantastic,' Ethan said sarcastically, as he looked around and saw that the only light came through cracks in the tin roof and a tiny slot window just above his eye level. 'So what is this place anyway? I mean, those aren't farm animals out there.'

Michael shook his head as he backed out of the cage. 'I'm not supposed to talk to you,' he said. 'Kessie will peel my skin off if I do.'

*

Ning felt weird as she ate breakfast. It was a Sunday and DESA's new term didn't start until tomorrow. So while most pupils wouldn't even arrive until the evening, Ning was already thinking about her exit strategy.

There was no point being at DESA if Ethan wasn't coming, but Ning knew CHERUB would make her stick around for a week or two, just so that the school didn't get suspicious about three newly arrived pupils who either didn't arrive or immediately disappeared.

As she ate rubbery scrambled eggs and tried to decide if she liked the Halal beef bacon, Ning hoped Amy would ask her to get expelled and let her be creative about how she did it: setting off the fire alarms, flooding the bathrooms, booting a basketball at a teacher's head.

'What's on your mind?' Alfie asked, as he sat down across the table dressed in jeans and a Lacoste polo shirt. His hair was slicked back and he had a pair of wraparound sunglasses balanced on top of his head.

'I was thinking that we could get kicked out if we climbed the big tree out front and egged the headmaster,' Ning said.

'Nice,' Alfie said. 'Why are you in uniform?'

Ning shrugged. 'I didn't realise. I thought we had to wear it all the time.'

'Have you spoken to Amy?' Alfie asked, as he stuffed an entire hash brown in his mouth.

Ning shook her head.

'Hot!' Alfie spluttered, as he spat a mound of greasy potato flakes back on to his plate. 'MFFF!'

'Gross,' Ning said, turning away as Alfie gulped orange juice to cool his mouth. 'You looked cool with the trendy shirt and sunglasses, but the food gobbing kind of spoiled it.'

'I'm dressed for golf,' Alfie explained. 'Met a couple of guys last night and they invited me for a round at eleven.'

'I've never heard of golf at school,' Ning said, smiling. 'Can you play?'

'Badly,' Alfie said. 'But Ethan's not here, so what else am I gonna do all day?'

'When you've finished pigging yourself we should go back to my room—'

Alfie interrupted and put on his thickest French accent. 'And make wild passionate love!'

'Double gross!' Ning said. 'And shut up. I'm *trying* to be serious.'

Ning looked around to make sure nobody else was nearby before continuing. 'We need to call Amy and see what's happening.'

Ning's room was a couple of minutes' walk from the dining-hall. Despite being modelled on a traditional

English boarding school, with big oak doors and gabled windows, DESA's buildings were only three years old. The corridors felt sterile and hummed with air-conditioning units fighting off the blazing heat outside.

'Mine looks out over the playing fields,' Alfie said, as he stepped inside and looked at Ning's room, and her half-unpacked stuff sprawled over the desk and bed.

Ning pushed her door closed, called Amy and put her iPhone on speaker so that Alfie could hear. She sat on the edge of her bed, and Alfie wheeled the chair over from the desk to be close.

'So we're stuck here for a bit,' Ning said, after all the boring hello stuff was out of the way. 'What happens now?'

'I'm trying to work on a strategy with Ted Brasker,' Amy said. 'It's not just that we've lost Ethan, he was also our best window into Aramov Clan operations.'

'And if Leonid's got Ethan, or had him killed, he must be about to make a move against Irena,' Alfie said.

'For sure,' Amy said.

'This may sound crazy, but what about Dan?' Ning asked.

'Who's he?' Alfie asked.

Amy knew the story because she'd debriefed Ning when she'd first arrived on CHERUB campus, but Ning told a short version for Alfie's benefit.

'Leonid Aramov and his goons kidnapped me and my stepmum. He tortured us both. Killed my stepmum once he'd forced her to transfer several million dollars out of her bank accounts, but by that time I'd managed to escape with Dan's help.'

'So Dan works for Aramov?' Alfie asked.

Ning nodded. 'He's only sixteen – seventeen now I guess. He works for the clan because it's the only work he can get. But he hates it and he risked his life to save me.'

'Interesting thought,' Amy said. 'We've been concentrating so much on Ethan that I'd not even considered trying to use another source inside the Kremlin.'

'I was holed up in Dan's apartment for a couple of weeks,' Ning said. 'I did have his mobile number and I called from the Czech Republic to tell him I was safe. But when I tried from Britain a few weeks later his number was dead.'

'Mmm,' Amy said, before a pause. 'If Dan does Leonid Aramov's dirty work, he probably has to change his mobile phone regularly to stop it being tracked. What about his address?'

'I don't know the exact address, but if you let me play with Google satellite maps for a while I'm sure I could narrow it down.'

'I'll have to speak to Ted Brasker and my boss, Dr D,' Amy said. 'But we urgently need to know what's going on inside the Kremlin, so we should definitely look into your idea.'

17. PERSUASION

Ethan's cage was only lit by a couple of shafts of moonlight. As soon as it got dark the stone floor of his cell came alive with cockroaches, and once in a while he jolted at the sound of something bigger – either a rat or some weird African equivalent that he'd never heard of.

The slim girl who brought Ethan plates of rice, spiced meat and fried banana was no older than fourteen. She spoke no English, but her smile was kind and when he'd quickly drunk the water in his jug she'd immediately gone to the tap to refill it.

In his desperate state, this small act of kindness had brought tears to Ethan's eyes. When he heard the door of the cage block open in the middle of the night he thought that the girl had come to check on him again, but when Ethan rolled on his mattress he saw a much larger body moving in the shadows.

'Not sleeping tonight?' Kessie said, laughing loudly.

He held a two-litre plastic beer bottle, and was absurdly dressed in wellington boots, striped pyjama bottoms and a Hawaiian shirt.

'I'll kill you quickly when the time comes,' Kessie said. 'As long as you're a good boy.'

Ethan couldn't see the point in being cowardly when it looked like he was going to die no matter what. 'What's your deal with Leonid?' he asked.

Kessie slugged from his big bottle before speaking. 'I was a poor boy. Came up from dirt! This place was nothing. I built it with my own hands and Leonid's planes move everything in and out.'

'So what happens here?' Ethan asked. 'I mean, they're not farm animals.'

'You want an animal, Kessie will get it for you. Dead, alive, stuffed or skinned. Ivory, leather, even powdered rhino horns for randy Chinamen! And then there are the game reserves. Rich men are too lazy to go into the bush and spend three or four days hunting an animal, so we breed in captivity and sell them to game parks. They stuff the parks so full of "wild" animals that even the fattest American ends up with a trophy to hang on his wall.'

'Sounds like you've got a good business,' Ethan said. 'And I suppose selling the animals to game parks makes the smuggling side look more legitimate.'

Kessie smiled. 'You're a smart boy, Ethan!'

'Leonid's not so smart,' Ethan said. 'People fear him, but my grandma's got more brains in her big toe. And she may be a sick old lady, but when she finds out she'll hammer you.'

'This has been planned carefully over months,' Kessie said, waving his arm dismissively.

'Give me a phone,' Ethan said boldly. 'I'll speak to my grandma. We'll give you double whatever Leonid's paying you to keep me down here. And my Grandma's gonna know by now, because I didn't turn up at the school.'

Kessie found this extremely funny. 'Leonid has the educational consultant in his pocket. The school will be told that you are sick and that you will not arrive for two to three weeks. Your grandmother will be told that newly arrived pupils are discouraged from contacting their families while they settle into a new school. So unfortunately, Ethan, nobody at the Kremlin will miss you until it's too late.'

Ethan was disheartened, but tried to keep it out of his voice. 'You should think about what you're doing. You've still got a chance to save yourself.'

Kessie found this so funny that he had to clutch his shaking belly. 'Oh, I will *torture* myself with worry,' he laughed. 'I will have *nightmares*. Here, have the rest of my beer. You deserve it for giving me a laugh!'

Kessie had to squash the plastic bottle to get it between the bars. When he threw it into the cage, it hit the concrete floor and the gassy beer foamed out over the floor.

'Sweet dreams, Ethan Aramov!' Kessie said, as he swaggered out of the shed. 'Sweet dreams!'

*

After his drunken chat with Kessie on the first night in the cage, Ethan's next four days were dominated by boredom and a dodgy stomach. His only visitor had been the girl who brought his food and water, and when Michael entered the cage block in the afternoon of his fourth day, Ethan backed up, fearing that Leonid had finally sent down the order to have him executed.

Oddly the prospect didn't scare him, because after days of hopelessness, dying just seemed like being put out of his misery.

'Your friend from the kitchen is right,' Michael said, masking his face with the top of his T-shirt as a much smaller lad took one step inside before rushing out.

Ethan looked baffled. 'What's the matter?'

'You stink this place up,' Michael said accusingly. 'Girl in the kitchen is refusing to bring your food down. Two-tonne hippos make less stink than you!'

Ethan spoke angrily. 'What do you expect? No clean clothes. No way to wash or clean out my bucket and the food hasn't been agreeing with me.'

'Back way up,' Michael said, as he unlocked the cell. 'You carry the bucket. I'm not touching your filth.'

Ethan quickly pushed his grubby socks into trainers and picked up his shit-and-puke-splattered bucket as Michael slid the barred gate. He'd kept little food down over the last couple of days and felt shaky as he walked out of the cage.

A greater shock came when he stepped into bright sunlight. After four days in twilight his eyes burned and he wrapped an arm over his face.

Michael gave the younger boy orders. 'Hose everything out with bleach, then go back to the house and get the stuff.' Then he looked at Ethan. 'Keep your distance.'

Ethan didn't see much for the first couple of hundred metres. But when his eyes began coping with the light, he found himself walking towards a fast-flowing river roughly ten metres wide. On the opposite bank a dozen men worked around huge open casks filled with chemicals, while fully cured animal hides and fur pelts were drying on wooden frames.

In contrast to Kessie's neat animal pens and modern farm buildings, the river was a dark brown mass, with debris from soggy newspaper to plastic pots clumped around the riverbank and chemical foam bubbling on the surface.

Ethan's destination was an open-air shower block, adjacent to a dormitory used by some of Kessie's workers. The showers were built over the riverbank, so the water drained through gaps between the slippery plastic sheeting that formed the shower floor.

'Wash good,' Michael ordered, as he pointed out grubby soap slivers on a wooden shelf. 'Scrub your clothes and clean out your bucket in the river.'

The process was awkward, with no towel and limited privacy. Ethan decided the best thing was to rinse the bucket out first. But as soon as he moved it towards the shower Michael turned angry.

'Are you stupid?' he shouted. 'You don't tip that

out in our shower! Take it down the bank and empty it in the river.'

Still feeling shaky, Ethan stepped over uneven rocks as he crept down towards the churning water. The current almost knocked him down when he dunked the bucket in the water.

Michael was extremely irritated and shouted, 'If you fall I'm not coming after you!'

But Kessie had ordered Michael to look after Ethan, so despite his harsh words Michael scrambled over the rocks and snatched the bucket.

'Get up there and shower,' he ordered, giving Ethan a gentle rap over the back of the head.

Ethan stripped and threw his clothes in a pile at his feet before pulling a cord to start the shower. The shower was fed with water from a rooftop tank, and warmed only by sunlight. With tepid water the grubby bar of soap didn't lather, but the shower was still the first thing in days that made Ethan feel like a human, instead of a caged animal.

By the time he'd lathered up his hair and let the foam run down his body, Michael had come back up the rocks with the rinsed-out bucket, but instead of looking at Ethan, Michael's eyes fixed on an attractive girl in her mid-teens.

As Michael spoke to the girl, Ethan began washing out his clothes. He couldn't understand their language, but Michael's smile and open stance, and the girl's hand on hip and over-the-top laugh, was obviously the body language of two people who fancied each other.

They were so into each other that Ethan looked about. Could he run away from the riverbank, cut between the two dormitories? Hop into his trousers and maybe find a bike or a car?

Ethan's escape plan was short-lived because one of the farm workers had come out of the dorm with a towel over his shoulder. He shouted something to Michael as he threw his towel over a hook.

Ethan was paranoid and assumed it was a warning about him looking around for an escape route, but it was the girl who looked upset and began hurrying away.

A brief conversation ensued in which the only word Ethan grasped was *Kessie*. The girl had been quite well dressed, and by the end of the conversation, Ethan was fairly sure that the girl was Kessie's daughter and Michael was being told to stay away from her.

'I've wasted enough time with you,' Michael said, scowling as he grabbed Ethan's soggy jeans off the plastic shower floor. 'Put these on and grab the bucket.'

Back at the cage block, Ethan found that the younger boy had not only swept out his filthy cage, but rather than moving him back into the cage with the wet floor, he'd moved Ethan's mattress into a different one.

The light in this cage was slightly better and a length of hose had been rigged up so that he could get water whenever he liked. There were also a couple of new personal items, including the toothbrush he'd been promised since he first arrived, soap, a towel and two pairs of badly frayed but freshly laundered undershorts.

'Now you've got no excuse to stink,' Michael said, still

moody after his telling-off at the shower block. 'You're lucky I'm not beating you.'

Ethan looked at the younger lad. 'I couldn't help getting sick.'

But the boy didn't understand and moments later Ethan was plunged back into semi-darkness. He felt feverish as he sat on the mattress, preparing to peel off his wringing wet jeans and hang them over the bars to dry properly. Apparently he had a few more days to live, because surely they wouldn't have bothered taking him for a shower if he was about to get a bullet through the head.

18. CHANCES

Amy and Ning could have hopped on a plane and reached Bishkek within a few hours of having the idea to find Dan, but there was a big difference between a routine *make-friends-with-Ethan-at-a-boarding-school* mission and the much more dangerous prospect of working undercover in Kyrgyzstan, where the Aramov Clan owned enough cops, soldiers and politicians to operate beyond the law.

Amy had taken Ning's idea to Dr D – her boss at the Dallas-based Transnational Facilitator Unit – and Zara Asker, the chairwoman of CHERUB. While Alfie stayed at DESA to cover the increasingly remote possibility that Ethan would eventually turn up there, Amy, Ning and Ryan flew back to London.

Over two exhausting days, Amy, Dr D and Ted Brasker from TFU, plus CHERUB's chief mission controller Ewart Asker, worked from CHERUB campus hammering out a plan for a two-pronged mission that would maximise their chances of finding Ethan and getting information on what Leonid was up to inside the Kremlin.

When they weren't involved with the planning side of things, Ryan and Ning worked with a CIA expert on Central Asia, learning about Kyrgyz culture, customs and language. Ryan's father had been Russian so he was fluent in a language spoken by more than half of the population in Bishkek, but Ning would have to get by with English and Mandarin.

There were only two direct flights a week from Britain to Kyrgyzstan, so the five-strong team had to fly to St Petersburg and spend a night in an airport hotel there before taking an early morning flight to Bishkek's Manas International Airport.

Amy had a long and successful career as a CHERUB agent behind her, but her experience of running undercover operations was limited, so the big Texan Ted Brasker would be in overall charge of the operation.

Ning and Amy would form one unit. Their task was to locate Dan, get as much information as they could out of him, and then try to recruit him as a spy. The second team, comprising Ryan and Instructor Kazakov, would try making a more direct approach to the Kremlin.

The Mission Control and Training departments at CHERUB were completely separate, but this particular mission had been put together at short notice and although Kazakov was a training instructor not a mission controller, his background in Soviet Special Forces meant he was better suited to the operation than any of the available mission controllers.

To avoid being seen arriving together, Ted, Amy and Ning flew up front in business class, while Ryan and Kazakov slummed it in the cheap seats. Kyrgyzstan didn't have a major tourist industry and Bishkek's only big international-class hotel was closely watched by everyone from the Kyrgyz Secret Service to traffic cops hoping to shake down tourists, so a CIA liaison at the American embassy had arranged more discreet accommodation.

Amy picked up a hire car and drove to a small hostel with Ning, while Ted, Ryan and Kazakov travelled by taxi to a rented house. It was two storeys, with grubby carpets and a whiff of damp, but its location was ideal, close to the road up to the Kremlin, and like the homes of most wealthy people in Bishkek the house was enclosed by a high security wall that gave them excellent privacy.

The local CIA liaison had also got hold of two inconspicuous Toyota Corollas. Upon arrival, Ted removed large backpacks containing advanced bugging and surveillance gear from one of the trunks.

'Nice equipment,' Kazakov said, as he watched Ted unzipping bags filled with all the latest gadgets. 'I hope your friend at the embassy was discreet when he set this place up.'

'I don't know the liaison and I'm not going to meet *her* unless something goes drastically wrong,' Ted said, as he held one of the latest ultra-light stab vests up to the light. It was Ryan's size, so he threw it his way. 'All I know is, she's done everything we asked her to do on very late notice.'

'True,' Kazakov said grudgingly. 'But the Aramovs have eyes everywhere and you yanks aren't known for your delicate touch in situations like this.'

Ted bristled, but Zara had warned him that Kazakov resented Americans because his brother had been killed by a US-supplied missile when he was fighting in Afghanistan.

'So what's the plan for today?' Ryan asked.

'There's nothing sophisticated about this,' Kazakov said. 'We wait until it gets dark, drive up to the Kremlin and see if we can get inside for a nose around. In the meantime, you might as well get some rest.'

Ryan arched his back and reached his arms up in a big stretch. 'All I've done for twenty-four hours is sit around in planes, hotels and airport lounges. The last thing I need is rest. I feel like a run, or a sparring session or something.'

Kazakov laughed. 'You can run around the garden, but I don't want you going outside the gates until we've got a better idea what's out there. But I'll spar with you if you like.'

As the last words came out, Kazakov charged forward. Ryan squealed and vaulted the couch but Kazakov got an arm around his waist. Ryan tried to spin out and hit Kazakov with a high kick, but the grey-haired Ukrainian knew that move was coming.

Kazakov neatly snatched Ryan's flying ankle and twisted it. Ryan's other leg buckled and he ended up with his back pinned to stained carpet and his ankles trapped painfully beneath his buttocks.

Kazakov smiled. 'You've lost sharpness since basic training. I might have to remedy that when we get back to campus.'

But to show he wasn't serious, Kazakov gave the tip of Ryan's nose a playful flick before letting him up.

As Ryan found his feet, he saw that Ted was killing himself laughing.

'What's so funny?' Ryan asked, as he pulled up his trousers.

'You,' Ted said. 'The *EEEEK* noise you made when Kazakov lunged at you. You sounded like a five-year-old.'

'Well he's five times my size,' Ryan said defensively. 'Why don't you two spar? After all, Mr Kazakov's ex-Soviet Spetsnaz, you were a US Navy SEAL. It'd be like, *The Cold War – Part Two!*'

'I could kick his arse,' Kazakov said, half seriously. 'But on this operation Agent Brasker is my commanding officer, so my training dictates that I should allow him to win, in order not to undermine the command structure of the operation.'

Ted smiled. 'Spoken like a true soldier. But on a serious note, Ryan, if you're not tired you can help me sort out all this equipment. I need to know what we've got, what you'll need for tonight's operation and what we need to pack up and send over to the girls.'

*

The last few days had been so frantic that Ning hadn't given much thought to her own emotions. But her eyes glazed over as the drive from Manas Airport to a hostel north of the city centre stirred up memories of the worst time of her life.

Over a few days the previous year, Ning had discovered that her stepfather wasn't an honest businessman but a criminal who'd tricked thousands of girls into becoming prostitutes. She'd then been forced to flee China and ended up in Kyrgyzstan where she watched Leonid Aramov's goons brutally torture her stepmother.

'We never heard anything about my dad, did we?' Ning said, as the hire car's sat-nav directed them past grim low-rise housing.

'No,' Amy said, touched by Ning's sadness but also slightly irritated because she was driving in a strange town and needed to concentrate. 'How do you feel about him?'

'It's odd,' Ning said. 'On the one hand, I know what my stepdad did to all those girls and it makes me sick. But I still think of him coming home from work and sitting in his recliner. When I was little he used to let me pour him whisky and Coke. I'd cuddle on his lap as he sat watching the news, with the ice cubes chinking in his glass.'

'Almost like two separate people,' Amy said.

Ning nodded in agreement, as the car turned on to a muddy track with a livestock market up ahead.

'Dead end,' Amy said, as she gave the sat-nav screen evil eyes and put the car into reverse.

After a while, Amy worked out that she'd mistyped a Russian character into the sat-nav and located the hostel down a side street that they'd already passed twice.

The hostel had begun life as a Soviet-style concrete office block. A sunshine-yellow paint job on the outside hadn't done much to make the building more enticing, but the inside was funky, with headlamps off old cars stuck to the wall behind the reception counter, piped rock music and a lively crowd of hardcore backpackers hanging around a communal kitchen right beside the main lobby.

Upstairs the shared toilet and showers were less enticing and Amy flung the window of their little twin bunk room straight open to get rid of a musty smell.

'It's like a prison,' Ning said. 'I guess we won't be here long, at least.'

'Quick shower, change clothes, grab a bite,' Amy said. 'Then I say we head straight back out to try finding Dan.'

19. LOCKS

Despite the clean-up, Ethan still got a new girl delivering his food. She was curvy, aged about twenty, with a tight T-shirt stretched over huge tits. Her manner seemed abrupt when she slid a plate between the cell bars, but to Ethan's delight she spoke English as she handed over a small plastic bottle filled with white powder.

'For your bad stomach,' she explained. 'It's made for cows but we use it too. Mix it in your food to mask the taste.'

'Your English is good,' Ethan said. 'Where did you learn?'

'We learn in school, but I polished it working as a pool guard at a resort in South Africa,' the girl explained. 'Lots of English speakers.'

Ethan wasn't sure what to say. 'So you're a good swimmer?'

The girl tutted. 'No, they made me a life guard because I can't swim.'

Boredom was driving Ethan insane, so he ignored the bad vibe and tried getting a couple more sentences out of the girl before she walked out and plunged him back into twilight.

'Is South Africa far from here?'

'I certainly wouldn't want to walk to the border,' the girl said, before putting a finger to her lips and making a shush sound. 'I'm not supposed to talk with you.'

Ethan was pleased with himself for wheedling out the fact that he was in a country that bordered South Africa, but the boredom was really getting to him and he shouted desperately as the young woman headed out.

'Please try and get me a book or something.'

When the door clanked he looked down at his food. After being taken out to shower the previous day, Ethan was starting to feel less shaky and his appetite was returning. He never got cutlery and his plate was always a disposable polystyrene job.

Until now, he'd only been given vegetables or meat off the bone so he was surprised to see a chop – possibly lamb, although with such a variety of animals on Kessie's ranch it might easily have been something more exotic.

Ethan picked up the chop and as he bit off his first chunk of meat he realised that the T-shaped bone running through the middle tapered down to a point. Maybe if he chewed all the meat off and sharpened the narrow end by rubbing it against the concrete floor he'd have himself some kind of weapon.

There were no detailed photographic street maps of Bishkek on the Internet, or in the CIA's database, but there were good-quality overhead satellite maps. While Ning didn't know the exact address of the apartment where Dan had hidden her, she knew that it was an X-shaped three-storey block, with two identical cousins nearby.

But Bishkek had hundreds of near-identical Soviet-era housing blocks, so Ning used other factors to try identifying it: a lake she'd seen when she peeked from a window of Dan's apartment and the fact that he had a car but chose to walk to the local market because it was very close.

Using this info, Ning had pinpointed an area in the east of the city, then picked out several X-shaped housing developments within a kilometre of a large oval street market.

Kyrgyzstan was one of the world's poorest countries and eastern Bishkek was one of the city's poorest zones. Amy drove past ragged people, on roads with potholes big enough to wreck a car's suspension if you took them too fast, or get you wedged if you went too slowly.

The first street they drove to was wrong, but Ning smiled as they neared the second of her pinpointed locations.

'This is totally it,' she said. 'Park over by that building.'

'You're certain?' Amy asked.

'I recognise the graffiti,' Ning said. 'And see all those plastic sheets behind the bins? There's an old man who lives in there, scavenging food out of the rubbish bins.'

'OK,' Amy said. 'But everyone will notice two foreigners arriving in a nice hire car. It's best if we park a couple of streets away and walk.'

The pavements – where they existed – were as much of an adventure as the roads. They were badly cracked and you had to step over open manholes whose metal covers had been stolen for scrap.

'I hope our car doesn't get wrecked,' Amy said, looking back. 'Dr D doesn't like it when TFU has to pay an unexpected bill.'

'I just hope Dan's not moved away,' Ning said anxiously.

The uneven stairs and whiff of piss stirred memories as Ning led Amy through a broken security gate and up to the first floor. Dan's apartment was the third from the stairs, and one of the few things that had changed since Ning was last here was that a large steel plate had been fitted over his door. There were also scorch marks around the doorframe, indicating some kind of attempted arson.

'He might have moved away,' Ning said warily.

'Only one way to find out,' Amy replied, as she pressed the doorbell.

She waited a full minute before ringing again.

'It's the middle of the day,' Ning said. 'He might well be at work.'

She crouched down to peek through the letterbox, but could only see into the dark confines of a fully enclosed metal box.

'Well, whoever lives here, they're not home,' Amy said.

Ning nodded. 'I didn't see Dan's car downstairs.'

Amy hadn't risked going through airport security carrying a lock gun, but she always kept a basic torque wrench and some old-skool manual lock picks in her make-up bag.

'Haven't done one of these in a while,' Amy said, as she inspected the deadlock. 'No sign of an alarm and it's pretty quiet around here. Do you think we should have a poke around inside?'

Ning nodded. 'If we find Dan's stuff, we'll be certain he still lives here. I'll keep my ears open for anyone on the stairs.'

Amy fumbled through pots of foundation and eyeliner before digging her lock picks out of her shoulder bag. She'd expected to have to put in quite an effort with the deadlock, but while the brand name of a reputable lock maker was etched on the plate over the keyhole, the mechanism inside was a cheap knock-off that yielded to a twist of the torque wrench and a slight jiggle of a lock pick. The latch was even easier.

'I suppose the counterfeit industry does have its upsides,' Amy said, as she gave Ning a smile. 'Let's go.'

Ning instantly knew that Dan still lived here just from the coat rack and the battered trainers by the door.

'Let's have a discreet rummage,' Amy said. 'Work out what he's been up to. And keep an eye out for a phone bill or a SIM card package. His new mobile number would be a godsend.'

The apartment only comprised a bathroom and a single room with a fold-out bed and kitchen units. As Amy passed the sliding bathroom door, a muscular arm shot out. It grabbed her around the neck and jerked her backwards into the bathroom.

But Amy was far stronger than her assailant expected and she released the arm by twisting the thumb digging into her neck, then swung back, catching a man's nose with the point of her elbow.

'It's Dan,' Ning shouted desperately as she caught a glimpse. But Amy was committed to a solid gut punch.

Dan doubled backwards into his bathroom and crashed into his shower cubicle. He was badly winded and he tore the shower curtain off its hooks as he fell.

Ning rushed forward as Amy sprang back.

'Dan, it's me!' Ning said.

Ning almost cried as she made eye contact with the young man who'd saved her life. Dan's happiness was veiled by pain and confusion, but even with blood dripping from his nose the beefy seventeen-year-old managed to smile.

'Why you here?' he gasped, speaking in stilted English.

Amy pulled a packet of tissues out of her bag. 'Give him those to stop the bleeding.'

'It's a long story,' Ning said. 'Why didn't you answer the door?'

'I was shower,' Dan said, as he used the edge of the sink to pull himself up. 'I sing in shower, so I not hear. When I step out, I watch the lock turn, although I never give anyone my key.'

Dan staggered out of his bathroom, wearing only underpants. One hand clutched his stomach and the other clamped the bloody tissues to his nose. Even in a baggy grey sweatsuit Amy was clearly a babe and Dan was shamed by his defeat as he walked up to his tiny dining table and sat down.

'You punch *really* hard,' Dan told Amy, as he looked her up and down. 'I watch many *Ultimate Fighting*. I think you could win there!'

With free weights, an X-box, big-screen TV, a very lax attitude to cleanliness and posters of naked women all over the wall, Dan's apartment looked more like the home of some macho nutter than the kind of lad who'd put his life on the line to save Ning.

'I hate that you come back here,' Dan told Ning. 'It's dangerous.'

'After I left I met good people,' Ning said, remembering that she wasn't supposed to specifically mention CHERUB under any circumstances. 'Amy works for the CIA. I brought her here because they need to know what's going on inside the Kremlin.'

Amy clicked into interrogator mode, and adopted her most soothing voice. 'I'm sorry if I hurt you,' she began. 'Ning tells me you're a good person who hates doing bad things. We need to know what's going on inside the Kremlin right now. And I'm in a position to help you, if you're prepared to work with us.'

'Help how?' Dan asked.

'Depends what you want,' Amy said. 'Money? Education? A new life? America is the richest country in the world, and right now you're in the fortunate position of having information that America wants.'

Dan's nose had stopped bleeding and he put his hands behind his head and laughed, showing off bulging shoulders and pectorals in the process.

'I don't think anyone knows what goes on in the Kremlin now,' Dan said. 'Irena, the big boss, is very sick. Nurse made a mistake with her cancer drugs. She's off her head. All is of a blur for her now.'

'When did that happen?' Amy asked.

'Last weekend,' Dan said.

Amy and Ning both realised that this timing coincided perfectly with Ethan getting kidnapped. Leonid was surely behind this 'mistake' with his mother's drugs.

'I lift weights with Boris and Alex Aramov,' Dan continued. 'They've always been much in love with themselves. Strut like big men. But right now they are no boasting. Very quiet, like they are pregnant with big secret.'

'What about Ethan Aramov?' Amy asked. 'Have you heard anything?'

Dan shrugged. 'Who is that?'

'He came here from California late last year,' Amy said.

'Ah!' Dan said. 'Skinny boy?'

Amy nodded. 'He's no bodybuilder, that's for sure.'

'I see Ethan three, maybe four times, but I never speak him. There is a beautiful girl called Natalka. I think she is his friend.'

'Right,' Amy said.

She already knew about Natalka through Ethan's online correspondence with Ryan, but the mention of her name was reassuring because it confirmed that Dan was being honest.

'You've already given us a lot of helpful information,' Amy said. 'Do you think you could talk to Natalka and ask what she's heard about Ethan? And stay close to Boris and Alex. Let me know as soon as you hear anything.'

Dan eyed Amy uneasily as he aimed a hand at Ning. 'I helped her because I didn't like to see her in pain. But what you ask is very different. Snitching against Aramov could get me killed. My sister killed and nephew killed too.'

Amy didn't let Dan's knockback affect her composure. 'Leonid Aramov is worth billions of dollars,' she said serenely. 'Dan, you live in this tiny apartment which people try to set on fire. I'm prepared to open a bank account for you. The opening balance will be fifty thousand dollars.

'You'll be paid two thousand dollars per week for as long as you're willing to help us. The money will be tax free, and if you and your immediate family wish to become United States citizens when this is all over, we can get that sorted too. So instead of a future pumping weights with Boris Aramov at the back of the Kremlin while you wait for Leonid Aramov's next set of orders, you could be sunning it in Miami or going to college in New York.'

'I need to think,' Dan said.

But Ning had lived in this apartment long enough to read Dan's face, and she felt sure that he'd been hooked by the beautiful girl offering everything he'd ever dreamed of.

20. PIPE

Ethan didn't get anything to read and the hours sitting in the dark with nothing to do were starting to scramble his brain. He made mental lists – ten sexiest film stars, ten favourite bands, ten best cars. He counted up to 17,492 and invented a game where he filled his mouth with water and spat it at bugs crawling across the floor.

That evening some of Kessie's workers socialised in a clearing behind the cage hut. Now that Ethan had a hose to flush his piss and crap into the drain, he could turn the empty bucket upside down and stand on it to look out of the window.

He rested his elbows on a ledge and watched a soccer game, lit up by the headlights of two tractors. There was a lot of boozing going on and players faced off every time a dirty tackle went in. Older ranch workers sat at the edge watching, and the girls from the kitchen sat in their own lively circle, gossiping and rebuffing the occasional sweaty footballers who came over to flirt.

Ethan didn't know what had gone on the day he'd been taken to the riverside shower, but the order had clearly been sent down that he needed to be checked on more frequently. Michael had delegated this task to the small lad who'd swept out his old cell, but he was something of a star on the football field, so it was his long-legged pal who came through the door at around ten p.m.

The boy was no more than thirteen, barefoot and wearing filthy nylon shorts and a Barcelona football shirt. Ethan had watched the lad charging around on the football field, mad keen but talentless. He was out of breath and sweat was beading up through his close-cropped hair.

The boy turned the lights on. It was far from floodlit, but Ethan was so used to dark that even the gloomy strip lights along the centre of the barn were enough to make him squint. The boy didn't seem entirely certain what checking on Ethan was supposed to involve, so after a brief-but-awkward stare he spun and bolted back outside.

Ethan stood back on his bucket and watched the boy approach Michael, who was playing in goal. Michael seemed satisfied with whatever he was told and the boy ran back on to the field to continue charging hopelessly after footballs.

The boy had closed the outer door of the building, but for the first time since arriving Ethan found himself alone in the cell with enough light to study his surroundings in detail. One of the cages at the far end was used to store tools and for the first time he properly appreciated how many bugs came out to crawl up the walls in the night.

Ethan was briefly intrigued by a metal handle sticking out of the floor close to the cage block's main entrance. This lever was designed so that all the animals on his side of the block could be let out to graze.

Each cage also had an override so that they could be locked individually, but as Ethan was alone and the handle was conveniently near the door, everybody who entered his cell used the lever. No human prison would be designed with such a simple locking system, but this place had been built to hold animals.

When Ethan grew bored with the novelty of the light he went back to stand on his bucket, attracted by what sounded like the biggest ruck of the night so far. But he was also a little thirsty so he grabbed the hose and gently squeezed its plastic trigger to shoot a drizzle of water into his mouth.

As the shouts outside reached a new peak, Ethan looked down his hosepipe, which ran ten metres to a tap at the opposite end of the barn. Then he spun and looked at the lever, seven metres in the opposite direction. His mind posed an obvious question:

Could he make a lasso from the hose and hook it around the lever?

There was no shortage of issues: the hose was attached to the tap head with a plastic fitting that didn't look like it would be easy to break off. And if he could break it he'd then face an extremely awkward throw, reaching out through the bars of his cage and trying to hook something over a lever more than six metres away, by somehow pulling it sideways. And what then? It wasn't like Ethan could run out into the street and hail a taxi.

He wouldn't be able to put the hose back on the tap once it was off, so even trying the plan risked a beating and worse conditions. But while Ethan wasn't sure how Leonid's scheme to take control of the Aramov Clan was supposed to work, he knew he was only being kept alive as a way to blackmail Irena if something went wrong. He'd been here for almost a week and it might not be long before someone came through the door carrying a gun instead of a plate of food.

After a deep breath, and a careful glance at the lever to make sure he wasn't insane, Ethan sat on the concrete floor, wound the end of the hose around both wrists, pushed his feet against the bars of the cage for leverage and started yanking with all his might.

*

Ryan and Kazakov packed their white Toyota Corolla with as much gear as they could find, putting the back seat down and filling the rear with suitcases, bedding, pillows and even a rusty old bike that they'd found in the garage of their rented house. The idea was to make it look like they'd left somewhere in a hurry with all their belongings.

They set off for the Kremlin just before eleven. The unlit road took them uphill, then broke down into a gravel-covered track for the final stretch into a valley basin illuminated by runway lights. Although the Aramovs mainly ran ex-Soviet military planes, it was a comparatively modern Boeing freighter that blasted over the pointed star on the Kremlin's rooftop as the Toyota stopped outside the lobby.

'You got our story straight?' Kazakov asked.

Ryan raised one eyebrow and replied in Russian. 'Sure thing, *Dad*.'

'You stay here in the car,' Kazakov told him, as he reached up and flipped the switch for the overhead light. 'That's so they can see you when I tell my story, but put your baseball cap on so they can't see your face.'

The Kremlin lobby always had a couple of burly armed guards on duty, but there was no formal system with IDs and Kazakov almost thought he'd bluffed his way into the building when one of the guards stepped into his path.

'Don't think I know your face,' the guard said, placing one hand on the compact machine gun slung around his neck.

'You wouldn't,' Kazakov said confidently, as he reached out to shake the man's hand. 'I'm Igor Kazlov. I was at a bar in Bishkek and a guy told me there might be security work available here.'

The guard looked down his nose at Kazakov and made a kind of snorting sound.

'You come here at this time of night to ask for a job?'

'I worked security at an oil installation in Kazakhstan. My contractor did a runner just before pay day. So I'm running on fumes, you know? Got my boy sitting in the car. Only enough money to keep things running for a day or two.'

The guard looked fairly sympathetic, and looked to his gun-toting colleague. 'Keep an eye on him.'

The guard headed past the fruit machines to the bar at the back of the lobby. There were plenty of people at the tables and vodka and beer getting consumed at a rapid rate, but the atmosphere felt as gloomy as the lighting.

Ryan looked on from the car as Kazakov stood waiting with his hands plugged into the pockets of his bomber jacket. After a couple of minutes, a chunky man wearing a bar apron strode back with the guard.

The barman's tone wasn't unfriendly, but the message wasn't what Kazakov wanted to hear.

'Hey,' the barman began. 'I understand your situation's grim, but you're out of luck here.'

'I'm experienced in security and close protection,' Kazakov said. 'Excellent references. But I'm so hard up right now I'll wash dishes if that's what you need.'

'We run a freight operation out of the airstrip,' the barman explained. 'Pilots, mechanics and the like are recruited in Russia or Ukraine. Menials like me are recruited locally, but jobs here are like gold and everyone comes in through personal recommendation.'

'Right,' Kazakov said dourly. 'Well is there any chance I can kip down in the bar. My son's got a bad chest and—'

The barman interrupted and his tone hardened. 'This isn't a flop house. The facilities are for clan employees and family members only. I've got customers waiting, so I must now ask you to leave.'

'Just one night,' Kazakov begged, but the barman was already turning away.

The bigger of the two guards now became aggressive, eyeballing Kazakov and putting a hand on his shoulder.

'We've been friendly so far,' the guard growled, 'but now it's time to leave.'

To emphasise this point, the other guard swung his gun around to face Kazakov's chest.

'No luck?' Ryan said, as Kazakov made it through the drizzle and opened the driver's door of the Toyota.

'Chances of this working were never that great,' Kazakov said. 'What have you seen out here?'

Ryan pointed beyond the car's bonnet. 'There's plenty going on down at the airfield, but I've not seen anything back in the hills.'

'So you fancy having a go?'

Ryan nodded, as Kazakov started the engine and crunched the car into first gear. While the car drove slowly over the gravel in front of the Kremlin's main lobby, Ryan unzipped the top of a small backpack, filled with handmade wire snare traps.

He rummaged beneath the traps, pulled out a small disc magnet and pushed it behind his ear. The magnetic field this created activated a tiny transceiver which had been tweezered into Ryan's ear canal before he'd left the house.

'Testing,' Ryan said, as the car began moving slowly away from the Kremlin.

Ted Brasker's voice came from a strange place inside Ryan's head. 'Hearing you loud and clear, boy.'

'We had no luck at the front door,' Ryan told Ted. 'Looks like I'm gonna have to go on a little hunting trip.'

'Remember what we discussed,' Ted said firmly. 'No stupid risks. If you get caught, stick to your background story. Can you remember it?'

'Ran out on my dad after a row. Hitched a ride out here to go hunting and then got lost in the dark.'

'Perfect,' Ted said.

Five hundred metres from the Kremlin a sharp uphill bend behind dense trees took the car out of sight of the lobby. Kazakov pulled over. If anyone had seen them, it would have looked like Ryan was getting out to pee in the bushes.

'Good luck,' Kazakov said, as Ryan slung his backpack over his shoulder.

Ryan's boots crunched the undergrowth as he scrambled into the trees and set off towards the Aramov stable block, aiming to get hold of the USB stick that Ethan had plugged into Leonid Aramov's computer.

21. BONE

Someone usually came and checked on Ethan in the middle of the night, but unless something out of the ordinary happened he'd have the next couple of hours to himself.

Breaking the length of black hose from the tap ten metres away was never going to be easy, but it was harder than Ethan expected because instead of pulling on the tap head, the hose just stretched.

When bracing against the bars failed, he stood up and pulled himself backwards with the plastic digging agonisingly into his wrists. He tried pulling and jerking the hose. Then he hit on the idea of stretching the hose as far as he could and knotting the end around one of the bars. Once the hose was stretched tight and tied to a bar at the rear of his cage, Ethan gripped the hose with both hands and pushed down with his entire bodyweight.

There was a whoosh, followed by a series of chimes as the hose clanked metal bars. Ethan dived back as the hose whiplashed, stinging his upper arm and narrowly missing his cheek as it flailed through the air.

There was the sound of water spattering the concrete up by the tap, but rather than snapping the hose from its joint with the tap, the hose itself had actually split into two pieces. All Ethan's effort was wasted if he didn't have enough hose to tie a loop and lasso the handle.

After a quick rub of the red welt where the catapulting hose had lashed his shoulder, Ethan pulled the hose arm over arm, counting lengths of one metre.

Luckily, the hose had snapped near to the tap and Ethan had enough hose to reach the lever. But he wasn't sure how much extra length he needed to make the loop and tie a knot. After a couple of attempts it was clear that tying a knot in a rubber hose is bloody hard, and that he'd come up short by the time he'd made it.

But Ethan's success in getting the hose had buoyed his spirits. He'd kept the chop bone he'd been served a couple of days earlier and had even sharpened the pointed end by scraping it across the concrete floor. He used this point to spear one of the cushions on his mattress. He then tore out a forty-centimetre strip of strong fabric and used it to knot a loop. But as he finished double knotting and gave the loop a tug to test its strength, a shaft of moonlight shot through the main door.

Ethan guessed someone had heard the noise and

that he was about to get busted, but he still lifted his mattress and hastily crammed as much hose as he could underneath it.

Kessie lumbered into the cage block, for only the second time since Ethan's arrival. He was as drunk as on his first visit and his safari trousers had an all-too-conspicuous damp patch around the crotch.

'Who was in here last?' Kessie asked furiously, in English.

Rather than looking at Ethan and the train of hosepipe sticking out of his mattress, Kessie stared angrily at the fluorescent lights, and the insects swarming around them.

'Some boy,' Ethan said weakly.

'A boy who hasn't seen my electricity bill!' Kessie shouted. 'That much I know for sure.'

And with that, Kessie flipped off the light switch and stormed outside.

While Ethan gasped with relief, Kessie stormed into the middle of the football match and began shouting that there would be no more parties on his ranch until people learned to turn off light switches and stopped wasting his money.

Ethan didn't understand Kessie's language, but he watched from the bucket as the lanky kid who'd left his lights on got grassed up by Michael. The terrified lad was dragged in front of Kessie, who choked him before knocking him cold with a knee to the head.

As the shocked ranch workers dispersed, leaving the lad sprawled unattended in the dirt, Ethan jumped down off the bucket and peered back into his now dark cell. He could see nothing at all, though he knew from experience that his eyes would soon adjust enough to see shadowy outlines.

Ethan appreciated the dose of luck, but throwing the loop of hose around the handle was going to be much harder in the dark. Once he'd fed the hose through the bars, he pushed his arm through, and for once in his life he was grateful for being skinny.

He began by whipping the hose gently until he could feel it laid out straight in front of his arm. Then he made a much stronger movement, pulling the whole hose backwards and sending it cracking forwards with a whipping motion.

By the third crack he was getting a feel for the kind of swing it took to make the hose flick up into the air. But in the near dark the only feedback he got on where the hose was landing was the difference in sound between the pipe hitting the floor and clanking off the metal bars.

After each crack, Ethan would tug the hose hoping that he'd snagged the lever. After thirty attempts the metal bars were cutting into his chest and his arm and shoulder ached. But his life depended on this, so he ignored the pain.

Forty minutes later he was still going. The sound of the hose slapping the concrete after each unsuccessful throw tormented him, and his arm hurt so bad that he had to take a break, lying on the mattress and moaning as he tried to ease the pain by massaging himself.

After ten minutes on his mattress, dripping with sweat and wishing that he'd had the sense to run some water into the bucket before breaking the hose apart, he gave it another go.

Cloud cover had moved away from the moon, giving him slightly better light. His third attempt made a tantalisingly different sound. Ethan realised that one edge of the loop was balancing on top of the lever, but when he pulled the hose it fell back to the floor.

Despite increasing pain in his arm, Ethan's throws were improving. The next time the loop caught the end of the lever he didn't pull back. With his heart in what was now a very dry mouth, Ethan made a little upwards flick with his wrist. It was enough to send a ripple along the snagged hose and make it move forward.

'Please, God,' Ethan whispered, as he tugged the hose and felt it pulling against the lever.

Success felt good, but there wasn't time to wallow in it. If the handle had had to be pulled towards him he'd now be on easy street, but it had to travel at an angle near perpendicular to the hose and he had no idea if the lever would budge when he pulled.

Ethan used the same brute force technique he'd devised when ripping the hose off the tap: stretching the hose back by winding the ends around his wrists and bracing his feet against the cell bars.

It seemed far more likely that the piece of cloth holding the loop of hose together would break this time, rather than the hose itself. There was a terrifying ripping sound, followed by a sudden slip, but as Ethan thought the loop was about to break there was a metallic thunk.

The sudden movement of the hose made him slip and as he lost his grip it lashed away through the bars, burning his right wrist before slithering across the concrete floor and out of reach. But Ethan was sure he'd reached the lever and he ignored the blood drizzling down his arm as he rolled on to his chest and crawled towards the cage door.

His palm squished a cockroach, but that didn't deter him as he reached his cell door. The door was designed to open automatically, but the spring that made this possible was furred up with dried-out animal waste, so Ethan still wasn't sure whether he'd pulled the lever far enough to set himself free.

The hose was out of reach, so there was no second chance. His heart banged as he tugged a bar and felt a shudder up his arm as the rusty mechanism moved freely. Ethan found his feet quickly and stepped out of the cage, half convinced that he was dreaming.

The piece of hose still attached to the tap had created a big puddle at the opposite end of the block and he picked it up and splashed his face before drinking four big mouthfuls of water. Being free gave Ethan a huge rush, but he was also overwhelmed by his situation. His body shook with a mix of fear and exhaustion as he took a deep breath and mumbled to himself.

'What now?'

*

After getting kicked off his first big mission, Ryan was keen to prove himself. Dan had confirmed that local kids occasionally dared one another to venture into the valley around the Aramovs' airbase, and never received anything more than a few slaps, unless they'd been caught stealing or vandalising.

But despite this reassurance, Ryan still felt well out of his comfort zone as he scrambled through the dark. Any kind of advanced equipment would make him seem like something other than a kid who'd stormed out of home to go hunting, so apart from his bag of traps and a water bottle he was relying on his BlackBerry for GPS navigation and the hidden ear-canal transceiver for communication.

'You good?' Brasker asked, through the earpiece.

'Bit soggy,' Ryan whispered as branches sprang back spraying water over his face.

'Stable's about four hundred metres ahead of you,' Brasker told him. 'Amy is in position and ready to pick you up at the top of the valley.'

'Understood,' Ryan whispered.

There was no avoiding a stretch of open ground on the final approach to the stables. He could have sprinted across in less than twenty seconds, but he had to stay in character as a lost kid, so he bumbled through the tall grass at nothing more than a brisk walk.

As he reached the cover of the trees he heard a horse moving slowly along the side of the stable block. The valley's sides were too steep for wheeled vehicles, so Aramov security teams patrolled on horseback, dressed in police-style uniforms with rifles slung over their shoulders.

The guard looked relaxed, giving no guidance as the horse made its own way along the gravel path. Ryan waited for the animal and rider to trot past, then circled around to the side of the stable block and the adjoining admin shed which contained Leonid's office.

'OK?' Brasker asked.

'Patrol,' Ryan said. 'Looks routine. I'm squatting against a tree, getting a wet bum.'

'Hot chocolate and cookies when you get home,' Ted joked.

Ryan watched the horse and guard come back into view as they headed uphill on the opposite side of the stable.

'Going in,' Ryan said.

As he got close to the admin block, Ryan noticed a four-wheeled equipment trolley standing outside a stable, illuminated by a clip-on lamp inside. There was a smallish woman in the stable, and a slender man wearing a blood-smeared apron.

'Looks like a vet,' Ryan said. 'I think one of the horses is giving birth.'

'OK,' Ted said. 'Withdraw by the quickest available route.'

'Negative,' Ryan said. 'They're at the far end of the stable. They'll never see me.'

'Ryan, your mission parameters are clear,' Ted said firmly. 'We're in hostile territory and your little-boy-lost cover story doesn't work once you start rummaging inside.'

'You're breaking up,' Ryan lied, as he took a few more

cautious steps along the side of the building. 'Can you repeat your last message?'

Ryan looked through the office's small square window, glimpsing Leonid's desk and some wall-mounted hunting trophies through slats in a wonky Venetian blind.

'Ryan, don't you bullshit me,' Ted said. 'We agreed, if there's anyone at the stables you back out. That is a direct order, do you hear?'

Ryan tipped his head back to look up at the sky and exhaled with frustration. If it hadn't been discovered, the USB stick that might have information on Ethan's location was on the other side of the wall, less than four metres away. But CHERUB agents who disobey their mission controllers don't last long, and with one black mark already on his record, Ryan was out of options.

'Understood,' Ryan said reluctantly. 'Heading up the valley.'

He gave a quick glance left and right before setting off, but after less than ten metres he heard a horse moving right behind, closely followed by a shout in Kyrgyz which he didn't understand. The bullet that whizzed over his head when he'd taken two more steps needed no translation.

As Ryan jolted, then dived at the ground, the mounted guard shone torchlight on Ryan's back and said more stuff he didn't understand.

'Russian!' Ryan said, as he rolled on to his back with his hands in the air.

The guard switched from Kyrgyz to Russian. 'Get on your feet, turn to face me.'

Ryan realised what he'd done wrong. The guard on the path and the light in the stable had distracted him and he'd failed to follow basic procedure and check out all sides of the building.

Ryan wasn't sure if the guard now pointing a gun at him was the same guy who'd ridden past on the hill, but he had no trouble identifying the well-built youth who strode up beside the horse armed with the long rubber cosh that Leonid had used to beat Ethan one month earlier.

'You're in a lot of trouble, kiddo,' Boris Aramov said, as he swooshed the cosh through the air.

'I'm just lost, sir,' Ryan said.

Boris shrugged. 'Don't really care why you're here, kiddo. There's no girls in town and nothing decent on TV, so I'll be putting some stripes on your back before we send you back to Mummy and Daddy.'

22. SUNGLASSES

After guzzling from the hose Ethan turned off the tap and walked over the puddled concrete to the cell at the back that was used to store farm equipment. Most of it was heavy stuff, like a sprayer unit and sacks filled with chemicals, but he found a hand fork with three nice sharp prongs and decided that it made a better weapon than his sharpened lamb chop.

Kessie's workers had retreated to their dorms after he'd beaten the young boy for leaving the cage block lights on, so Ethan stepped out into cool night air and a deserted landscape. He had nothing but the clothes on his back and the little fork.

The only things Ethan knew about his location were that he was in a country that bordered South Africa and that he'd seen a sizeable town out of the plane window on his final approach to Kessie's landing strip.

He wasn't sure what direction the town was in, but he did remember the sewage flowing downriver when he'd been taken to the showers. It seemed logical that he'd find the source of the filth if he went in the direction it came from.

Ethan had spent some of his lonely hours inside the cage considering what he might do if he did somehow escape. No disguise would hide the fact that he was a white kid in a black country and he'd concluded that his only realistic strategy was to find somewhere with a phone and call Irena, or anyone else he could get hold of inside the Kremlin who wasn't loyal to Leonid.

Ethan had no watch, but he reckoned it was about 1 a.m. Provided nobody sighted him leaving the ranch, that gave him two hours before anyone came looking for him, and maybe four and a half before it started getting light.

He moved quickly towards the river, then jogged along the bank until he could hear voices inside the dormitory blocks. No bridge spanned this part of the river, but there were a couple of spots where Kessie's men crossed using a combo of stepping stones and planks resting precariously on boulders.

The stench of the churning brown water made Ethan heave and the slippery rocks and planks were tricky in darkness, but he felt safer once he reached the quieter side of the river, and he found himself walking between the huge barrels in which animal pelts were being cured.

A bashed-up Mitsubishi pick-up offered some temptation, but Ethan had no idea how to jump start a car and his only driving experience was when his mum gifted him a track session in a single-seat race car with automatic transmission.

The ground Ethan crossed now was open, but nobody worked at night so he felt safe until he got close to the steel posts and barbed wire that ringed the whole of Kessie's ranch. The yellow and black signs were written in a language Ethan didn't understand, but the symbols of thunderbolts and stick figures getting zapped made it obvious the fence was electrified.

Ethan studied the point where the fence crossed the river. The foul water had been neatly boxed in with concrete so that the perimeter fence could go along the top. Luckily the water flowing at the edge beneath the bridge looked shallow and Ethan decided to risk it.

Fighting the urge to puke, he crouched under the bridge and sploshed through shallow water as his trainers flooded. The smooth concrete below his Nikes was slippery with algae, and he had to keep his head down because the water went over the concrete bridge at peak flow and maggots were hatching in the brown scum deposited on the ceiling.

As Ethan straightened up and climbed the overgrown embankment on the outside of Kessie's land he could see the manned security gate at the ranch's main entrance about three hundred metres to his left. The road out of the ranch went for about four hundred metres before joining a four-lane highway running parallel to the river.

Ethan decided it would be best to set off towards town by going along the overgrown stretch of land between the highway and the river, although it was really dark and he worried that he'd lumber into a snake, crocodile, or whatever it was that lived in this part of the world and liked biting lumps out of humans.

Ethan had to avoid being seen as he crossed the well-lit road out of Kessie's ranch, so he kept low and headed for the highway. As he got closer, he saw a kind of informal terminus in a dirt patch where the ranch's access road met the highway.

A few motor rickshaws stood with their drivers hoping to pick up a ride, but at this time of night the traffic was mostly men being dropped off after a night in town. Some were alone, some in twos and threes. All looked wasted and most dived into the bushes to urinate as soon as they'd paid their drivers.

Ethan had to avoid the terminus, and as he didn't dare cross the access road either, he'd have to back up a couple of hundred metres and cross to the other side of the highway. Perhaps he'd even stay over there, because the more he thought about the riverbank, the less appetite he had for walking it.

The four-lane highway was a mere back road compared to the freeways Ethan rode every day in California, but although the traffic was light most drivers went as fast as their vehicles allowed and many didn't bother with headlights.

Ethan squatted in reeds close to the road and watched the speeding traffic, trying to decide whether he should cross two lanes and stop in the median, or wait longer for a gap in all four lanes and run straight to the far side.

He was about to sprint to the middle when he was startled by a retching sound in the reeds nearby.

When a set of headlamps flashed the scene, Ethan saw a young woman, standing with her legs far apart, spewing her guts up. When she straightened up, she mopped her face with a tissue but only managed a couple of drunken steps before sitting down and making a low sob.

Ethan crept closer, and the next set of headlights showed him a badly swollen right eye and fresh claw marks across the girl's face. He felt pity and wondered why she'd been beaten, but the girl had put her clutch bag down beside her and it offered the tantalising possibility of cash and maybe even a mobile phone.

Fear, time pressure and a mass of critical decisions made Ethan desperate. It was like a maths problem that he didn't have the brainpower to solve and in the end he acted on impulse, setting off fast and reaching down to make a running grab at her bag.

To Ethan's surprise, the drunken woman sprang at him. She got one arm around his waist and flipped him. Ethan slammed down hard and the puke soaked into his back as the growling woman put an arm across his throat.

'You should join a gym, white boy,' the woman snorted, speaking decent English as she thumped Ethan in the gut. 'Weakling, grow some muscles!'

Ethan gasped for air as the woman smirked. She'd drunk so much that her sweat smelled like booze and for the first time Ethan studied her properly. Her long nails meant she was no farm girl and based on the way she was dressed he thought that she might be a prostitute.

'What you doing out here, white boy?' the girl asked.

Ethan couldn't answer until she took the arm off his throat. 'I need to get into town,' he croaked.

'White boy? Out here?' the girl said suspiciously.

Her eyes were like dark glass balls and Ethan was starting to think there was something stronger than alcohol in her system.

'I saw you were sick,' Ethan croaked. 'I thought you might need help.'

The girl snorted as she increased the pressure on Ethan's neck. 'You tried to steal my bag, you piece of shit. Not that I'd be stuck out here if there was any money in it.'

'Hey, Amina!' a man shouted.

'Shit,' the girl said, as she rolled off of Ethan. 'One move and I'll kick your arse.'

'Amina,' the shadowy figure wading through the tall grass shouted again. Then he said a bunch of stuff in his own language and whatever it was made the girl hiss.

'Is he the guy who beat you?' Ethan asked.

'Wow, you must be a detective,' the girl said as she reached across Ethan's body and picked the three-pronged fork out of the dirt. 'Yeah, I'm Amina.'

Amina still looked hopelessly drunk as she stumbled to her feet. The man coming their way was no taller than Ethan, but he packed a ton of muscle. He was dressed for a night out, in a purple shirt with ruffled front and uber-bling gold-framed sunglasses with mirrored lenses.

He held tattooed arms out wide as if to apologise and Amina staggered forward into his arms.

'Baby,' she said warmly.

The man closed in for an embrace, but an instant before they touched Amina took the fork out from behind her back and rammed it sideways under the man's ribcage. As she burst into a crazy spitting rant, the man crumpled. He clutched his guts as Amina stamped down, puncturing his thigh with the point of her high-heeled shoe.

As the man wailed, Amina menaced him with the fork as she took a wallet from the back of his trousers and a pack of cigarettes and a mobile telephone from his shirt pocket. Amina roared one final threat, before turning back towards Ethan with a bunch of local currency flapping in her hand and speaking in English.

'I'm riding back into town, white boy. Might need a little help with my balance though.'

Ethan thought for half a second before stepping up to the girl. She was heavier than him and he near-buckled as she put her arm around a shoulder that was already knackered from using the hose as a whip.

With arms around each other's backs, Ethan and Amina started a clumsy walk towards the waiting rickshaws a couple of hundred metres away.

'These will suit you,' Amina said, smiling as she reached across and almost poked Ethan's eye out with the man's mirrored sunglasses.

'He your boyfriend, or what?' Ethan asked, as the glasses settled on his nose.

'Cousin,' Amina said. 'Dragged me out of a club in town and started beating on me cos I was dancing with some guy he has beef with.'

Amina was all over the place and Ethan started getting nervous as they reached the line-up of motor rickshaws. There were no farm workers within fifty metres, but if any of Kessie's men pulled off the highway he'd be screwed.

The rickshaw driver at the head of the queue looked slightly curious about the combination of a drunk girl and skinny white teenager. But a fare was a fare so he didn't ask questions.

'Where in town?' Amina asked Ethan.

'Anywhere but here,' Ethan said, as he helped her climb into the rickshaw's cramped rear seat.

Amina yelled an address as the driver revved his engine and let out the clutch, making his lightweight vehicle shoot forward with a two-stroke roar and a plume of oil smoke.

23. MARCH

Boris Aramov had dismissed the armed guard before grabbing a handful of Ryan's hoodie and frogmarching him towards the Kremlin.

'Ryan, stay calm,' Ted urged, through the hidden earpiece. 'Stick to your story, you've got nothing to worry about.'

'Gonna beat you *good*,' Boris said, as he lashed out with the cosh, blasting Ryan in the back of the legs.

It was enough to make Ryan stumble, but his thick denim jeans took a lot of the sting out.

'I can do whatever I like with you,' Boris teased. 'Break your face, burn up your nads with a blowlamp.'

Ryan had read briefing documents on all of the Aramovs, but there was still something chilling about Boris' casual sadism. He'd assumed Boris was taking him all the way to the Kremlin, but Ryan got pushed through a broken wire fence into the exercise yard and nudged towards the weight stack at its centre.

It was drizzling and past midnight, but there was a fit blond guy doing bicep curls with 30kg dumbbells.

'Hey, Vlad,' Boris said. 'Why you out so late?'

'Can't sleep,' Vlad said, shaking his head.

'So have you met my new toy?' Boris asked, as he yanked Ryan sharply backwards. 'I'm gonna have some fun, teaching him that straying on to Aramov turf has painful consequences.'

Boris aimed the cosh higher, making Ryan yelp as it thumped his lower back.

Ryan hadn't resisted up to now because Dan had said he'd get a few slaps and a warning not to come back. But he'd already taken five whacks and Boris was only warming up.

It was drizzling hard as Boris shoved Ryan face down over a puddled weight-lifting bench, then wrenched his head back.

'Nobody knows you're here, do they?' Boris teased. 'And even if I kill you, who's got the balls to come after me?'

Then Boris turned and spoke to Vlad. 'Get me a couple of seven point fives.'

Vlad knew better than to argue with Boris, who was backing away from the weight bench. It was the first time Boris had given Ryan space and he used the opportunity to look around. The rear of the Kremlin was in plain sight less than a hundred metres away and Amy was supposed to be waiting for him at the top of the eastern side of the valley about a kilometre away.

Ryan thought about rolling off the bench and making a run for it, but Boris and Vlad were both older than him and in good shape, so there was every chance that one or both of them would either catch him or alert the security teams. He really needed to disable them.

While Ryan thought this through, Boris had gripped a 7.5kg dumbbell in each hand and swung a couple of test punches with them.

'You'll kill him with those,' Vlad warned.

Boris gave Vlad an angry scowl. 'You don't tell me what to do.' Then he clanged the two dumbbells like a boxer touching gloves and began closing on Ryan. 'By the time I've battered you with these babes, you'll be *begging* me to kill you just to stop the pain.'

Ted could hear some of what was being said. 'Ryan, you've got to get out of there.'

'Oh I hadn't thought of *that* idea,' Ryan muttered, as Boris pulled back his fist.

Ryan rolled off the bench as Boris launched a savage punch with the metal dumbbell. The blow slammed the padded bench as Ryan hit the floor beside it. Boris couldn't grab Ryan with the dumbbells in his hands so he straddled the bench and tried pinning Ryan to its side using his legs.

But Ryan grabbed the end of the bench and pulled his body forward. As he stood up, Boris caught him in the ribcage with a dumbbell. Ryan stumbled sideways into the weight rack, badly winded.

'Feisty one, eh?' Boris said, with a massive grin on his

face. 'Now I'm *definitely* gonna kill you.'

Boris' next swing was an uppercut, but the weight of the dumbbells made him slow and Ryan was able to spin out and shield himself behind the weight rack. Boris tried adjusting his aim mid-punch, but he didn't reach Ryan and his fist slammed into one of the racked dumbbells.

The crash of metal on metal sent a shockwave up Boris' arm. The pain made him drop the dumbbell from his right hand, as a 32.5kg weight near the bottom of the rack broke loose and rolled towards his foot.

Ryan had barely got his breath back after the rib blow and the pain was excruciating, but he had to go for it. Using the top of the weight rack as a pivot point, he launched a spectacular roundhouse kick that connected with Boris' temple.

As Boris stumbled, Ryan grabbed one of the little 4kg dumbbells from the top of the weight rack and gave it a two-handed swing. As Boris recovered from the first blow, the second one smashed him in the base of his chin with enough force to dislocate his jaw.

Boris was unconscious, but Vlad had moved behind Ryan, getting an arm around his chest and lifting him off the ground. With arms flailing and feet off the ground, Ryan turned his head and sunk his teeth into Vlad's enormous bicep.

The pain wasn't bad enough to make Vlad let go and Ryan found himself being pushed forward towards a weight bench, with Vlad's blood in his mouth and all the air being crushed out of his chest.

Ryan was hoping to use Vlad's forward momentum to roll him over his back as soon as his feet got back on the concrete, but before it got to that stage Vlad aimed a side punch at the same part of Ryan's ribcage that Boris had bashed with the weight.

The pain this caused was so bad that Ryan suffered a momentary blackout. When he came to he was sprawled across the bench, but Vlad stood two paces back, yelling in agony. With no idea how this had happened, Ryan launched a quick back kick, planting his muddy boot in Vlad's guts, then he spun and planted his other boot between Vlad's legs.

Vlad was down on his knees as Ryan stumbled forward and grabbed one of the 7.5kg dumbbells that Boris had dropped. Ryan took a big backswing and smashed it ruthlessly into Vlad's temple. Ted's voice had been going for a while, but only now did his brain have time to tune in.

'Ryan, speak to me,' Ted was yelling. 'Ryan, Ryan?'

Ryan spun around, making sure that nobody else was coming his way. 'I'm on my way up the hill,' he told Ted. 'Ten minutes, fifteen tops.'

'Roger that,' Ted said, sounding relieved.

Ryan didn't have time to hang about, but he was still mystified as to why Vlad had let him go. He glanced around curiously, but it was only when he looked at the front of his hoodie that he saw the spike of bloody plastic sticking through a torn pocket.

When Ryan tapped the pocket he realised that his BlackBerry was in bits. Boris' first blow with the weight had smashed the back cover of his phone, and then a broken shard of plastic had stabbed Vlad's fist when he'd punched him.

Adrenalin had kept Ryan going during the fight, but he struggled for breath as he started to run.

'I'm in agony,' Ryan told Ted as he stepped through the torn fence of the exercise yard and headed up the side of the valley at jogging pace. 'I reckon I've cracked a couple of ribs.'

24. KANYE

Ethan tried to keep his white face out of sight as the
motorised rickshaw blazed down the highway for ten
minutes. The outskirts of town were populated with
tightly packed huts, but further in Ethan saw rows of
copper-roofed houses and an environment that might
have passed for one of Los Angeles' shabbier suburbs.

The infrequent signs were written in English and the
local language. They told him that he'd entered *East
Kanye*, heading for *Town Centre & Government Square*. It
was the early hours of the morning so the streets were
quiet, apart from occasional blasts of light and noise as
they passed bars or discos.

Amina's head rolled from side to side as the open-
sided vehicle cruised, but a pothole jolt woke her up and
she took a few moments to work out where she was.
After a quick row with the driver, they cut down a dirt

track and took a left through the deserted stalls of a street market.

'Here,' Amina said, pushing money in the driver's hand as they came to a sharp stop.

They were on the edge of a market, with a band playing a lively dance down the street and a three-legged dog hunting for scraps. All around were shopfronts with brightly painted signage and closed metal shutters.

As the rickshaw made a tight U-turn and blasted off, Amina took a couple of steps and crashed into a stack of plastic crates.

'Which way?' Ethan asked.

He propped her up and she led him to a metal door at the side of a bright yellow shopfront. After a fumble with her key they moved to a steep and extraordinarily narrow staircase with electrical wires taped crudely to the walls.

Amina was groaning as Ethan helped her up the stairs. He jumped when a door opened up on the landing, but it was a little old dude in flip-flops and boxer shorts. He started saying something in the local language, but switched to English when he saw Ethan's white face.

'A boy your age should be ashamed!' the man hissed. 'Keep the noise down.'

Amina gave a wild stare and squeezed her breasts provocatively. 'Mind your business, you dirty old goat.'

'I'll call the cops on you!' the old man said. 'See if I don't.'

As Amina tried to give an *up yours* gesture she

overbalanced and hit her head on the stair rail.

'God has punished you!' the old man said happily, as Amina swore. 'Dirty slut!'

Ethan had a job getting Amina up the last three steps and when she finally got her door unlocked, she sprawled out on the floor just inside the door. The apartment was shabby but clean, with lots of cushions over the double bed and family photos pinned to the peeling turquoise walls. Ethan was surprised by a clothes rail hung with neatly pressed blouses and grey skirts, and a diploma on the wall that read *Amina Malhaspa – Botswanan Institute of Structural Engineers.*

'You want some water?' Ethan asked.

But Amina was still and when Ethan lifted her arm he realised that she'd passed out. He put one of the cushions under her head, then opened the fridge and helped himself to a can of Pepsi.

The bubbles were nectar for his dry throat, but the back of his T-shirt was soaked in Amina's puke and his shoulder was more painful than ever. After giving himself two minutes to drain the can and catch his breath, Ethan stepped over Amina and peeled her clutch bag out of her hand.

Any crappy mobile would have been OK, but he was delighted to find a nice-looking Samsung smartphone in the purse. The phone had several missed calls. Ethan ignored them and pressed the map application, followed by the *find me* icon.

The reception was only down on two bars. The first map took almost two minutes to load, and even longer when he zoomed out to see that he was near the centre of Kanye, Botswana, fifty kilometres from the South African border and less than three hundred from the city of Johannesburg.

Armed with this info, Ethan decided to call the Kremlin, but although he knew the main switchboard number and the extensions for most of his family members, he was stumped because he didn't know the country code for calling Kyrgyzstan.

He tried opening the web browser on Amina's phone, but he couldn't even get Google to load. After his third *No Data Connection* message Ethan jumped as the phone started playing a harpsichord ringtone.

He answered without thinking and the voice on the other end was roaring in the local language. The only words Ethan understood before he hung up were *white boy* and some choice English swear words.

After failing with the Internet, Ethan decided to try calling information. He didn't have the number so he decided to have a rummage through the apartment to try and find any information or leaflets.

A drawer beside the bed was stuffed with household bills. Ethan found some Orange Botswana phone bills near the top and some digging took him to a *Making the most of your new phone* leaflet.

The dual-language pamphlet had the information number and after a couple of minutes on hold he got put through to a directory enquiries service. Ethan grew frustrated as the Indian man on the other end .explained that he could only give specific numbers, not answer queries about country codes.

After a bit of brain bending, Ethan got the number for his old school in Bishkek and used the country code from that to dial the Kremlin. Kyrgyz telephone exchanges give out a bizarre shrill ringing sound that always reminded Ethan of an elephant trumpeting. He'd never thought he'd be this grateful to hear it and after three rings he reached an automated switchboard, which spoke Russian.

'Please enter the correct extension number, or press 00 to leave a message.'

Ethan pressed 519 to speak directly to Irena, but it just rang until the switchboard cut him off.

'Press one to leave a message, or two followed by the extension number to try another line.'

Ethan had to think fast. Natalka was extension 315, but it was unlikely that she'd be able to get direct access to Irena up on the sixth floor. In the end he picked 522 to speak to his uncle Josef.

This tall simple-minded man was Irena's oldest son, and Ethan's uncle. They'd never really interacted because Ethan found Josef slightly creepy and his uncle's conversation rarely strayed beyond favourite TV quiz shows and tedious stories about how he was the only person who knew how to fix the Kremlin's heating system.

'Hello,' Josef said.

Ethan didn't want to sound too excited. He didn't know Josef well, but Leonid was staging a coup and Ethan suspected that Josef was the kind of man who'd keep his head down and side with whoever won.

'It's Ethan. I know it's early, but I need to speak to Irena and I can't get through.'

'She's been sick,' Josef said. 'That crazy nurse, Yang, poisoned her. Is there a problem at your new school?'

'Josef, this is really complicated. You said Irena's been poisoned. Is she able to talk?'

'She's over the worst, but she's still weak. And I don't know what time it is in Dubai, but it's five in the morning here.'

Ethan hadn't thought about the time difference. But he hoped to spin it in his favour.

'Irena always wakes up really early, Josef. *Please*, just go and wake her up. I *swear* she'll want to speak with me.'

'I'd get Leonid to speak to you, but he's at the hospital.'

Ethan wasn't sure he'd heard right. 'What's wrong with him?'

'Leonid's OK, but some crazy intruder attacked Boris. His jaw is smashed, so they've taken him to the hospital in Bishkek.'

'Wow,' Ethan said. 'But listen, Uncle, I really, really, need you to go wake up Irena.'

'She's a sick old lady,' Josef said. 'I'm not waking her up just because you're homesick.'

Ethan heard a bleep, and saw *Low Battery* flash across the phone's screen. He felt like screaming. 'I've *got* to speak to her.'

'I'll take a message,' Josef said. 'I'll make sure that

Irena calls you as soon as she wakes up, but I'm not going to disturb her.'

Ethan reconsidered: maybe he *could* tell Josef what was going on, especially if Leonid wasn't in the Kremlin. But he felt reasonably secure inside Amina's apartment and decided that it would be less risky to wait for a couple of hours.

'Have you got a pen and paper?' Ethan asked. 'Take this number, and promise me you'll get Irena to call the instant she wakes up.'

Josef took a while getting the number down.

'As soon as she wakes up,' Ethan repeated, just before hanging up.

The phone gave another *Low Battery* warning, but Ethan had spotted the charger when he'd been searching for the phone pamphlet. Once he'd plugged the charger in he wondered what else he could do. Apart from the Kremlin, the only other number that Ethan had committed to memory was his old friend in California.

There probably wasn't much Ryan could do, but Irena wouldn't call back for at least an hour and Ryan might even have found something about what Leonid was up to in the hacked files he'd sent through before leaving the Kremlin.

Ethan calculated the time difference between Africa and California and reckoned that Ryan would most likely be sitting at home doing his homework after school. But the phone cut straight to voicemail.

'Hi, you've reached Ryan Brasker's mobile. I'm probably out with a hot chick or sorting out some science problem that NASA can't solve. But leave a message and I'll get back to you when I can.'

25. EMBED

'Ryan, I can't help you if you don't stop acting like a baby,' Amy said firmly.

'I'm not acting,' Ryan shouted. 'It bloody hurts!'

He was lying on the couch at the house the CIA liaison had rented. His hoodie was pulled up to his nipples and Amy loomed over his bloody abdomen with a pair of tweezers.

'Shouldn't a proper nurse be doing this in a hospital?' Ryan asked.

Amy gave a cheeky smile. 'The only decent hospital within two hundred kilometres is the International in the centre of town. But right now, it's a safe bet that Boris Aramov is in the emergency room there. So unless you want to bump into him, shut up and keep *still*.'

Amy moved in with the disposable tweezers from the medical kit. She gripped the bloody end of a plastic shard roughly the size of a pen lid.

'Hold your breath, and on three,' she said soothingly. 'One . . . two . . . three.'

'JEEEEEEEEEEEEEEEEEEEESUS Christ!' Ryan screamed.

The pain made his legs shoot up and he almost kneed Amy in the head as a trickle of blood ran out of the splinter hole.

'Can't see any more splinters,' Amy said, as she dropped the lump of plastic into a coffee mug, then dabbed Ryan's wound with a cotton wool pad.

'Are you sure my ribs aren't broken?' Ryan asked.

'I don't have an X-ray machine handy, but if your ribs are bruised the hospital would strap them up. If your ribs are broken the hospital would strap them up. So what's the difference?'

'I could have punctured a lung,' Ryan said.

Amy smirked. 'Ryan, if you'd punctured a lung you'd be coughing up blood, and you certainly wouldn't have run a kilometre up the side of the valley.'

'How's the patient?' Ted asked, as he stepped into the living-room holding a glass of clear, fizzing liquid.

'Just got the last splinter of BlackBerry,' Amy said. 'I'll give it ten minutes for his wound to clot, then I'll wipe off the worst of the blood and put some strapping on.'

'Stitches?' Ted asked.

Amy shook her head. 'It looks a mess, but it's nothing major.'

'Nothing major!' Ryan spluttered. 'I'm in agony here.'

'Tip this down your throat,' Ted said, as he

passed the glass across.

Ryan took the glass and gave it an experimental sniff.

'Soluble Neurofen,' Ted explained.

'Isn't there morphine in our medical kit?' Ryan asked.

Ted and Amy both burst out laughing.

'Ryan, you are officially the *worst* patient ever,' Amy said. 'Morphine's basically heroin. I might give you a shot if you'd had your legs blown off, but regular painkillers will do for what you've got.'

Ted was smiling, but gave Ryan a reassuring tap on the shoulder. 'You did great out there, fighting off those two apes.'

Ryan took an experimental sip of the drink. It didn't taste as nasty as he'd expected.

'The night was hardly a huge success,' Ryan said. 'Plans A *and* B failed. We haven't got the USB stick and I almost got killed. And don't accept *anything* that your pal Dan tells you from now on.'

'Dan's OK,' Amy said. 'You were unfortunate to run into Boris the psycho instead of a regular Aramov security guard.' She dipped a hand into their first-aid box and came out with a packet containing another pair of sterile tweezers.

Ryan recoiled. 'I thought you were done.'

'Turn your head to face the wall,' Amy said. 'I've still got to get the com unit out of your ear.'

*

Ethan had spent ninety minutes hovering nervously around Amina's little apartment, with her snores as the soundtrack. He was waiting for Irena to call back, but the only time the Samsung rang it was an incomprehensible rant, presumably from the dude Amina had stabbed with the hand fork.

If Kessie's people hadn't missed Ethan already, they would do soon, and while the apartment was safer than being out on the street there was a rickshaw driver and a man with a stab wound who'd know where to look if word got round that he was searching for a white boy.

While Ethan waited for his call he took off his trainers and squeezed as much stinking river water out of them as he could. Amina was stockier than him, but she was about the same height and he put on a pair of her dry trainer socks.

Replacing his puke-spattered T-shirt was trickier because most of Amina's stuff had girly designs and was shaped to stretch over her bust. But he dug out a *Johannesburg University* sweatshirt that didn't look too absurd when he pulled it over his head, and hoped Amina wouldn't be too pissed off if she woke up and saw him wearing it.

When he was sick of pacing about, Ethan crashed on Amina's cushion-covered bed and stared at the Artexed ceiling, trying to get his head straight. The most intriguing thing to come out of his conversation with Josef was the fact that someone had beaten Boris up, and Leonid being at the hospital with him.

The idea of calling Leonid's apartment would normally have been absurd, but if Leonid, Boris and – hopefully – Alex were all at the hospital there was a good chance Andre was home alone. And as Andre worked hard at being Ethan's friend and had a close relationship with his grandma, he might be the one person who'd go and wake Irena up for him.

The clock on the Samsung told Ethan that he'd now been waiting two and a quarter hours for Irena to call back, and a four-hour time difference meant it would already be getting light in Kyrgyzstan. So should he wait and see if Josef came through, or risk calling Andre?

First he called Irena's number again and got no answer. Josef's line went to answerphone, so Ethan took a deep breath and punched in 00 to go back to the Kremlin switchboard, then hesitated briefly before tapping the extension number for Leonid's apartment.

On the fourth ring, Ethan almost chickened out and pressed *end call*. On the fifth Andre picked up, as he'd hoped.

'Hello?'

Ethan didn't want Andre to blurt his name, so he put on a deep voice. 'I'd like to speak with Leonid Aramov.'

'He's at the hospital. If it's urgent I can pass a message.'

'Is there another adult home?' Ethan boomed, convinced that he was doing the worst *grown-up* voice in recorded human history.

'I can go downstairs and get my mum,' Andre said.

Ethan dropped the accent. 'Andre, it's me, Ethan.'

'Hey!' Andre said brightly. 'How's your school? I really wanted to call you, but Dad said nobody's supposed to speak to you in the first few weeks, to stop you from getting homesick.'

'Listen, Andre, something really bad has happened

and I've got to talk to Grandma right now. Do you know if she's awake?'

'She always moans that she can't sleep and gets up really early,' Andre said. 'Did you hear that her crazy nurse gave her the wrong drugs? She was unconscious for two days.'

'I got a message saying that she was sick,' Ethan said. 'How is she now?'

'Almost back to normal when I saw her last night,' Andre said.

'So do you think I can speak to her? I know it's early but it's really important.'

'Dad had her moved into your room so we could keep an eye on her until a new nurse arrives. Hang on a second.'

Ethan heard doors and footsteps as Andre walked out into the hallway. It was ironic that Irena might have picked up if he'd called his own extension and a relief when the next voice he heard was his grandmother's.

'You're not supposed to be speaking to me yet, are you?' Irena said brusquely.

Irena had always defended Leonid, so Ethan had to phrase his next words carefully.

'Grandma, I never got to the school in Dubai. Leonid diverted my plane. I'm in a place called Kanye in Botswana.'

Irena sounded shocked. 'Kessie's place?'

'Yes,' Ethan said. 'They've been keeping me in a cage on Kessie's ranch but I just escaped. Leonid's planning to take over the clan. I don't think your nurse poisoned you, I'm sure it was Leonid.'

Irena was struggling to take all this in. 'No . . . He wouldn't.'

Now Ethan spoke firmly. 'Grandma, I'm *in* Botswana. If you don't believe me, call the school in Dubai and they'll tell you that I never arrived. Leonid killed my mum. He tried to poison *you*, and he's sent me down here so that he could blackmail you if something went wrong.'

'Blackmail how?' Irena asked.

'All I know is that he's trying to get control of your money.'

Irena's tone suddenly changed. 'Is he?' she yelled furiously. 'I could never understand the mistake with my dose. Yang was a sweet nurse and I've had the same pills for months. The doctor said the overdose should have killed me. Luckily that medicine makes me nauseous and I vomited before most of it got into my system.'

'Leonid had to make it look like an accident,' Ethan said. 'A lot of your people don't like the idea of working for him after you're gone, and he'd have real problems taking over the clan if everyone thought he'd murdered his own mother.'

'And ironically, I've been telling those very people that Leonid's bark is worse than his bite,' Irena said. 'The evening before the overdose, he badgered me into signing a whole bunch of documents as I was trying to go to sleep.'

'Did you sign them?' Ethan asked.

'Yes,' Irena said, sounding distressed. 'I'm *exhausted*, Ethan. This never would have happened before I got sick. And your mother . . . You suspected Leonid all along, didn't you?'

'Don't worry about that now,' Ethan said, as he heard his grandmother sob. 'We need to act fast, especially while Leonid's away from the Kremlin at the hospital. Do you think you can help me get out of here?'

'I know people in the diamond racket in those parts,' Irena said. 'But if Leonid has taken control of my bank accounts . . .'

'I was suspicious about what he's been up to, so I put a spy program on both his computers,' Ethan said. 'With any luck they'll have recorded information on where the money's gone. If we can get his banking details we can transfer the money back to you, or change passwords to lock Leonid out of his own accounts.'

'Get them how?' Irena asked.

'There's a stick in the computer in Leonid's office, but I think the important one is in his computer at the stables,' Ethan said. 'Send Andre, nobody will suspect him. An FTP site is used to distribute files online. If you upload, the files will be waiting for me as soon as I get somewhere with a fast Internet connection.'

'It will be done,' Irena said.

'But I need to get out of here before I can help you,' Ethan said. 'I'm a white kid in a black town and Kessie's got teams out searching for me.'

'I know a couple of good bush pilots,' Irena said. 'Just keep your head down. My hands shake too bad to write much, so Andre's going to take your number and I'll call you back when I've made arrangements.'

'One last thing,' Ethan said. 'I'm not sure if you can trust Josef. I asked him to get you to call me a couple of hours back, but he didn't.'

'Let me think on that one,' Irena said. 'I'm passing the phone over.'

Andre sounded confused. 'I've got a pen,' he said. 'What's my dad done?'

'Speak to Grandma,' Ethan said. 'But don't act all innocent. You know what a bastard he is and Alex and Boris bully the shit out of you.'

'I'm not on their side,' Andre said firmly. 'So what's this number?'

As Andre wrote down Amina's mobile number, Irena shouted for Josef in the background. Ethan wasn't sure this was the right move, but he couldn't control everything and while Irena might have had a blind spot when it came to Leonid, she hadn't built the Aramov Clan without being a smart operator.

Ethan felt safer with Irena on his side, but this was only a baby step and there was no certainty he'd be able to get out of Kanye or reverse the progress of Leonid's coup. As Ethan ended the call and pocketed the Samsung, he saw that Amina had sat up a little, while screwing up her face because of a bad taste in her mouth.

Ethan ran a glass of water. 'Here,' he said.

Amina looked curious as she took the glass, then she looked pissed off. 'Why are you wearing my university shirt?'

Ethan got out of answering, because at the same moment Amina touched her swollen eye and winced with pain.

'Why are you still here?' Amina said. 'I guess you're a gentleman, at least.'

'What do you mean?' Ethan asked.

Amina smiled at Ethan's naivety. 'You didn't try screwing me while I was unconscious.'

'More water?' Ethan asked, as Amina drained her glass.

Amina nodded as she massaged her aching temples. 'There are pills in the cupboard above the microwave. Get me those as well.'

Ethan refilled the glass and opened the cupboard, but as he reached for an old ice cream tub filled with sachets and pill pots he heard feet on the stairs. It was too fast to be the old guy who lived across the balcony and when he took a step back and peered out of the window there was a near-new Toyota pick-up right outside.

'Shit,' Ethan said.

Someone shouted from the landing outside. 'Amina, open up.'

But before she'd even turned around, the door took an enormous boot and swung into the room. Ethan recognised Michael from the ranch, closely followed by a couple of heavies. He turned back to the window and wondered if he could make the jump to the ground floor without breaking his legs.

26. SOLDIER

Once Ryan fell asleep, Ning, Amy, Ted and Kazakov gathered around a bar unit in the kitchen and tried figuring out what to do next.

'Sun'll be up before long,' Kazakov said, breaking into a yawn as he peeked between mildewed curtains with bunnies on them.

'Pulling the USB sticks and bugging Leonid's office was our best shot at finding Ethan,' Ted said. 'Amy, do you think there's any way Dan could get it for us?'

'I can ask him,' Amy said, as she caught Kazakov's yawn. 'But we have to make a decision. Do we pressure Dan into taking a big risk now, or view him as a longer-term asset?'

'He works for Leonid and he pumps iron with Boris and Alex,' Ted said, nodding thoughtfully. 'As keen as I am to find what's on those memory sticks, if we ask Dan to do something risky right now, we might freak him out and lose him for good.'

Ning sighed. 'So what *can* we do about Ethan?'

Kazakov spoke. 'Security at the Kremlin isn't magnificent. Give me forty-eight hours and four Special Forces guys and I'll get your memory sticks.'

Ted shook his head. 'You might get your team in, but the Aramovs either own or scare the shit out of everyone with any kind of authority in these parts.'

'We could use a chopper to fly our men in,' Kazakov suggested.

'Not practical,' Ted said. 'Kyrgyzstan is land-locked. We'd have to ask about six foreign governments for permission to fly over their land to get there. Even if you could do that without someone tipping off the Aramovs, there'd be a massive diplomatic shit storm afterwards. The Aramovs are connected right up to Politburo level in China and they're very chummy with the Russian security service and air force.'

Kazakov realised he was wrong and put up his hands. 'I guess if we could wade in and tackle the Aramovs head on, we would have shot their planes down long ago.'

'Exactly,' Ted said. 'And let's not forget, if we do this correctly Dan will become a valuable intelligence asset inside the Aramov Clan. He may not be a family member like Ethan, but I'd bet that he has more day-to-day involvement with Leonid Aramov's dealings than Ethan does.'

'So, where do we all go?' Ning asked.

Ted thought for a couple of seconds. 'Amy can stay

here in Bishkek to work as Dan's controller. I'll stick with her until our procedures and equipment are running smooth. Kazakov, you can go back to campus with Ning and our little wounded soldier in the living-room.'

'Makes sense,' Kazakov said.

Ted looked at his watch. 'The Aramovs have eyeballs everywhere, so after the incident last night, it's best if Ryan and Kazakov skip town ASAP. Rather than risk a scheduled flight, I'll charter a jet to take you as far as Dubai and you can pick up a regular flight back to the UK from there.'

'Me too?' Ning asked.

Ted nodded. 'Dan wasn't the only one of Leonid's goons you met when you were here with your stepmother. Amy and I can handle Dan now that you've found him and made the introduction.'

'How long for a jet?' Kazakov asked.

'CIA transportation should have planes on standby in Afghanistan,' Ted said. 'I'd guess four to five hours, so pack your bags now then you might as well grab some sleep.'

'Dan could be a huge help to us, Ning,' Amy added. 'If he turns into a valuable intelligence asset it'll be a big feather in your cap.'

'Might even be a navy shirt in it,' Kazakov teased.

Ning smiled at the compliment and liked the thought of getting promoted so soon after basic training.

'Try not to get Dan killed though,' she told Amy. 'He went against his own people to save my life, so I'm fond of the guy.'

The ground looked hard and Ethan had never made a jump from half this height before. The weird thing was that he wasn't scared of getting beaten, or of dying. What he couldn't stand was the thought of mind-bending days back in the cage with nothing to occupy his mind.

Michael reached through the open window and got fingertips to the Johannesburg University sweatshirt, but Ethan threw himself out and fell for what felt like an hour. His legs collapsed when he hit the ground. Intense pain drove up into his thighs and when he tried moving his right leg it made an involuntary twitch.

He was right by the Toyota's back wheels. There was a guy sitting in the driving seat, and the biggest of Kessie's goons was coming back down the stairs that led to Amina's apartment. He was so vast that he had to turn sideways and held up the fitter men trapped behind him.

Ethan crawled a couple of metres before he started feeling something in his leg. He used a stack of empty crates by a shopfront to pull himself up and started to jog with his right leg almost lame. A pistol got fired into the air as a warning, but Kessie wanted him alive so Ethan kept going.

The Toyota pick-up had started its engine and a couple of goons had now pushed past the fat arse and made it on to the street. These guys yelled as the driver put the Toyota in reverse and aimed it towards Ethan.

Ethan heard the pick-up coming and realised that

either the driver didn't know what he was doing, or that Kessie wasn't actually bothered if he came back alive. His right leg hurt like hell, but the shock of a charging car overrode the pain and he broke into a proper run.

With the Toyota less than ten metres away, Ethan turned out of the road and cut down an alleyway between two buildings. One building seemed to be an auto workshop, because the alleyway was piled up with rusty wheel hubs and empty oil cans.

The guy driving the Toyota swung the steering wheel and tried to follow, but the alleyway was barely a car's width and there were sparks and a massive crunch as the pick-up reversed into the corner of a building, cracking a breeze-block wall.

Ethan couldn't tell if three or four guys had been running after him, but they were all shouting and giving the pick-up driver abuse. Little kids were screaming and lights were coming on in windows above the shops.

Two of Kessie's goons scrambled over the wedged pick-up to keep up the chase. As the second one jumped down off the pick-up's crumpled tail there was a shotgun blast. The lead runner, who'd got within a few metres of Ethan, screamed with pain and fell down. Ethan heard shotgun pellets ricocheting off the alley walls but nothing hit home.

Ethan dared a backward glance and saw an enormously fat woman in a nightshirt. She stood on the roof of the damaged shop, aiming a shotgun down at Kessie's men and threatening to blast anyone who moved before the cops arrived.

While the shopkeeper kept the men around the crash site in place, the second guy who'd made it over the pick-up straddled his stricken friend and kept up the chase. Having one guy after you is better than four or five, but it was still a grown man versus a thirteen-year-old with a screwed-up leg, and the guy was closing fast.

The alleyway ended at a wooden fence, but local kids had made a hole at the bottom and Ethan was slim enough to crash through. Now he was in a broader alleyway that ran parallel to the shopping street, with a health clinic right in front of him.

While his larger opponent pulled himself over the fence, Ethan eyed a mound of junk. A pair of stray dogs barked behind as Ethan grabbed a stick of laminated timber, which looked like it had been part of a wardrobe or kitchen cabinet. One end formed a long point where it had been snapped.

As Kessie's goon dropped down off the fence and caught his balance, Ethan charged in and speared him in the gut. The goon had a cartoonish expression of shock when he looked down disbelievingly at twenty centimetres of wood embedded in his stomach.

Someone a couple of buildings across yelled for the barking dogs to shut up as the goon crumpled into the dirt and started coughing blood. Once the initial shock passed, Ethan peeked through the hole in the fence, making sure nobody else was coming.

Apart from his clothes, the only thing Ethan had on him was Amina's phone. Money or a weapon would be useful, but the goon was still thrashing about so Ethan grabbed a chunk of rubble off the junk heap and took a shuddering breath before swinging it at the guy's head.

The first swing made a hollow thud and sent the goon sprawling on to his back. Ethan had never been a violent person, but after all the shit he'd been through he found a degree of satisfaction in hurting one of his former captors.

Ethan's hands trembled and he was sure he'd killed his enemy as he searched the pockets of his shorts. There were some coins and some fifty-and one-hundred-pula notes, plus a cheapo Nokia phone, and a twenty-centimetre utility knife in a sheath tied to a belt loop.

One of the dogs had come within a couple of metres and as Ethan hobbled away it closed in and began licking the warm blood.

27. GEEKS

Tons of weird stuff had happened to Ethan since his mum had died, but wandering dark streets in a Botswanan town, holding a knife in bloody hands, took the prize. He knew he was in Kanye, but not where in Kanye, and his priority was to get as much distance between himself and the last place where Kessie's boys had seen him.

Ethan crossed a busy road and limped uphill into a well-maintained housing development. It could have been California, with three-car garages and palms down the middle of the road. There was even private security and he dived behind a wall as the little Suzuki patrol vehicle rolled past.

Amina's Samsung rang as the patrol car's rear lights faded. Ethan adjusted his position so that he was sitting on the edge of a brick driveway and was pleased to see *international* flashing on the screen.

Irena spoke, but she didn't sound like the bedridden cancer patient Ethan had known at the Kremlin. This was the iron lady who'd changed the Aramov Clan from an organisation that smuggled Western cigarettes on muleback, to a billion-dollar empire that owned more than sixty aircraft.

'How's it going?' she asked.

'I had to leave the apartment in a hurry,' Ethan explained. 'I'm on the street. It's a nice area, but I'll need a hiding place before it gets light.'

'Listen good,' Irena said. 'My bush pilot friend is on your case. There's a lot of diamonds smuggled out of your area, so he knows it well. Two kilometres up the main road north out of Kanye there's a derelict boarding school. Apparently it moved to a new facility eight years ago. Try getting there before daylight and hiding out in the school buildings. The old playing fields are used as a landing strip by smugglers. My contact has got to fly from South Africa, but he should be able to land there within four hours.'

'Sounds good,' Ethan said. 'I'm not sure exactly where I am right now, but this phone has maps if I can get a data connection. What's going on where you are?'

'Andre got the USB keys. I've also put in a call to my main bank in Russia. Eighty-two million euros was electronically transferred out of various accounts over the past week.'

'Damn,' Ethan said. 'All of the data on Leonid's computers is encrypted, but the spy software captures screenshots while they're in use, in their unencrypted state. If Leonid used either of his computers to access online banking facilities, or to type up notes of his passwords, we should be able to get the money back.'

'I've also rounded up some muscle that I can trust,' Irena said. 'They're searching Leonid's office and apartment for any paperwork relating to what he's been up to. I've got security teams stationed on the sixth-floor lifts and their orders are to grab Leonid and bring him to me the instant he arrives.'

'Is he still at the hospital?' Ethan asked.

'He was when I called half an hour back to ask after Boris,' Irena said.

'How is he?'

'His jaw is shattered. He'll probably have to go abroad for treatment.'

'But Leonid doesn't know I'm free?' Ethan asked.

'Not as far as I know,' Irena said. 'If he gets wind of it he might go into hiding rather than show up here to face me.'

'The less he knows, the more chance we have of getting your money out of his control,' Ethan said. 'I doubt Kessie will be in any hurry to let Leonid know I've escaped.'

'Agreed,' Irena said. 'Now the thing is, Andre plugged the USB stick into my computer. He says there are hundreds of files, but he can't open any of them.'

'The files are stored on the key in a compressed and encrypted format,' Ethan explained. 'That way it looks like a bunch of corrupted files if someone stumbles on them by accident. The files need to be unzipped using a software tool that I've got stored on my FTP page.'

Irena sounded frustrated. 'Ethan, I don't know about this stuff. Andre's trying, but he's not a computer whiz like you.'

Ethan sighed. 'If you upload the files and get me to a computer with a fast Internet connection I can open them up no problem. Is there nobody you trust at the Kremlin who knows about computer stuff?'

'There's an aircraft mechanic who fixes the network and backs up our server, but he's one of Leonid's people,' Irena said. 'Your mother handled all of our IT stuff. I should have recruited a replacement after she died – after Leonid murdered her – but I've been sick the whole time.'

'Get the plane to take me somewhere with fast Internet,' Ethan said. 'Get Andre to start uploading the files on the USB keys to my FTP site. Once I've decrypted them all, it would be useful to have someone brainy to help me go through the information.'

'Understood,' Irena said. 'You keep safe out there.'

Ethan laughed a little. 'I'll try my best. And you be careful too. Leonid's not exactly Mr Popularity, but he still has friends around the Kremlin.'

*

Ryan's sides ached as he swung his legs off the couch and sat up. When he threw the duvet off his lap, he saw that he'd slept in one sock, a bloodstained T-shirt and briefs. His mouth was dry so he padded through to the kitchen where Ted sat at the table playing Pac-Man on his laptop.

'Old skool!' Ryan said, as he found one of the less grubby glasses in the cupboard and filled it from the tap.

'How you feeling?' Ted asked.

Ryan shrugged and gulped water. 'Depressed, I guess.'

'You're a kid,' Ted laughed. 'What have you got to be depressed about?'

'I wanna be someone at CHERUB,' Ryan explained. 'But I got kicked off my first mission after shoving Dr D and I didn't get the USB stick last night. So I doubt my name is gonna top any lists the next time mission control is dishing out a juicy mission.'

'I can think of worse prospects than being stuck on CHERUB campus,' Ted said, smiling. 'Great facilities, good education and lots of babes. Speaking of which, how is your love life?'

Ryan laughed awkwardly as Ted lost his last life and gave his laptop a frustrated shove.

'Grace still wants to kill me and most of the other girls on campus think I'm a pig because I broke up with her by SMS.'

Ted laughed. 'You're a good-looking guy, you'll win 'em back. And didn't Grace see you when you were back on campus doing your Kyrgyzstan prep?'

'I was pretty busy,' Ryan said. 'She had lessons and I took most meals up to my room to avoid a confrontation.'

Ted found the idea of Ryan hiding in his room avoiding a girl funny, but he didn't want Ryan getting annoyed so he changed the subject.

'The others all went upstairs to grab some sleep,' Ted said. 'There's a jet coming in to take you, Ning and Kazakov out of the country. It's due in at noon, so you've got a while to pack up and make yourself presentable.'

'Cool,' Ryan said.

'I had the devil's job booking it. The mobile phone signals here are poor. I ended up using a satellite phone, and even then I couldn't get a secure channel because TFU have got air-conditioning problems in Dallas.'

Ryan looked confused. 'Air conditioning?'

'Dallas is hot,' Ted explained. 'Computer servers are hot. When the air conditioning fails in the server room at TFU headquarters all the servers go into thermal cut-out. The system was supposed to be up and running within an hour, but TFU's not a big organisation. There's only one technician on duty and she told me the same thing three hours ago.'

'That's crap,' Ryan said, shaking his head as he pulled up his T-shirt and peeled back the dressing over his abs. 'I think it's scabbed over.'

Ted took a peek and nodded in agreement. 'You'll be fine in the shower if you don't rub your scabs too hard. I'll fix you a new dressing when you come out, and *don't* leave the shower tray all bloody when you're done.'

'I'm not a total slob you know,' Ryan said cheekily. 'And speaking of communication difficulties . . .'

Ryan had spotted his BlackBerry, on top of the washing machine where he'd dumped it the night before. The half of the case that hadn't splintered was buckled, the screen had two big cracks and everything was smeared with dry blood.

'There were a couple of spare phones amongst the equipment we brought out the back of the Toyota,' Ted said. 'Grab one if you want.'

Ryan shook his head as he turned the BlackBerry over in his hands. 'I've got a bunch of contacts on this phone and it's loaded with the special software for logging into TFU and accessing my Ryan Brasker persona. You think I might be able to get it going if I clean the dried blood off?'

'Worth a shot,' Ted said. 'But don't worry too much. I've already let Dallas know that your phone's dead. And I'm sure the CHERUB tech department can have a new cell up and running by the time you get back to campus.'

'Sounds good, boss,' Ryan said as he put his empty glass in the dishwasher and headed for the door. 'Guess I'd better go and scrub up then.'

28. LUNCHBOX

Amina's Samsung wasn't getting the best signal, but Ethan managed to get GPS connected and downloaded enough location maps to work out that he was in the centre of Kanye. He needed to trek about six kilometres to reach the derelict school.

He made it to the edge of town as dawn broke, with a thumping headache and a ballooning right ankle that shot pain up his leg on every step. The last stretch on the road north was going to be a real problem. Not only was it getting light, but the broad verge alongside the road offered limited cover.

Ethan limped through the bush land off to the sides, ducking behind trees or bushes whenever he heard traffic. He got his first sighting of some of Kessie's goons in over two hours as they climbed out of a Nissan 4×4 close to a school bus stop.

Over a dozen kids milled about waiting for their ride and a machine-gun-toting goon electrified them by waving a big wodge of money.

Ethan was behind bushes twenty-five metres away. He couldn't follow because the goon spoke in Tswana, but waving money, excited kids and the phrase *white boy* made it obvious that he was offering a reward for anyone who found him.

The kids seemed really excited as the Nissan drove off. Ethan reckoned the school bus was imminent and decided to wait it out rather than risk being seen moving through the bush, but that option crashed when a lad of about eight gave a much older boy a cheeky kick up the arse before sprinting off in Ethan's direction.

Ethan held his breath. The little lad was less than five metres from Ethan's hiding spot when the big one brought him down with a rugby tackle. There was a shower of dust and stones as the little kid tried to kick free, but the bigger one had a good hold and lifted him up over his head.

'AAARGH!' the little kid yelled as the big one ran forwards and lobbed him into a bush.

Ethan had no choice but to scramble back as the little kid crashed through branches less than two metres away. A girl was coming over, yelling something along the lines of *leave him alone he's only little*, and at least three boys were jogging towards the scene to get a better view of the action.

With his bad leg, Ethan wouldn't be able to outrun anybody and he crawled into the next patch of bushes, sure that someone would spot him soon.

The little kid was furious about his excursion through a bush, but only his pride was injured and he bounced up and squared off against a much bigger opponent. However, the other lad was at least five years older. Any fist fight would have been so one-sided that the bigger kid burst out laughing and turned away.

While all this was going on, there was some shouting from up near the bus stop and a trail of dust coming off a shabby blue bus that had a plastic model of Jesus on the cross mounted between the headlights.

The kids boarded noisily as Ethan felt relieved. He was about to move off when the 4×4 with Kessie's goons aboard shot past heading back towards town. Then he spotted a black Justin Bieber lunchbox.

Ethan opened it up and realised that he was starving when he saw two pieces of fruit, a carton of squash and a cling-film-wrapped parcel of what seemed to be mostly rice, with black beans and stuff in it. The rice stuff looked nasty, but he pushed the straw into the drink carton and guzzled it before setting off.

*

Ryan, Ning and Kazakov felt tense as they headed into the luxurious private jet terminal at Manas Airport. Their flight was being run by the CIA's transportation unit and the US embassy had sent a driver to collect them, but the Aramov Clan had a lot of pull in these parts and for all they knew the clan had circulated Ryan and Kazakov's description to every corrupt official in town.

Customs waved them through with nothing more than a bag X-ray and a little golf-buggy-with-trailer contraption glided them out to a waiting jet. The plane belonged to the CIA, but was logoed up with the name of an obscure Turkish aircraft leasing company.

'Nice,' Ryan said, as he eyed the luxurious interior.

His sides hurt and he'd been dreading the four-hour flight to Dubai, but he was pleased to see six huge recliner seats in which he'd be able to lie flat.

Ning took the seat across the aisle from Ryan and was amused as he pulled a slide-out table across his lap and produced a freezer bag filled with bits of his broken-down phone.

'If you want to check your messages you can pop your SIM card in my phone for a minute,' Ning suggested.

Ryan shook his head as he tipped out the parts. 'I scraped the dried blood out of the battery compartment before we left. It might work.'

'You'll get issued a new one when you get to campus,' Ning pointed out.

'I know,' Ryan said. 'But I started trying to fix it and now I'm kind of determined. Plus, I've got a whole bunch of music and contacts stored on this one.'

Ning gasped with mock shock. 'You mean to say you *didn't* back your phone up regularly in accordance with CHERUB procedures?'

'Who does?' Ryan grinned, feeling a jolt as the plane started its taxi towards the runway.

Kazakov was fiddling with the seat in front as Ryan pushed the battery into his phone. Ning smirked as

Ryan pushed on the phone's battery cover. He then had to use a straightened hairclip to reach inside the case because the on/off button hadn't made it back from the Kremlin.

The phone's ringer had been damaged and instead of nice swoopy onscreen logos and a soothing little tinkle sound, Ryan got the top two-thirds of a cracked screen and a fart sound.

'It's gonna work!' Ryan said, holding up crossed fingers. 'Come on, you little beauty.'

Ning enjoyed the mini-drama as Ryan's phone booted up. He entered his pin and watched as *searching for network* flashed onscreen.

'Aren't you a clever boy!' Ning said.

Ryan nodded, but just as he got a connection a red-haired stewardess came out of the tiny galley at the back with a tray of drinks.

'I'm afraid you'll have to turn that off,' she said firmly. '*All* electronic devices need to be off during take-off and landing. You can use the plane's Wi-Fi connection once we're airborne.'

Ryan looked narked as he took a glass of fresh-squeezed orange juice off the tray.

'How come you never hear about planes dropping out of the sky because someone left their mobile phone on?' he asked.

'I don't make the rules,' the stewardess said, as she handed Kazakov a double whisky and Coke.

Kazakov smiled at the stewardess, then looked back and gave Ryan and Ning his *do-as-you're-told-or-I'll-make-you-*

run-laps-till-you-puke look, which they both remembered from basic training.

It was a little plane, so rather than use the intercom the co-pilot leaned out of the cockpit door. 'Sorry to rush you folks with those drinks,' he said. 'But we've been given our take-off slot and we'll be airborne in around seven minutes.'

*

Back in California, Ethan had always got a spooky feeling when he came out of his after-school chess club and walked deserted corridors. The derelict boarding school on the outskirts of Kanye was like the same feeling multiplied by a hundred.

The main gate was padlocked, with a faded sign forbidding trespassers and giving the address and contact numbers for the school's new site. But while the gates stood firm, scavengers had cut out whole sections further along the fence to sell as scrap, and Ethan got in by stepping on to a knee-height wall and making an excruciatingly painful jump into tangled grass on the other side.

The school buildings were modernist concrete, eaten away by weather and gradually getting swallowed by nature. Wading through waist-height grass took Ethan to a broad ramp leading up to what had once been the school's main entrance. Now there were weeds growing through cracks and an arm-sized lizard basking in the early sun.

The doors were off their hinges and Ethan wasn't surprised by the graffiti and broken glass inside. The bullet holes and shell casings were more alarming. Perhaps a resentful pupil returning to blast holes in his old school, or a shoot-out between smugglers using the airstrip.

The inside looked less treacherous than the overgrown bush around the school building, so Ethan cut through. Glass crunched underfoot as he walked through the school's main lobby. He passed decaying signs in English as he headed towards the light on the opposite side of the building. After going up four stairs he found himself in a room with a panoramic view over the playground and playing fields.

This had clearly been the staffroom, and while anything of value had been stripped out, there were still timetables and rotas on a noticeboard and a cupboard with *Pupils' Asthma Medicine* written on the door.

When Irena had mentioned that the playing fields were used as a landing strip, Ethan had imagined that the planes landed on the overgrown pitches. In reality long grass made for dangerous landings, so they'd been nuked with herbicides, leaving a barren dirt strip.

Ethan stepped outside through what had once been a fire door, and gave the rusted handrail a shake before deciding to trust the metal steps. A sign at the base of the stairs pointed to changing-rooms and a science block and as Ethan wanted to walk no further than he had to, he decided to head to the changing-rooms and wait there until he heard the plane.

He only made three steps before a shout came from the roof over the staffroom.

'Ethan Kitsell?' a man shouted.

He was silhouetted against the sunlight. Dressed in ragged shirt and shorts. Maybe thirty years old, with a Kalashnikov rifle and some ropes slung over his shoulder.

Ethan remembered seeing something on the Discovery Channel saying that Kalashnikovs weren't very accurate. He thought about running, but at the same time he was curious because none of Kessie's men would know his American name.

'I am Brian,' the man said, as he moved to the edge of the roof. 'I've tried sending you SMS.'

From this angle, Ethan could see that the man had a satellite phone in his hand.

'There's not much signal out here,' Ethan said.

'I am in contact with your pilot,' Brian explained. 'I was hoping you'd be bigger because we need to clear the runway.'

'I don't understand,' Ethan said, still not entirely sure that he should trust this stranger.

Brian made an athletic jump from the roof above the staffroom, hindered only by the loss of a flip-flop in midair.

'You'll see when you get closer,' Brian said. 'Your ankle is badly swollen.'

'It's agony,' Ethan said.

'But I may still need your help,' Brian said. 'If I'd known you were injured I would have brought a friend.'

Brian started walking at a brisk pace, with Ethan struggling to keep up. The problem became clear when they got past the changing-rooms: there were more than a dozen concrete blocks strewn across the runway, each one carefully camouflaged in paint that closely matched the earth.

'If it lands here before the blocks are moved your plane will be destroyed,' Brian explained.

'So you know the people who maintain this runway?'

Brian shook his head. 'My father is an old friend of your pilot. The people who control this strip won't like it at all if they know we're landing here.'

'Kessie?' Ethan asked.

Brian shook his head. 'Kessie has his own strip. Much better than this one.'

'Diamond smugglers?'

Brian smiled. 'Let's just say, I've been promised a *lot* of money for doing this and I've got no intention of sticking around long enough to meet any bad guys.'

29. BLOCKS

Ethan was weedy and with his ankle all puffed up he was worse than useless. Veins bulged and sweat bristled as Brian hooked ropes through holes in the concrete blocks and used all his strength to drag them clear of the illicit runway.

Ethan sat on the changing-room steps. Brian's satellite phone rested on the paving slab beside him as he stared with increasing alarm at an ankle that was double normal size and excruciating to move or touch.

The Samsung rang. He'd learned to screen calls for Amina, but the display flashed *international* so he answered.

'Grandma?' Ethan shouted. 'The signal's really weak out here. You're breaking up.'

'It's me, Andre,' the voice on the other end said. 'I'm trying to upload my dad's files to the FTP site, but it's really slow and it keeps crashing.'

'Shit,' Ethan said, as Brian lost his footing in the dry earth. Brian had managed the first few blocks OK, but was now on the point of exhaustion.

'So what can I do?' Andre asked.

'It's probably the Kremlin's shitty satellite connection,' Ethan said. 'You need a driver to take you into Bishkek. Go to a web café. Natalka knows the good ones.'

'I don't know where Natalka is.'

'Just get a driver to take you to Dordoi Bazaar,' Ethan said. 'There's loads of web cafés with fast connections. Even if you can upload stuff on that satellite link, it's going to take hours.'

As Ethan said this the satellite phone started ringing. 'I've got to go, Andre.'

Ethan ended the call and got a much clearer voice through the bulky satellite phone.

'Brian?' a man with a heavy South African accent said. There was an enormous jet engine roar in the background.

'It's Ethan Aramov. Are you my pilot?'

'Yes I am, and it's good to hear your voice, young man! I'll be over Kanye in around ten minutes. What's your situation?'

'Brian's hauling the blocks. He's got three to go.'

The South African laughed. 'Tell him to get his black arse moving. Your grandma wants you in Sharjah super-fast and our fuel situation is marginal.'

'I'll tell him,' Ethan said.

Brian had noticed Ethan on the phone and was running over.

'The pilot will be here in ten minutes,' Ethan shouted, flashing two sets of five fingers.

Brian looked dubious. 'That's cutting it close. Tell him to look for the all-clear signal.'

Ethan relayed the message and hung up. As soon as the phone was away from his ear, Ethan heard the distant roar of the approaching plane. As it grew louder, Brian crashed forward into the dirt as he tried moving the penultimate block.

'Jesus,' Brian shouted out furiously.

Ethan looked up and saw that the rope Brian had been using to pull the blocks had snapped.

'I've got another piece in my car,' Brian shouted. 'I'll go get it. Call your pilot and tell him there's a delay. If that fails, get out on the runway and make a signal like this.'

Brian raised his hands above his head and crossed his arms. 'If they land on the blocks it'll rip off the undercarriage.'

As Brian sprinted back through the school towards his car, Ethan finally sighted his ride. The plane's silhouette was pencil thin, with sharply raked wings. But the most extraordinary thing was the noise. Six months living at the Kremlin had acclimatised Ethan to the racket made by old Soviet jets, but this one was on a new level.

Ethan grabbed the sat phone. It was a chunky device, with a small black-on-grey LCD screen that seemed primitive compared to a modern touch phone. He didn't have the number to call his pilot, but he expected to find a call log or last dialled setting. But the sat phone was set to Japanese, or Korean, or something and the menus were entirely made up of weird kanji characters. By the time Ethan realised he needed help Brian was out of sight.

The plane was getting bigger and the noise was almost beyond comprehension as Ethan levered himself up and began limping towards the landing strip. There was still no sign of Brian so he looked up and raised his hands over his head to make the *don't land* signal.

Ethan felt like his eardrums were going to explode as the pilot aborted the landing and throttled up to gain height. The satellite phone rang moments later.

'What are you dick heads playing at down there,' the pilot shouted.

'Brian's rope broke,' Ethan explained, as he looked around for any sign of Brian's return. 'There's still two blocks on the runway.'

'Christ!' the pilot shouted. 'I'm coming around for another approach. He's got eight minutes.'

Ethan was relieved when he saw a guy coming down the steps out of the staffroom. But while he was black and dressed in shorts and a pale shirt, Ethan realised it wasn't Brian when he got closer. And when he looked back he saw Michael from the ranch running across the landing strip towards him.

'Hands up, you little shit,' Michael shouted, as he pulled a pistol and closed Ethan down. 'You killed

Kessie's cousin. He's gonna torture you bad for that!'

Ethan could barely stand, let alone run, so he put his hands into the air. He guessed they'd already nabbed Brian, or maybe he'd seen them coming and run off. But this theory got proved spectacularly wrong when a bullet punched through Michael's head.

As the gunshot echoed, Ethan backed away from a mist of blood. A second shot took out the other one of Kessie's goons with a bullet between the shoulders. While the dead goon twitched in the dirt, Brian dropped from a ground-floor window, with his Kalashnikov poised and a new coil of rope around his shoulder.

'There was another guy in the pick-up,' Brian said, as he handed Ethan the rifle. 'I've no idea where he is, so you cover my back. OK?'

'I've never shot a gun before,' Ethan said.

'It's on single shot,' Brian said. 'You've got eight rounds. Do your best.'

As Ethan limped back to the runway with the gun, Brian threaded the rope through the penultimate block and made a groaning sound as he started hauling it off the landing strip. The jet was getting really loud and coming back into view.

The last block was fifty metres further on and as Brian hooked up the rope, Ethan saw figures moving, at least one inside the school building and more coming around the side towards him.

'Brian,' Ethan shouted, as he moved to take cover behind the changing block. 'There's loads of them.'

As Brian finished dragging the last block, he sprinted

back across the dirt runway towards the changing-rooms. The satellite phone rang as he snatched the gun from Ethan.

'Are we clear?' the pilot asked.

'Blocks are clear,' Brian told the phone. 'We've got hostiles on the ground, but I'll cover them.'

Brian interrupted the call and spun around. He fired a shot that went through the open changing-room door, out of a shattered window and into the chest of a man closing in from about thirty metres. After that Brian rolled around the side of the building and took a couple of seemingly wild shots at the school.

'When the plane stops moving, you jump on my back,' Brian told Ethan.

Ethan was shaking and Brian put a hand on his shoulder.

'It's not as bad as it looks,' Brian told him. 'There's four or five of them left, but I'm a soldier and they're farm boys.'

To prove his point, Brian leaned around the side of the building and took a shot up through one of the school's shattered windows. Ethan didn't even understand how Brian had seen the movement, but a scream indicated that he'd scored a good hit.

As the plane came out of the shadows, Ethan was staggered by the noise, and impressed by an all-silver TU-22 supersonic bomber. It was a fifty-year-old Cold War relic, and even though Ethan didn't know exactly what it was, he loved the fact that he had the only grandma in the world who could dispatch one of these babies out on a rescue mission.

Ethan was convinced he'd be suffering some permanent hearing damage if he made it out of here alive because it felt like someone was trying to drill inside his ears. The bomber had thrown up a curtain of warm dust and in the confusion Ethan missed Brian's signal to jump on to his back and found himself being thrown over instead.

Brian wasn't big, but he was driven by some Herculean force as he ran through the hot dust, with a gun around his waist and Ethan over his back. The noise of the old bomber made it impossible to know if anyone was shooting at them.

Thirty seconds after leaving cover, Ethan found himself being carried through clearer air. A chain ladder had been thrown over the side of the plane, but Ethan's ankle would have been too weak to climb it so Brian raised him as high as he could and someone inside the cockpit grabbed him under the arms.

Ethan wanted to thank Brian, but as soon as he'd been relieved of Ethan's weight, Brian ducked under the aircraft's fuselage and scrambled out the other side into the surrounding bush. At least Ethan felt confident that he'd be able to get away from Kessie's farm workers.

As the clear plastic cockpit slid shut around his head, Ethan found himself being pushed into the third of the aircraft's three single-file seats.

As the bomber started a slow turn, the helmeted co-pilot pulled elastic straps of a breathing mask over Ethan's face and spoke in frantic Russian, pointing to a five-point harness. The cockpit shook as the co-pilot fitted the harness, and as Ethan buckled his he realised he could hear the pilot and co-pilot's voices through built-in speakers.

'Engines, fuel, check. Position check. Short take-off, alignment check. Full thrust on my mark.'

Ethan had been on enough flights to know the difference between the lumbering take-off of a heavy passenger jet and a smaller plane, but this was more like being launched off the top of a rollercoaster.

His neck snapped backwards as the pilot opened the throttles. All kinds of lights and warnings started to flash as the plane shot forward and then up into a near-vertical climb. A big red light with a picture of a two aeroplanes colliding was blinking right in front of Ethan's face.

'Are we OK?' Ethan shouted anxiously. 'It's lit up like Vegas back here.'

The co-pilot laughed. 'Nothing back there has worked for at least fifteen years. Just don't touch *anything*.'

As suddenly as the aircraft had taken off, they burst through cotton wool clouds. Unlike any other plane he'd been in, the cockpit surrounded Ethan on all sides and he felt like he could almost reach out and touch them.

'Sorry if that was a little bumpy,' the pilot said. 'Some of the smugglers in these parts have rocket-propelled grenades, so it's best not to stay on the ground for any longer than you have to.'

Ethan's ears hurt and his ankle was completely

buggered, but he was off the ground and hopefully back in control of his own destiny.

He laughed as he looked sideways out of his visor. 'It's absolutely damned beautiful up here.'

30. FTP

Ryan enjoyed a chance to chill out as the CIA jet swept over the Kyrgyz mountains. The stewardess served up warm baguettes and plates of nibbly stuff like crab cakes and spring rolls. There was chocolate mousse and mini donuts for dessert and after the stewardess swept crumbs off Ryan's lap he reclined the seat and watched *Fast Five* on the seatback entertainment system.

After the movie Ryan peed and decided to try connecting his BlackBerry to the plane's Wi-Fi. The bottom third of the display was dead, but almost all the keys worked and he cracked up laughing when he noticed a text message from Grace.

'Ning,' he said, as he reached across the aisle and gave her a poke.

She looked slightly irritated as she paused her movie and pulled off her headphones. 'What?'

'This is from Grace. *Just found out you were on campus for three days. When you get back next time I'm gonna cut your tiny little balls off and feed them to the campus guard dogs.*'

Ning smiled, but then shook her head. 'Buy her a gift when we get to Dubai Airport. Breaking up by text message was shitty.'

Ryan tutted. 'Grace wanted to rule my life! I couldn't fart without asking her permission.'

'I'm not talking about *why* you broke up with her,' Ning said. 'I'm talking about the *way* you did it.'

'I suppose I could get her a box of chocolates or something. I'm gonna have to see her again at some point and it might stop her from going too mental.'

'What I don't understand is, why go out with her a second time when the first break-up was such a nightmare?'

'Boobs,' Ryan admitted. 'I was sitting in the back of the taxi after the you-know-what incident. She was coming on to me, she was wearing a really tight top and I was snogging her before I even knew it.'

'Classy story,' Ning said, grinning.

'So who do you fancy on campus?' Ryan asked.

'If I fancied someone on campus you'd be the *last* person to know,' Ning said.

As Ning said this, Ryan entered the special code into his phone that switched to his Ryan Brasker identity. He'd had so little contact with Ethan over the past six weeks that he was used to seeing an empty inbox.

When he saw that Ethan had left two voice messages his first thought was that it was old stuff somehow dragged up by the dodgy phone. But both messages had today's date.

'Mr Kazakov,' Ryan shouted excitedly, as he leaned forward and tapped the top of his head.

Kazakov looked like he wanted to rip Ryan's head off as he leaned out the side of his chair and looked back.

'Don't poke my head,' he snapped furiously.

'I've got two voice messages from Ethan,' Ryan explained. 'I need your laptop.'

Kazakov looked surprised. 'Can't you just listen to them?'

Ryan shook his head. 'There's no mobile signal up here. I've just got e-mails from the TFU communication centre in Dallas saying that I've received two voicemails. If you give me your laptop I might be able to log in and download the voice files. I could try it on this phone, but with the back bashed in it probably won't sound too great.'

Kazakov opened an overhead locker.

'I'm sure Ted or Amy would have us know if anything important had happened,' Kazakov said.

'Ted told Dallas that I was offline,' Ryan said. 'But they were still having nightmares with their computers when we left for the airport and both of these messages were sent before then.'

Ning chimed in. 'So we've got no idea if TFU would have noticed these messages when the servers came back up, or passed them along to Ted or Amy?'

'Precisely,' Ryan said. 'And I'd rather be safe than sorry.'

'Technology,' Kazakov said grumpily as he passed Ryan the laptop. 'If I had my way we'd all live in the treetops.'

It took ages to get Windows booted up on Kazakov's elderly laptop. While Ryan tapped in the settings to connect to the aircraft's Wi-Fi, Ning tapped out e-mails on her iPhone asking Amy and Ted if they knew about Ethan's messages.

'Looks like at least some of the servers are back up,' Ryan said, as he logged into TFU and located the copies of the voice messages.

The in-air Internet connection wasn't the fastest and Ryan, Ning and Kazakov spent two minutes staring at the laptop screen, watching a spinning wheel and the word *buffering*. Eventually Ethan's voice came out of the loudspeaker.

'Turn it up,' Ning said urgently.

'Ryan, it's me, Ethan. This is so messed up. You're probably gonna think I'm bullshitting, but I'm not, I swear. I'm in a place called Kanye in Botswana. My uncle hijacked my plane to Dubai and I've been kept in an animal cage, but I've just escaped. I'm trying to call my grandma but she's not replying. If you get this, call me back cos I'm pretty desperate.'

'Jesus,' Ryan gasped, as he clicked to start buffering the second message.

'What's the number?' Ning asked. 'Maybe if the plane dropped height, we could pick up a mobile signal and you could call him back.'

'For all we know TFU are already working on this,' Ryan said. 'I can't call Ethan until we're sure they've not already sent him texts or e-mails under my identity.'

The second message started to play. *'Ryan, it's me again. I've spoken to my grandma now and she's gonna try getting me out of here. Looks like my crazy uncle tried to kill her and rip off all her money. My cousin Andre is uploading all the spyware data to our FTP site. If my grandma can get me out of Kanye I'll take a look myself, but if you get a chance can you log in and try finding any info on Leonid's banking or money? And if you can help, I swear it won't go unrewarded. I don't know where you are, but please call me if you can.'*

'At least he's not dead,' Ryan said as he ran hands through his hair.

'So,' Ning said, before pausing to get her thoughts together. 'Leonid Aramov ripped off his own mother's money and tried to poison her. And by now, his secrets are probably being uploaded to an FTP site.'

'We can't be sure that the spyware has captured anything useful,' Ryan said. 'But hopefully the team in Dallas are working on Ethan's uploads right now.'

'So we have access to this FTP site?' Kazakov asked.

Ryan nodded. 'I signed up to the FTP site when I needed to transfer the spyware files to Ethan. I've got all the admin passwords, so Ethan can't lock me out even if he wanted to.'

As Ryan spoke, he flipped through menus on his busted BlackBerry looking for the web address and password for the FTP site. When he finally logged in using Kazakov's laptop, the screen filled with yellow envelopes, each one representing a folder of information.

'Looks like they had problems,' Ryan said, as he

pointed to the first few online folders. 'Judging by the upload time it was taking six or seven minutes between each file, but if you scroll down you can see new files being uploaded much faster.'

Ryan scrolled to the bottom of the FTP site page. Ning and Kazakov looked on as new envelopes popped up every few seconds.

'So Leonid's data is being uploaded as we speak?' Kazakov asked.

Ryan nodded. 'Looks like cousin Andre found a nice speedy Internet connection.'

Ryan opened up a new tab in his web browser and typed *Kanye Botswana* into Bing Maps, just to see where it was.

Kazakov looked at the stewardess sitting up back. 'Do you know when we're due to land?'

'Just under an hour,' she said.

As the stewardess answered the co-pilot came out of the cockpit. 'Is there a Ryan Sharma on board?' he asked.

Ryan put his hand up. 'Guilty.'

'I've got Amy Collins on the sat phone. She says it's urgent.'

The phone was wired into the aircraft's cockpit, so Ryan had to stand in a cramped space behind the pilot's seat with the curly-corded handset at full stretch.

'Amy,' Ryan said.

'Ryan, this is *beyond* huge,' Amy said excitedly.

Ryan gasped. 'You didn't know about Ethan's messages?'

'I didn't,' Amy said. 'Neither did anyone at

headquarters in Dallas. Ted asked them to forward any communications from Ethan to his laptop, but I guess it's only forwarding newly arrived messages. These ones must have come through while the servers were down.'

'Are they working on it now?' Ryan asked.

'You bet they are. I just hope we're not too late, because if Leonid has stolen his mother's money, that psycho now has effective control of the Aramov Clan.'

'How do you figure that?' Ryan asked.

'Wages,' Amy said. 'Fuel bills, bribes, aircraft maintenance, rent. If Irena can't pay her bills, the Aramov Clan is nothing but a few million bucks' worth of tatty aircraft and a lot of pissed-off staff.'

'So if you control the money, you control the clan,' Ryan said.

'And it's dodgy money,' Amy said. 'It's not like Irena can drop into Bishkek police station and file a complaint. Right now, Leonid probably has the money. Ethan wants to find Leonid's passwords and bank account details so that control over it passes back to Irena. But if we get to the passwords before Ethan, we might be able to lock out Leonid *and* Irena.'

'Nice,' Ryan said, as he nodded. 'We steal the money, the Aramov Clan can't pay its bills.'

'Exactly,' Amy said. 'And with Irena dying and Leonid a raving psychopath the instability might tear the entire organisation apart.'

Ryan laughed. 'Is there a navy CHERUB shirt in that?'

'Could be,' Amy said. 'But don't start counting

chickens. We're not even sure that the spyware has captured Leonid's banking passwords.'

'We should have a big speed advantage over Ethan,' Ryan said. 'He'll be looking through the uploaded files on his own.'

'The CIA's top hacking team is about to start work,' Amy said. 'But I still want you to get in touch with Ethan as soon as you can. Irena might give him information about her financial dealings that we won't have, and she'll have had Leonid's office and apartment searched. For all we know, there's a full list of passwords sitting in his desk drawer.'

Ryan's vision blurred as he looked at all the cockpit dials and screens. 'I'm not usually the nervous type,' he said. 'But this is *immense*. I hope I don't put my foot in it with Ethan or something.'

31. SHARJAH

As Ryan, Ning and Kazakov closed on Dubai, the TU-22 bomber flew at three times the speed towards Sharjah Airport, ten kilometres north.

Ethan asked the South African pilot about his plane and got a half-hour spiel on how he'd bought up TU-22s from Libya and Iraq and cannibalised them for parts to keep two high-speed planes flying.

'I'm the only supersonic smuggler on earth,' he boasted. 'Take any two points on the globe and this bird can get between them in under fifteen hours. I've even flown film stars, so they can attend movie premieres on two different continents in the same night.'

'Did you get autographs and stuff?' Ethan asked.

'You can't really,' the pilot said. 'It's not professional.'

Everything in the TU-22 was noisy, but at least the landing was less brutal than take-off. They taxied a few hundred metres from Sharjah's main runway to an unmarked hangar with three characteristically tatty Aramov cargo planes inside.

Ethan had no documents and he was concerned by the sight of a customs official as the co-pilot helped him down a set of wheeled steps.

Alongside the customs man was a slim woman dressed in a business suit. She handed Ethan a brand new Kyrgyz passport, which already had the entry stamp for his arrival. The document appeared completely genuine, with a photograph taken from his Facebook profile.

While the customs official dealt with the two South African pilots, the slim woman led Ethan briskly towards an office at the back.

'You're struggling with that ankle,' the woman said, speaking English with a slight French accent. 'I'll arrange a wheelchair, and I'll take you to the hospital later to get it looked at.'

'Who are you exactly?' Ethan asked.

'I'm Ruby,' the woman said. 'I'm an accountant, and I run the Clanair operation here in Sharjah. I've known your grandmother for many years and we've been in touch over the past few hours. Your cousin Andre is still uploading files and your grandmother has faxed across some banking details. I'm no computer buff, but hopefully my accounting background can help you locate the relevant information.'

'I was wondering how fast money can be moved between banks,' Ethan said. 'Is it instant?'

'It depends on the country, the bank, the amount of

money involved. Your best bet is to target accounts to which Leonid moved the largest sums. If you can't move the money back to your grandmother's accounts, try changing his passwords to lock him out.'

'You think he'd have used Internet banking?' Ethan asked.

'That's a near certainty,' Ruby said. 'Almost all business banking is done over the Internet these days.'

'That's good for us,' Ethan said. 'Provided he didn't do it on a computer we don't know about.'

By this time they'd exited the hangar, passed along a short corridor and were stepping into a small office with a single PC and a big window looking out over the runway. Ruby had already logged the computer into the FTP site and set it to download all the files.

'I've installed the decryption program but I haven't accessed any of the spyware files because I'd need your key,' Ruby explained.

'No problem,' Ethan said, as he lowered himself into an office chair. 'Can I get a drink? Coke or something?'

'Sure,' Ruby said.

As Ruby headed out, Ethan looked at the keyboard and screen. After animal cages, planes and African towns there was something soothing about sitting in front of a Windows desktop with a mouse in hand.

The spyware files were coming through in date order. So far there were 370 data files and 3,700 screen shots from the computer at the stable, plus a file that had logged every keystroke typed into the computer.

Ethan decided to begin by targeting files and

screenshots from the hours immediately after Irena had been poisoned, as Ruby came back into the room holding a laptop, a can of warm Pepsi and a sheath of faxes.

'How can I help?' she asked.

'Is the laptop on the same network as my PC?' Ethan asked, as he finished entering his key and clicked a button to start decrypting files.

'It is,' Ruby said. 'This is my office and my laptop.'

'I've never done this before,' Ethan said. 'But if I start going through the documents Leonid accessed, you can look through the screen captures.'

'What about the weblog?' Ruby asked.

Ethan looked confused until he scrolled up the screen and found a file called *weblog*.

'I didn't know that was there,' Ethan admitted.

'Well I'm no spy,' Ruby said. 'But if the key log file logs keystrokes, the weblog file probably records all the websites Leonid visited.'

Ethan was starting to like Ruby and finished her sentence. 'So we hunt through looking for the URLs of online banking sites. Then we look at the key logs and screenshots from the same time period and with any luck we'll be able to capture Leonid's login details.'

Ruby began flipping through the faxes, and read something off one of them. 'Irena thinks Leonid has a friend at a Russian bank called Industrial Trust. So let's search for that website first.'

As Ethan decrypted the weblog file, Ruby found the website for Industrial Trust on Google and clicked through to the bank's customer login screen.

'Search the weblog for the Industrial Trust website,' Ruby said.

Ethan opened the weblog file up in Microsoft Word and did a search. The document was twenty pages long and it jumped to a bunch of references to RITB on page sixteen. Until this Ethan hadn't even been sure that Leonid used this computer for banking.

'Holy shit,' he said, as he looked back at Ruby. 'I'll get the key log for the time he logged in, you check the screenshots.'

The Industrial Trust banking site used drop-down menus to prevent logins being detected by a simple key logger program, but the spyware also recorded screenshots of whatever Leonid did.

'Looks like his password is *IlOvmyself*,' Ethan said, as he studied the key log.

But Ruby had less success with the screenshots. 'When you log into the online banking it asks for three digits from your security number,' she explained. 'I've got the third, seventh and ninth digits here, but if we try to log on it'll ask for different ones.'

'Crap,' Ethan said. 'Let's hope he's logged on more than once.'

He checked through the log files and found two more Industrial Trust logins. When Ruby checked the drop-down screenshots she managed to get digits one, two, five and eight of Leonid's security number.

Ethan wrote what they had on a Post-it note:

'We could try logging in,' Ethan said. 'There's a decent chance that it won't ask for digits four or six.'

Ruby nodded in agreement. 'We've got nothing to lose. It won't lock us out after one failed attempt.'

Ethan opened a web browser and navigated to the Industrial Trust login page. He entered Leonid's password. He was satisfied when a green tick appeared and a little box slid open.

'Please enter digits two, three and nine of your security code.'

'You're in luck,' Ruby said brightly.

Ethan swigged his Pepsi as he entered the numbers using the drop-down boxes and pressed *enter*.

A banking home screen appeared with *Welcome Leonid Aramov* written at the top. Below it was a listing of five different accounts. Three were in euros, one in Russian roubles and one in US dollars. The rouble accounts seemed to have the big numbers in them.

'Any idea about the exchange rates?' Ethan asked.

'It's around thirty roubles to one US dollar,' Ruby said. 'Nine hundred and eighty-four million roubles is around thirty-two million US dollars.'

Ethan smiled. 'So that's almost half of Grandma's missing money right here. Get me the details of one of my grandma's accounts. I'll try and transfer it back.'

Ruby read details of one of Irena's accounts from a fax message. Ethan tapped the details in the transfer screen and hit *send*, but a warning box popped up on the screen.

Transfers in excess of 2,500,000 roubles require further verification. Please contact your personal banking representative for full details.

'Shit!' Ethan said, as he looked around the screen. 'I guess we could do it two and a half million at a time but it would take a while.'

'And the bank's fraud protection systems would pick that up in a heartbeat,' Ruby said.

'OK,' Ethan said, as he clicked on the *change details* button. 'Let's try something else.'

A screen opened up where you could change any personal details after you'd re-entered the password and a mother's maiden name. He tapped the screen.

'I don't know what Grandma's name was before she got married, but we can find that out. This is the tricky part.'

Ruby leaned forward and read the text aloud. 'All changes to personal details must be confirmed via e-mail.'

'So,' Ethan said, jerking with pain as his ankle caught the edge of the desk. 'It looks like Leonid's set up a Gmail account. We're going to need to access that before we can change his passwords, so let's go through the logs and see if he's accessed it over the last few weeks.'

32. DUBAI

Kazakov, Ryan and Ning had touched down in Dubai a few minutes before Ethan's arrival in Sharjah. But while Ethan had gone straight to a hangar, the instructor and CHERUB agents found their arrival at the private jet terminal coinciding with the departure of Dubai's Crown Prince, so they were forced to wait aboard their plane for a full half-hour.

'My mobile's dead,' Ning said impatiently. 'There's no airport Wi-Fi. It's like someone's blocking all the signals.'

'That's exactly what's happening,' Kazakov explained. 'Wireless and cellphones can be used to trigger bombs, so when very important people move around they switch off all the networks.'

Ning nodded. 'All these Arab leaders are shitting their pants after the uprisings.'

'It shouldn't matter much,' Ryan said. 'TFU is a pretty small set-up, but Amy said they've got a crack CIA hacking team working on this now.'

'Your personal touch with Ethan might still be vital,' Kazakov said.

As soon as the Crown Prince's jet was in the air, the ground crew rolled steps up to the plane. A few seconds after that, the Wi-Fi network kicked in and signal bars started reappearing on cellphone screens all over the airport.

It was two in the afternoon in Dubai, which made it 3 a.m. in California, where Ethan thought Ryan was. Normally Ryan would avoid calling when he ought to be asleep in California, but the situation was critical so he risked it.

While Ryan logged into the Ethan identity on his wrecked BlackBerry and made a call that would reroute through TFU headquarters in Dallas and appear to be coming from the USA, Ning called Amy for an update.

Ryan was stepping into the airport's marbled VIP lounge as Ethan answered.

'I just got your messages,' Ryan said. 'Your life is *insane*. Are you safe?'

Ethan sounded distracted. 'It's good to hear your voice, Ryan! I am safe. I'm in Sharjah in the United Arab Emirates.'

'Sharjah,' Ryan said, astonished to find that Ethan was less than twenty kilometres away, and had travelled from southern Africa in the time it had taken them to move half that distance from Kyrgyzstan.

'Ryan, no disrespect,' Ethan said. 'But I'm in the middle of some serious shit. I'll call you back when this is over.'

'I can help you,' Ryan said keenly. 'You said something about the FTP.'

'It's all good, bro,' Ethan said. 'Well, my shoulder's agony, my feet are blistered and my ankle is up shit creek, but Grandma found an old Russian bomber to get me out of Africa and now I'm hacking up Leonid.'

'I can totally help you with that,' Ryan said. 'It's the middle of the night, but I don't care.'

'I've got an accountant on the case with me. I'm in Leonid's online banking and I've just cracked his Gmail account. I'm sorry, but I'm hanging up.'

Ryan tried thinking of one last-ditch way to get information out of Ethan, but the line went dead.

'Cocky little bastard,' Ryan complained.

Ning was still on the phone with Amy. It sounded like things were going OK, but Ryan and Kazakov had to wait until Ning hung up to get a full report.

'There's a CIA team working on the spyware files,' Ning explained. 'Leonid has divided his mother's money between at least ten banks. They've already transferred a few million dollars out of one account and they're working through the rest. How was Ethan?'

'Sounded pretty chipper,' Ryan said, as an expression of concern spread across his face. 'He must be accessing different accounts to the CIA team. Sooner or later he's going to log into something and find that we've been there first.'

They'd almost reached the customs desks when Kazakov had a realisation. 'Did I hear you say Sharjah?'

'You did,' Ryan said.

They had to break for a moment as they flashed passports at a customs officer. Kazakov got asked if Ryan and Ning were his own kids, and after explaining that he was their tutor and that they were travelling on to Britain they got waved through.

'I've got a text from Ted saying that we're booked on a flight to London in a little over three hours,' Kazakov said, as they stepped on to a downwards escalator into the transit hall. 'But we're not getting on it.'

'Why not?' Ning asked.

'It's important that we get control of all of Irena's money,' Kazakov said. 'Ethan's got to change Leonid's passwords to *something*. And if we can get hold of Ethan, I'm sure I can tease the new passwords out of him with a little gentle persuasion.'

'Shouldn't we check with Ted or Amy first?' Ning asked.

'I'll let them know what I'm doing,' Kazakov said. 'But it's not like they're going to say no, is it?'

The trio stepped through automatic doors into muggy air. There was no taxi rank, but a smartly dressed chauffeur dashed across the tarmac and gave a little bow.

'Limousine, sir?' he said brightly. 'Which hotel, sir?'

'Sharjah Airport,' Kazakov said. 'Quick as you can.'

The trio didn't waste time putting bags in the trunk and lobbed them all into the back of the stretched limo.

Although the long car looked cool from the outside, Ryan was disappointed by a shabby interior that smelled vaguely of wet dog.

Kazakov pressed the button to raise the privacy screen and looked at Ning as the driver vanished behind a rising leatherette wall.

'You're faster with those smartphone keyboards than me,' Kazakov told Ning. 'We know the Aramovs have a base at Sharjah. An office, maybe even their own hangar. Get me an address.'

'The Aramovs' more reputable flights are run as Clanair,' Ryan said. 'It'll probably be under that.'

Ning only took a few taps to get an exact address for Clanair's Sharjah Airport hangar, but the traffic was horrendous and they took fifteen minutes just to reach the main road out of the airport. Amy called Ning just as they turned on to the expressway heading towards Sharjah.

'It's not looking that great,' Amy said dejectedly. 'The CIA team has taken control of eight of Leonid's bank accounts and TFU in Dallas are trying to get a couple of accounts inside the European Union frozen under money-laundering laws. But the big money was in Russia and it looks like Ethan beat us to it.'

'So much for the CIA's team of experts,' Ning said.

'Ethan must have been tipped off by his grandmother,' Amy said. 'It seems he went straight for a bank called Industrial Trust and unless Irena's a lot poorer than we thought, Ethan's now got control over the vast majority of her money.'

As Amy spoke, Kazakov gave Ning a signal to pass the phone over.

'We're on our way over to the Clanair hangar to find him,' Kazakov said. 'I'm sure a little Spetsnaz-style persuasion can wring a few passwords out of a thirteen-year-old.'

*

Andre had just got back from a web café in Dordoi Bazaar when Ethan called to speak with Irena.

'Ruby's added it all up,' Ethan told his grandmother. 'She reckons eighty-six million was transferred out of Leonid's accounts. I'm currently controlling accounts with seventy-three million in them.'

'You're a good boy,' Irena said softly.

'Passwords got changed on some of the minor accounts before I got to the other thirteen million,' Ethan said. 'Leonid must have been tipped off somehow.'

'Must have,' Irena said thoughtfully. 'I'll know soon enough. My spy at the hospital says he's on his way back here.'

33. SHOWDOWN

People moved aside as Leonid and Alex Aramov strode through the Kremlin lobby. One of the guards asked how Boris was doing and Leonid almost ripped his head off.

'He'd be doing better if the security teams around here didn't have their heads up their arses,' he barked.

There was a woman with a cleaner's cart waiting for the lift.

'Get the next one,' Leonid ordered, as he shoved past her. 'Ugly old bag.'

Even the lift seemed scared of Leonid and the doors closed obediently, without any of their usual shuddering back and forth. When he got to the sixth floor Leonid strode purposefully out of the lift towards his apartment, with Alex two paces behind.

'Mr Aramov, I must ask you to stop right there.'

Leonid looked back and was surprised to see two bulky men with handguns at the ready.

'Where did you two monkeys come from?' Leonid roared. 'You work downstairs, you pricks.'

The bigger of the two men took a step forward. 'I'm going to have to ask you to hand over any weapons you may be carrying.'

'Hands off,' Leonid shouted.

As Leonid turned back, he saw another big guy push Irena into the hallway in her wheelchair.

'Have you lost it, Mother?' Leonid shouted. 'Swallowed too many pills again?'

'Shut up,' Irena ordered. 'Take the gun out from under your jacket. Do it slowly or I'll tell them to shoot you.'

'She's high on painkillers,' Leonid told the guards. 'You can't listen to what she tells you.'

'I know you tried to kill me,' Irena growled. 'But you messed that up, like so many other things. Now open your jacket and drop the gun. Alex, the same goes for anything you're carrying.'

Leonid grimaced as he took his gun out and placed it on the carpet between his boots.

'Kick it across,' Irena said.

Leonid did as he was told and one of the heavies swooped in and picked the gun up.

'Both of you take your boots off,' Irena ordered. 'You've been known to keep knives down there.'

Leonid pulled off his boots, but Alex was only wearing trainers. Once they were both unshod the bodyguards patted them down.

'What kind of boy tries to kill his own mother?' Irena asked bitterly. 'Let's go to my room.'

The bodyguards stayed close behind as Leonid took the short walk down the hallway to Irena's living-room. Andre was there, and tried making himself invisible by backing up to a mirror over a fake fireplace.

'Sit,' Irena said.

Leonid smiled. 'It doesn't matter that you're alive, Mum. Your money's long gone and your goons had better think hard if they want to see next month's wages.'

Irena smiled back. 'You transferred my money, but you're not as clever as you like to think you are. Everything you typed on your computer was logged. Every web page you visited. Every security number and password. Over the past couple of hours we've changed all your passwords and begun transferring the money back to my accounts.'

Leonid's face drooped. 'You're paranoid. I didn't try to kill you.'

'Do you know how pathetic that sounds?' Irena asked. 'If you were anyone other than my son you'd be dead in a ditch already.'

Leonid pushed his hands into the pockets of his leather jacket and looked like a sulky kid. 'I want control,' he shouted. 'I've worked for the clan since I was thirteen years old.'

'Pity you didn't use all that time to grow up,' Irena said. 'You were a selfish child who became a selfish adult.'

Leonid hesitated for a few seconds before dramatically playing his final hand. 'If you want to see your grandson alive, you'll back off.'

Irena raised one eyebrow. 'Which grandson would that be?'

'Ethan.'

'He seemed perfectly fine when I spoke to him ten minutes ago,' Irena said. 'And fortunately he inherited his mother's brain. He's long suspected that you killed his mother. Ethan put the spyware on your computers to try and prove it.'

Leonid didn't know what to say to his mother, so he turned on Andre. 'What's your part in this?' he shouted. 'Did you betray your own father?'

Andre looked frightened, but spoke defiantly. 'You killed your sister, you kidnapped Ethan and tried to kill Grandma. How am *I* the disloyal one?'

'Don't take it out on a ten-year-old,' Irena said firmly. 'You have one hour to pack your things. You can take a plane to wherever you want to go, but if you set foot in Kyrgyzstan or interfere with clan affairs I'll come down hard. You'll receive a monthly allowance that will enable you to live comfortably. Alex and Boris are loyal to you and must leave with you. Andre and your ex-wife can make up their own minds.'

'I'm staying here,' Andre said instantly.

'This isn't over,' Leonid hissed. 'Everyone inside the clan knows you're past it.'

'Maybe I am past it,' Irena said. 'But that doesn't mean they want to work for you.'

'Bitch!' Leonid spat.

Irena's eyes were misting over as she reached for the plastic mask attached to an oxygen cylinder under her chair.

'My own son,' she said softly. 'You appal me.'

Leonid roared with laughter. 'Our planes are responsible for half the heroin on the streets of Europe. You deliver cluster bombs to psychopaths. Girls get kidnapped and sold as sex slaves. You taught me everything I know, Mother.'

'You don't speak to me like that, *boy*,' Irena shouted. 'Bring him here.'

Leonid was no weakling, but the bodyguards were twice his size.

'Kneel,' Irena ordered, as Leonid was held in front of her. Then she looked back at Andre. 'Get your grandfather's dagger from the mantelpiece.'

Andre trembled as he took the knife from the shelf. His grandfather had been a boy soldier in the Red Army and he'd stolen the dagger from a dead German officer. It smelled oily and the button on the leather sheath popped as Irena pulled the knife out and pushed its tip against Leonid's throat.

Leonid tried moving away, but the huge guards had him clamped.

'If I live much longer I expect I'll regret letting you go,' Irena told Leonid. 'But in my heart you're *still* the boy who sat on this floor playing Lego with Josef and Galenka.'

Leonid smiled. Andre gasped with relief, because

while he didn't think much of his dad he didn't want to watch his throat get cut either. But Leonid's smug grin needled his mother, so she tugged his ear, then slashed down with the knife, cutting it clean off his head.

The move was swift for someone so frail and the guard was so shocked by the spurting blood that he let Leonid go.

Leonid screamed, as blood gushed down the side of his neck. He made a lunge at Irena's wheelchair, but the bodyguards grabbed him under the arms and slammed him into the wall.

'One hour to pack,' Irena shouted. 'Stick a bandage around his thick head and don't let him out of your sight until his plane's off the ground.'

Irena made a little sob, as all the blood and stress sent Andre into a dry heave.

'Somebody take this away,' Irena said, as she dropped her son's ear at her feet. 'And get a cleaner up here to scrub the blood out of this rug. I'm very fond of it. It really ties the room together.'

*

The limousine was on the access roads around Sharjah Airport when Ryan's phone rang. *International* flashed on the display.

'Hey, man,' Ethan said.

'It's him,' Ryan mouthed, as he made a shush gesture.

Ning and Kazakov both nodded, and leaned forward trying to listen in.

'Ethan, buddy! How's it hanging?'

Ethan sounded really happy. 'I just shoved it to my

uncle Leonid, big time.'

'Seriously?' Ryan said. 'What happened?'

'He tried to rip my gran off. But I had the spyware on his computer. I got up in all his banking and e-mail. Locked him out of a bunch of accounts. Transferred a bunch of money back to my grandma.'

'Sweet,' Ryan said. 'Leonid must be furious.'

'Last I heard he was heading back to the Kremlin and my grandma was gonna nail his arse.'

'So where are you now?'

'This lady Ruby who works for my gran is driving me to a hospital in Dubai. I jumped off a building in Kanye and messed up my ankle pretty good.'

'You're heading to Dubai,' Ryan said, more for the benefit of his fellow passengers than anything else.

Meantime, Ning had typed something in the notes app on her phone and held it in front of Ryan's face:

ASK HIM ABOUT THE PASSWORDS!

'I finally feel like something good is about to happen in my life!' Ethan said. 'I can't get Mom back, but at least I won't have this Leonid thing weighing me down.'

Ryan couldn't ask Ethan for his passwords directly, but he had an idea.

'Just make sure you don't forget all those passwords you changed,' he said jokingly.

Ethan laughed. 'No fear. I sent them all to a safe place. And I hope I didn't piss you off earlier, but you called when everything was manic.'

'Not at all.'

'I've gotta go, I'm pulling into the hospital,' Ethan said. 'I'll call tomorrow or something and we can have a proper chat.'

'For sure,' Ryan said. 'Keep in touch.'

'Always, mate.'

As Ryan ended the call, Kazakov pressed the intercom button to speak to the driver. 'Turn it around. We're heading back to Dubai. I'll let you know where in a moment.'

Ryan spoke to Ning. 'Ethan said he sent all the passwords to a safe place. You can be sure that doesn't mean he printed them off and put them in the post.'

'What online accounts does he use?' Ning asked.

'Skype, Hotmail and Facebook mostly,' Ryan said. 'We've got his login details for all of them. Sir, can I borrow your laptop again?'

'Knock yourself out,' Kazakov said, before leaning forward and digging his laptop from the mound of baggage in the middle of the car.

The computer was in sleep mode, and as Ryan opened the lid and connected it to a local 3G network, Ning used the browser on her phone to try finding a list of hospitals where Ethan might have ended up. As the traffic looked bad in both directions and Ethan had arrived already, she figured that the hospital had to be near the border between the Emirates of Sharjah and Dubai.

'I reckon it's one of two hospitals,' Ning said. 'Both less than five kilometres from here.'

As soon as Ryan connected the laptop to the Internet he logged into his CHERUB agent portal, in which he stored data relating to his missions. It took a few seconds to locate the file named *Ethan*, which contained all Ethan's known login and online account details.

Once he had Ethan's passwords, Ryan logged into Ethan's Hotmail. The inbox contained tons of spam, the outbox had nothing recent, but there was an unsent message in the draft box. Ryan clicked it and saw a list of bank names, passwords and security numbers.

'I've bloody well got it,' he shouted jubilantly.

Ning leaned over to see and gave Ryan a grin. Ryan called Amy, but Ted answered.

'She's in the toilet,' Ted explained. 'Can I help?'

'I've got the lot,' Ryan said. 'I just spoke to Ethan. He was on the way to a hospital and he said he'd sent the passwords somewhere safe. So I logged into his Hotmail and they're all there in an unsent draft.'

'Nice to get a bit of luck for once,' Ted said. 'E-mail the list through to Dallas. They'll pass it on to the experts at the CIA, who can change all the passwords and lock Ethan out.'

'Copying and pasting as I speak,' Ryan said.

'This all sounds great,' Ted said. 'But we can't be certain this is *all* the information we need to access the accounts. So your job is to track Ethan down.'

'Ethan thinks I'm in California,' Ryan said. 'My cover's shot if he sees me here.'

'Stay in the background then,' Ted replied. Then jokingly, 'Or see if the hospital shop does balaclavas.'

34. NEWS

Amy called Ryan back as they approached a mirrored-glass hospital building, surrounded by a huge half-empty parking lot.

'I've got good news and good news,' Amy said cheerfully. 'Which do you want to hear first?'

'Guess it'll be the good news then,' Ryan said.

'Dubai has a centralised patient management system that the CIA can access at will. Ten minutes ago, a record got created for a new patient called Ethan Aramov. He's at Gulf Medical Institute.'

'Perfect,' Ryan said. 'We're heading into their parking lot.'

'He's in accident and emergency, bay sixteen. Preliminary assessment is that his condition is non-critical and he's due to be seen by a Dr Patel within fifteen minutes.'

Ryan relayed the news to the others in the limo before Amy continued.

'Second piece of good news: we got into Industrial Trust Bank using the passwords you hacked from Ethan. He couldn't transfer money out in chunks greater than two and a half million roubles, but that only applies to interbank transfers. So our boffins found a US-based advertising agency that does its Russian banking through Industrial Trust and transferred the entire nine hundred million roubles to them.'

'So the Aramovs are gonna be flat broke,' Ryan said.

'We've got them by the balls,' Amy agreed. 'Dan's inside the Kremlin, and says he'll be in touch as soon as he hears anything.'

'Nice update, Amy,' Ryan said. 'Everything's going our way at last.'

The car had pulled up at the hospital's visitor entrance. As Ning started dragging the bags out, Kazakov pulled his wallet from the back of his trousers and offered the driver a credit card.

'Cash only,' the driver said.

Kazakov waved some euros.

'AED,' the driver said furiously.

'I haven't been to a cash machine yet, there must be one inside the hospital,' Kazakov explained. He looked stressed as he turned to Ryan and Ning. 'Have you kids got any Arab Emirates dirhams on you?'

'I gave the last of our money to Alfie before we left,' Ning answered.

The driver was ranting as he climbed out of his car. 'I

not like your custom,' he shouted, as he frantically wagged a pointing finger. 'First you say Sharjah. Then hospital. Then you have no money.'

After the dim limo interior, Ryan got blinded by low sun as he helped Ning pull out their luggage. They were on a kerb close to a taxi rank and a set of automatic doors. When a hospital security guard in fluorescent vest heard the driver shouting he came striding over.

'Is there a cash machine inside?' Kazakov asked.

'No money!' the driver shouted.

It was hard to work out exactly why the driver was so angry and he kept yelling as the hospital security guard pointed out a cash machine inside the visitor's lobby, less than fifteen metres away. With all the noise and his mobile ringer more or less screwed Ryan almost missed the next call on his BlackBerry.

'Hello,' Ryan said.

'Long time no speak,' Dr D said.

Ryan gulped.

Dr D was the petite, screechy-voiced head of TFU, which made her Amy and Ted's boss. The last time Ryan had spoken to her, it had been a furious row over whether she should have allowed Ethan to be dragged off to Kyrgyzstan.

The row had ended with Ryan giving Dr D an almighty shove, which got him kicked off the mission and earned him five hundred hours working in the recycling centre when he got back to CHERUB campus.

Dr D's decision had almost got Ethan killed, but it now looked like a triumph, with Ethan safe and TFU on the verge of bringing down a criminal empire.

'How's it going?' Ryan asked uncomfortably.

'Let's start with a clean sheet,' Dr D said. 'The past has passed. We all do things we regret.'

'We're having a good day,' Ryan said. 'I guess.'

'We are,' Dr D said cheerfully. 'And much of our success is down to you. I'm en route from Dallas Fort Worth to Dubai, but it's going to be morning before I arrive. I understand you've tracked down Ethan?'

'Yeah,' Ryan said. 'Though I guess we don't really need him now I've got all the passwords.'

'Oh yes we do, baby!' Dr D said. 'We have the Aramovs where we want them, but how we play the next stage is critical. Get it wrong and the big snake turns into a nest of little ones.'

Ryan had learned this lesson in basic training. Whether you're talking about a neighbourhood drug gang, a terrorist group or even a rogue government, it's relatively easy to take out the top dog. But without a proper plan to dismantle an organisation you end up with a bunch of unstable splinter groups that are even more dangerous.

'Taking the Aramov Clan apart should take somewhere between six months and two years,' Dr D explained.

Ryan was distracted because he could hear Kazakov and the driver rowing inside the hospital building. Apparently Kazakov had an overdraft and his ATM card wasn't doing the business.

'I've got another card in my luggage,' Kazakov shouted. 'Let me go back for it.'

'I want police!' the driver was shouting.

Ryan spoke to Dr D, as he pulled a small Velcro pouch out of his jeans. 'Hang on, I need to save Kazakov from getting arrested.'

Ryan dashed inside the hospital and handed Kazakov a cash card. 'Six, four, nine, eight,' he told him.

'Sorry,' Ryan told Dr D as he headed back out through the automatic doors into the setting sun. 'You were saying?'

'The first step is for you to approach Ethan. You can tell him that you've been working with us without mentioning the existence of CHERUB. Then you'll explain that we now control Irena's money.'

'Ethan's gonna hate my guts,' Ryan said.

'Probably,' Dr D agreed. 'But you can appeal to his moral side. The Aramov organisation is responsible for some pretty horrific stuff.'

'I can try,' Ryan said uncertainly. 'I understand about winding the clan down gently, but I still don't get why Ethan's so important.'

'Irena thinks Ethan just saved her organisation. Right now, she'll pick up the phone when Ethan calls and listen to what he says. Irena is too cautious to take calls from complete strangers, and our only alternative would be to make contact by sending Amy and Ted to the Kremlin to ask for a meeting.'

'And Irena might just have them shot if she loses her rag,' Ryan said.

'Precisely,' Dr D said. 'So once we have Ethan onside – or at least firmly under our control – we'll use him to approach Irena and give her an ultimatum.'

'Poor bloody Ethan,' Ryan said. 'Everyone manipulates him. Me included.'

'I'm not proud of that,' Dr D said. 'But everything that we've done to Ethan has been for the greater good. When this is over we'll make sure he's OK.'

'So what's Irena's incentive to do what we say?' Ryan asked.

'Irena spent almost her entire adult life building up the Aramov Clan,' Dr D explained. 'If she lets us gently take control and wind clan operations down, her family will be protected and she'll be allowed to live out her final days in a reasonable level of comfort.'

'And otherwise?' Ryan asked.

'Without money, the Aramov Clan will be paralysed. Airports like Sharjah won't even let a plane take off if the refuelling bill hasn't been paid. People loyal to Leonid might try staging a coup, but he doesn't have the money to make the organisation work either. Irena will get sicker and sicker and her family will be at risk as the clan crumbles into anarchy.'

'But *we* don't want anarchy either,' Ryan pointed out.

'True,' Dr D said. 'Which is why this whole situation has got to be handled delicately.'

'So when do I approach Ethan?' Ryan asked. 'Now?'

'No,' Dr D said. 'Ethan's going to be exhausted, and I need time to work out the finer points of our strategy. Tell Kazakov to stay at the hospital. Right now your team's job is to make sure Ethan isn't moved out of the hospital and to track him if he is. I'll be back in touch when I know more, OK?'

'Right,' Ryan said, as he looked inside and was much relieved to see Kazakov handing the limo driver some local currency. 'Speak soon then, I guess.'

35. KUBAN

The Gulf Medical Institute's building was flash, with glass atriums and automatic doors everywhere you stepped. Every patient had a private room and the broad palm-filled corridors had comfortable nooks for visitors, filled with sofas, vending machines and TVs showing rolling news.

Back in Kyrgyzstan, Amy had used the CIA's hack into the Dubai healthcare database to track Ethan's progress. After an X-ray confirmed that his ankle wasn't broken, he'd had numerous scrapes and cuts treated before being wheeled to his room.

Ethan was put on an intravenous drip because his African stomach ailments had left him badly dehydrated, and after a nurse had strapped his swollen ankle she told him that he was being kept overnight for observation and gave him a strong sedative so that he could sleep off the worst of his pain.

Ruby the accountant stayed with Ethan until just after 9 p.m. Amy looked for a local British or American intelligence agent who could keep an eye on Ethan, but nobody was available so Ryan, Ning and Kazakov sprawled out on sofas in the visitors' area, with the door of Ethan's room in plain sight, ten metres down a hallway.

None of the trio had slept properly the previous night, and all three were in a zombie-like state. Kazakov fuelled himself up with bitter vending-machine coffee and told the kids that they could sleep. This wasn't easy with staff and patients coming by to drop coins in the machines, but Ryan managed to crash with his feet propped on a glass table. Ning wasn't so lucky and ended up flipping through the neat rows of upmarket magazines, with her eyes blurring whenever she tried to read.

'I need the loo,' Ning told Kazakov as she stood. 'Do you want a drink or anything while I'm up?'

'I'm good, thanks,' Kazakov said.

Ning only half needed the toilet. Mainly she was sick of sitting around and wanted to stretch her legs. There was a double-height space with a fountain at the corridor's far end. The shutters were down on a pair of food kiosks and there was a janitor emptying out the bins, but she found the rushing water soothing and dipped her hand into a chloriney jet and made it splash over her face.

As Ning did this she noticed two men, dressed near-identically in tight jeans and black leather jackets. She kind of recognised one of them, but dismissed it as a symptom of exhaustion until she put a name to the face:

Kuban.

He was one of Leonid Aramov's henchmen and he'd led the torture of Ning's stepmother. She didn't fancy taking on the two bulky men who'd just strode through the automatic doors leading down a corridor to Ethan's room, so she whipped out her mobile and dialled Kazakov.

'Two bad guys coming your way,' Ning said rapidly. 'You'll see them in a few seconds.'

Ryan was in the middle of a dream where he was scoffing a big KFC bucket when Kazakov jerked him awake.

'Ning says there's two guys coming,' Kazakov told him. 'I'm gonna try heading them off.'

Ryan rubbed his eyes and stood as Kazakov stormed down the corridor towards two men.

'Can I help you gentlemen?' Kazakov asked.

Kazakov's build and Ukrainian accent meant that Kuban and his giant associate instantly assumed that he was a security guard working for Irena.

'You can help by getting out of our way,' Kuban said, as his larger companion took a step closer to Kazakov.

'I can't allow that,' Kazakov said, as he cracked his knuckles. 'Let's be sensible, eh?'

Kuban's companion opened up his jacket and pulled out a handgun.

'This sensible enough for you?' he asked.

Kazakov instinctively reached towards his belt as he

took half a step back. But he'd come straight from the airport, and his trusted hunting knife was buried somewhere inside a wheelie bag.

Ryan couldn't actually see the gun as he looked on from the lounge area, but it was unlikely that Kazakov would back off for any other reason. He thought about heading across to defend Kazakov, or maybe finding a weapon and trying to ambush the men as they came past, but their goal was to protect Ethan so he hurried across the hallway and backed into Ethan's room.

Kazakov raised his hands in a surrender gesture, but Kuban and his pal couldn't risk having Kazakov come after them, so as Kuban held a gun right in Kazakov's face the massive dude slid a metal knuckleduster over his hand and delivered a vicious punch to the temple.

'That hurt,' Kuban laughed, as Kazakov crashed down, unconscious.

'He's lucky we didn't have a silencer for the pistol,' the big dude added.

Ryan felt queasy as he studied Ethan's room. The space was dark and Ethan snored gently, with the drip needle in his arm and his bad ankle raised in a sling to reduce the swelling. The en-suite bathroom had a broad sliding door designed for wheelchair access and Ryan nudged it open with his foot as he walked around the bed.

Ethan woke with a start as Ryan grabbed him under the armpits and started dragging him off the bed, then howled in pain as the drip needle got ripped out of his arm.

'Shut up,' Ryan said firmly.

Ryan's bruised ribs were agony as he dragged Ethan off the bed towards the bathroom.

'Ryan?' Ethan said, almost off his head because of the sedative. 'How did you get here?'

'Long story,' Ryan replied. 'Have faith. I need you to work with me.'

As Ryan dragged Ethan into the bathroom and slid the door shut, Kuban burst into the room, followed by the big guy who was dragging the unconscious Kazakov by his ankles.

'Where is he?' Kuban asked, before noticing the bathroom.

Ryan flipped the lock across the bathroom door. He dumped an extremely confused Ethan at the back of a walk-in shower and swept the privacy curtain across to hide him.

'They're Leonid's guys,' Ryan whispered. 'Don't make a sound.'

The toilet door had a safety lock which could be turned from the outside with a coin or screwdriver. Kuban hunted for change in his trousers as Ryan flipped the lock and slid the door halfway open.

Ryan spoke in Russian. 'What do you want?'

Ryan was the same age as Ethan but he didn't much look like him and he was dressed in jeans and T-shirt, rather than nightwear. What happened next depended on how well Kuban and his accomplice knew Ethan, and Kuban's expression was confused at best.

'Why are you here?' Ryan said firmly. 'Do you know who I am?'

This bolshiness made Kuban's mind up and he snarled, 'I know who *you* are. And I wouldn't want to stand in your shoes when Uncle Leonid catches up with you.'

The big dude didn't seem so certain. 'Is that him?' he asked.

'Room six one nine,' Kuban said, pointing at the number on the door as he gave Ryan sight of his gun. 'Your bodyguard's out for the count and you're coming with us.'

*

Ning had seen Kazakov knocked down and got a more distant view of Ryan crossing into Ethan's room. She tried thinking of some action she could take herself, or of running to hospital security, but she couldn't decide and ended up calling Amy.

'If they've got guns you stay back,' Amy said. 'Try and get some information on their vehicle.'

'Right,' Ning said.

As Ning spun around she was shocked to see Ryan being frogmarched between Kuban and the big dude. She was impressed by Ryan's identity-switching feat, but he'd exposed himself to a huge amount of danger.

The goons led Ryan through a set of swinging doors marked *staff only*. After giving them a few seconds to get clear, Ning jogged across the hallway and poked her head between the doors. She could hear footsteps clanking down metal stairs, but she was distracted by a shout from behind. It made Leonid's men stop and look up, but they didn't see Ning because she'd backed into the corridor.

'Hello?' Ethan shouted.

Ning looked behind and saw Ethan crawling out into the hallway, almost fifty metres away.

'Nurse?' Ethan shouted.

Ning wanted to go back to Ethan and Kazakov, but Ryan was in the most immediate danger, so she ventured back on to the staircase. As she crept back on to the landing a door slammed at ground level two flights below.

Kuban must have had a getaway driver because Ning heard a vehicle shoot off seconds later. By the time she'd crossed a bay filled with bales of dirty linen and stuck her head out into the night the number plate was a blur and all she could see were rapidly receding tail-lights.

Ning called Amy again as she raced back up the stairs. 'Dark-coloured people carrier,' she said. 'That's all I've got.'

'I'll try getting someone out there,' Amy said.

'This is a big mess,' Ning said. 'Ryan's kidnapped, Kazakov's spark out. I'm all on my own.'

'Stay calm while we think this through,' Amy said, not sounding terrifically calm herself. 'There should be an intelligence liaison at the British or American embassies who can send some people to help you out.'

When Ning got back into the hospital corridor she saw nurses disappearing into Ethan's room. She walked briskly, but didn't run because she didn't want to make it obvious that she'd been involved with what had happened.

Ning stopped when she reached the nook with the sofas, which was still piled up with the luggage they'd dragged out of the limo. The knuckleduster-enhanced punch that had knocked Kazakov out had broken his skin and there were dots of blood along the corridor and a sinister trickle running through the door of Ethan's room.

A second nurse was bolting down the corridor, wheeling a trolley to take Kazakov for emergency treatment.

'Possible fractured skull,' a nurse explained. 'He's a big bugger, ready?'

The nurses put the trolley to its lowest setting, then dragged Kazakov out into the corridor before rolling him on to it. A couple of other patients had heard the commotion and stood in their doorways watching.

'We've got to deal with this man,' the nurse said, as she leaned into Ethan's room. 'Stay right there. Someone will be here to clean you up and reconnect your drip.'

As the nurses wheeled Kazakov down the long corridor, Ning approached Ethan's room. She found him lying sideways on the bed, hunting for something.

'Hey,' Ning said. 'Are you OK?'

'Pretty freaked out,' Ethan said, sounding stoned. 'I think I just had a religious experience. I need to call my grandma. Can you help me find my mobile phone?'

'Religious experience?' Ning asked.

'There's this guy,' Ethan said. 'He's like my guardian

angel. He saved my life twice when I lived in California. My uncle sent some guys to kidnap me and this dude just came out of nowhere and saved me again.'

Ning half smiled. 'Ryan's *certainly* not an angel,' she said.

Now Ethan looked really confused. 'You know Ryan?'

'Yeah,' Ning said, as she looked around the room and spotted a wheelchair. 'I can't go into details, but there's a chance those guys will work out that Ryan isn't you and come back here for another look.'

'Who are you?' Ethan asked. 'This feels like some weird shitty dream that I can't wake up from.'

'I know that feeling,' Ning said, as she kicked the brake off the wheelchair. 'You're just in for observation, aren't you? You won't go dying on me if I get you out of here?'

'Out of here where?'

'Good question,' Ning said, as she rolled the wheelchair up to the bed. 'But it's definitely best if you're not lying here when Kuban comes back for you.'

'And you just popped out of nowhere,' Ethan said, as Ning slid him across the bed and lowered him into the wheelchair. 'Are you an angel too?'

36. WAREHOUSE

Ryan had made the decision to impersonate Ethan in an instant. Part of it was bravery, but there was also guilt in the mix, because he felt terrible about all the stuff Ethan had been put through.

The people carrier drove through deserted 3 a.m. streets and they wound up somewhere near Sharjah Airport. It was a run-down building full of office suites. Ryan tried to hide his fear as Kuban, the big dude and the driver marched him up two floors, then down a long corridor, passing doors with company names on them.

The plaque on suite 2019 said *China Pacific Holdings*. Ryan guessed that it was one of the dozens of small companies that the Aramov Clan used to disguise their illegal operations. Kuban tapped a code into a blipping burglar alarm and set strip lights ablaze by flicking a bank of switches.

The carpet tiles were peeling and there wasn't much furniture. Six identical desks with tatty drawer units underneath them, a kitchenette and an area full of industrial racking stacked with file boxes. Five desks were empty; the one closest to the window had an elderly Mac Pro computer, plus a telephone and a fax machine.

'I can make this as hard or as easy as you like,' Kuban said, as he leaned forward to switch the computer on. 'You stole your uncle's passwords and took his money. Now you must get them back.'

When you're being interrogated, the first rule is to try and dictate the pace, so Ryan kept quiet. He considered telling Kuban that he wasn't really Ethan, but while Kuban could probably make some calls and establish the truth, chances were that a heavy villain like him would kill Ryan sooner than leave a potential witness alive.

'Are you deaf?' Kuban asked, as the driver shoved Ryan towards an office chair and wheeled him in front of the Mac. 'Answer when I speak.'

The Apple logo was on the screen and Ryan rocked the chair from left to right as the computer booted up.

'You've gotta be brave to mess with Leonid Aramov,' Kuban said. 'I'll give you credit for that.'

Ryan kept silent until the Mac desktop came up. Kuban nudged the mouse across the desk towards him.

'If I don't see some action in three seconds this will get nasty,' Kuban said. Then he slammed his palm against the desktop for dramatic effect.

Ryan grabbed the mouse and opened up Safari web browser.

'What do you want me to do?'

'You know what I want you to do,' Kuban shouted. 'The bulk of the money was in Industrial Trust. So start with that one.'

Ryan took his time Googling Industrial Trust. Then he clicked on a link to a Bahamian bank with a similar name. He hoped to fiddle around with that site for a few minutes before pretending to realise his mistake, but Kuban instantly sussed the ruse.

'Do I look that stupid?' Kuban asked. 'How about a taste of what happens when people screw with me?'

Kuban pointed to the huge dude. 'Give the brat a wash.'

The giant grabbed Ryan's collar and hoiked him to his feet. He then drove Ryan forward and used his head to bash open a small blue door that led into a washroom. There was a strong stench of piss and the urinal had a bin-liner taped over it and an out-of-order notice.

Ryan found himself being thrust into a toilet cubicle. His legs were swept from beneath him and the huge dude suspended him by the neck of his T-shirt. The garment was ripping around the neck, but before it had a chance Ryan found his head getting thrust into the toilet bowl.

The water was dark yellow where someone had taken a piss and there were cigarette ends bobbing about. Ryan found his face squished against the inside of the bowl, with his hair dangling in the yellow water. His bruised ribs were pressed painfully against the toilet bowl and he moaned with pain as his tormentor hit the flush.

A torrent of disinfectant-blue water engulfed Ryan's face and ran inside his nostrils.

'How's the weather down there?' the big dude said cheerfully, as he closed the toilet lid on Ryan's back and pushed down hard.

Ryan was struggling to breathe. He wanted to cough, but his lungs were under pressure and his taste buds were exploding from a bitter substance designed to stop kids accidentally drinking the toilet cleaner.

As the cistern gurgled, the big dude added to Ryan's torment by adding the weight of his knee.

'MFFFF!' Ryan said.

The big dude pulled up Ryan's head.

'You saying something, kid?' he taunted. 'Because this is *nothing*. It can get a hundred times worse if you mess us about. Understand?'

Ryan was coughing and the disinfectant was making his gums burn, but he eventually managed to splutter, 'I understand.'

The washroom door opened and Kuban leaned in. 'Was there a nice big turd waiting for him?'

'Afraid not,' the big dude said.

'Maybe next time,' Kuban laughed. 'Stick him back in front of the computer.'

Ryan's hair dripped and his nose and mouth were on fire as he got shoved back towards the living-room.

He had an idea as he sat in the chair and put his hand on the mouse.

'I can't remember,' Ryan said, trying his best to look meek and honest. 'Every account has security numbers and passwords and stuff. When I did this at the hangar I had notes and stuff sent through by my grandma.'

'Are the notes back at the hospital?' Kuban asked.

'No,' Ryan said, shivering as a big drip trickled down his back. 'It's all back at the hangar.'

'Ruby's office?'

'Yeah, I think so,' Ryan agreed.

Kuban turned and looked at the driver. 'How far are we from the hangar?'

'Ten minutes at this time of night.'

'Will it be empty?'

'There's always a guard, and mechanics working through the night more often than not. But I have an identity badge, so it shouldn't be a problem.'

'Get over there then,' Kuban said. Then he looked at Ethan. 'Explain what he's looking for and where to find it.'

'Can't we bring the boy with us?' the big dude asked.

Kuban shook his head. 'He has to stay out of sight. There's only three of us and we don't know what forces Irena can muster.' Next he glanced at Ryan. 'Tell them what they're looking for. And it'll be more than a bog washing if you're lying to me.'

Dealing with two of Leonid's goons would be better than three, but dealing with only one would be best of all.

'Ruby locked some paperwork and stuff up,' Ryan said. 'The list of new passwords I wrote out. Plus a bunch of faxes that my grandma sent through.'

'Locked up in what?' Kuban asked. 'A safe?'

Ryan didn't want to say a safe because that might be off-putting. Also the driver sounded like he knew the hangar so he couldn't be too specific.

'I don't think it was a safe,' Ryan said, keeping things as vague as he dared. 'It was a kind of . . . Like a metal cabinet.'

The driver nodded. 'I think I know what he means. Ruby runs Sharjah operations. There's a fireproof cabinet at the rear of her office. It's used to keep aircraft registrations and maintenance logs.'

Kuban nodded. 'Can you get inside it?'

'I'd have to get hold of a crowbar or something,' the driver said. 'I've got tools at my apartment.'

'Where's that?'

'Two minutes' drive.'

Kuban thought for a second. 'Both of you go,' he said, to Ryan's delight. 'I can look after the kid and you might need some muscle to force the cabinet. If that doesn't work, we'll need to find where Ruby lives and grab her.'

'She probably left her contact details with the hospital,' the driver pointed out. 'They might have already told her that Ethan's disappeared. If they have, she'll be on red alert.'

Kuban rubbed his forehead, looking stressed. 'You'll have to be careful, but Irena can't have many people she trusts around here. The guard we took out at the hospital didn't even have a gun.'

'True,' the driver said.

'You're both big boys, use common sense,' Kuban

said. 'And keep me in the loop in case Leonid calls.'

The big dude nodded as the driver pulled his car keys out.

'Be less than an hour with any luck, boss,' the driver said.

Ryan checked the room out as the pair left. The only obvious weapon was a big red fire extinguisher, but it was on the opposite side of the room near the exit.

'They'd better find something,' Kuban told Ryan. 'Leonid's a mental case, so don't think being an Aramov will save your arse.'

'Can I take a piss?' Ryan asked.

Kuban couldn't resist making a joke. 'But you just came out of the toilet.'

As Kuban smirked, Ryan stood up and walked towards the toilet.

'Hey,' Kuban shouted. 'Did I say yes?'

Ryan stopped walking. 'You want me to piss my pants?' he asked.

Kuban shook his head and made a *get on with it* sweep with his hand.

Ryan hoped that Kuban would let him go alone, but Kuban kept a foot in the blue door. Ryan glimpsed himself in the mirror and was alarmed by the redness of his stinging eyes. The cubicle floor was puddled after his dunking and he looked for a weapon as he started to pee.

The only things in sight were a spare toilet roll on the ledge of a frosted-glass window and a wooden-handled plunger. Although Kuban looked tough, Ryan had two advantages. First, Kuban had no idea that Ryan was a CHERUB agent who'd done advanced combat training. Second, Kuban couldn't use his gun because he wanted the passwords.

Ryan flushed, then as he zipped his jeans he spun around and bolted the door.

'Open it, dick head,' Kuban shouted.

As Kuban shoulder-charged the door, Ryan grabbed the plunger and pushed the wooden end through the window. He had no sleeve to pull down and protect his hand, so he ripped his T-shirt over his head and wound it around his hand. He grabbed a long glass shard as Kuban's third charge snapped the bolt off the door and sent him crashing sideways into the cubicle.

Ryan swung with the shard, making a long slash across Kuban's cheek and slitting his right nostril. As Kuban instinctively raised his hands to cover his face, Ryan dropped the glass, braced one hand against either side of the cubicle and launched a two-footed kick.

Kuban slammed against the back of the cubicle as Ryan took a step forward and threw a nose-crunching punch. Three fast punches finished Kuban off and Ryan straddled his unconscious frame to exit the cubicle.

He unzipped Kuban's jacket and ripped out a bulging wallet before spotting a gun holstered inside his jacket. Ryan pushed it down his jeans and looked conspicuous as he exited the office with a bulging gun, stinging red eyes and blood-spattered hands.

He moved into the corridor and jogged to the nearest set of stairs before pulling out his wrecked BlackBerry.

He called Ning, but all he got was an engaged tone.

When Ryan got down to ground level, he exited through a revolving door into a parking lot. It was the middle of the night. There were less than five cars spread over two hundred spaces and none of them was the people carrier he'd arrived in.

Ryan was half sure he'd seen a car key bulging out of Kuban's wallet. After confirming and pulling it out, he noticed a Volkswagen logo on the fob and pressed the door opener as he walked towards a silver Passat with a hire company logo inside the windscreen.

There was a satisfying bleep and a flash of indicator lights. CHERUB had taught Ryan basic driving skills, but he'd yet to do the week-long advanced driving course and he didn't feel entirely comfortable as he settled into the driver's seat of the big car. He spent a couple of minutes adjusting the mirrors and familiarising himself with the main controls.

Ryan thought he'd done something wrong, because there was a weird chirping sound when he pushed the *engine start* button. It took him a couple of seconds to realise that it was his wrecked phone playing a garbled version of his usual ringtone.

Ning's voice was on the other end of the line when he'd dug it out of his jeans and answered.

'You're OK?' Ning asked.

'I've had better nights, but I feel better for battering Kuban,' Ryan said. 'Where are you? Where's Ethan?'

'I've got Ethan in a wheelchair,' Ning said. 'I didn't want to leave him in the hospital in case those thugs worked out you were faking and came straight back. I ran about half a kilometre from the hospital and now I'm in a parking lot around the back of some place that sells air conditioning. I was just on the phone to Amy. She said it's too risky getting a taxi, so she's trying to get someone from the British embassy to pick me up.'

'I've got wheels,' Ryan said, as he peered at the car's centre console. 'There's no sat-nav in here, but there's a map book under the seat. I'm gonna drive for a few kilometres just to get out of here. Text me your location and I'll work out how to get to you.'

37. CANCER

Ryan managed to negotiate Dubai's near-empty streets and picked up Ning and Ethan.

'Two angels!' Ethan said, as they helped him into the back of the car. But he was losing his battle with the sedatives and he was spark out before Ryan had even driven out of the parking lot.

It was ten the next morning when Ethan woke up. It felt like a hotel room, but was actually part of a villa. He was still dressed in hospital-issue pyjama bottoms. He had a bandage around his upper arm where his drip had been ripped out.

He peed in an en-suite bathroom before finding his way out into a large double-height living area. Ning sat in a black leather lounger, catching up with some homework on her laptop.

'Your ankle's gone down,' Ning said, before turning

back to shout. 'Ryan!'

'Hey, mate!' Ryan said, as he jogged in. He was barefoot and wore damp swimming shorts and a T-shirt. 'You want some breakfast?'

'I want to know what's going on,' Ethan said. 'If you're *not* my guardian angel then I don't know what the hell you are.'

Ryan wasn't going to tell the whole truth and admit to the existence of CHERUB, but he'd been briefed on what he should say when Ethan woke up. The idea was to tell the truth about tracking Ethan after his mother died, but to continue hiding the fact that Ryan, Amy and Ted had all originally been sent to California to make friends with Ethan and learn about the Aramov Clan.

'Do you ever get an itch at the base of your right buttock?' Ryan asked.

Ethan looked confused as he reached around and pointed at his bum. 'Right here. How did you know that?'

'When your mother died, the CIA worked out that she was really Galenka Aramov. They planted a tracking device in your buttock. About eighty-five per cent of people who end up with one report some mild irritation.'

'Mild,' Ethan blurted. 'I've spent *hours* scratching down there.'

'It's about the size of an aspirin, and you can't really feel it because the outer layer has a similar texture to body fat,' Ryan explained. 'The idea was to track you back to Kyrgyzstan and then start investigating the people your grandmother used to smuggle you out of the USA.

'Trouble was, the tracker device failed. So my dad got a call and I was asked to help keep track of you through Facebook and e-mail. They sorted you out with secret phones when you were in hospitals getting your arm fixed.'

Ethan was brainy and understood how he'd been manipulated while living at the Kremlin. 'So the spyware wasn't your idea at all? The CIA wanted you to plant it so that they could find out what was on my uncle's computer.'

'Yeah,' Ryan admitted.

Ethan crashed back into an armchair and sounded upset. 'I thought you were my friend,' he said angrily.

'They put a lot of pressure on me,' Ryan said. 'You *are* my friend, Ethan, but when the CIA come knocking on your door they can be very persuasive.'

'Like how?' Ethan asked.

Ryan shrugged, before spinning a carefully planned lie. 'When the CIA wants you to jump, you jump or else. I didn't want to get involved, but they threatened my dad's businesses with a big tax investigation. They even threatened to fit me up on some robbery charge and have me shipped off to juvenile offenders.'

'So when I was into Leonid's bank accounts yesterday, it wasn't his people in the system locking me out of the other accounts, it was the CIA?' Ethan asked.

'Yeah,' Ryan admitted. 'You never should have got any money at all. But we – I mean the CIA – had a server crash that delayed everything by a few hours.'

'I still got most of the money,' Ethan said proudly.

Ryan shook his head. 'You left a draft message in your Hotmail with all the passwords. The CIA have transferred all the Industrial Trust money to their own accounts now and locked you out of the others.'

'Shit,' Ethan said.

'I thought you hated your family in Kyrgyzstan,' Ryan said.

'I guess I've made a couple of friends there,' Ethan said. 'And without any money . . .'

'That's kind of what we want to talk about.'

Ethan didn't really take this in because he'd thought of something else. 'But why were *you* here last night, at the hospital?'

'They flew me in from California because they thought you'd have an easier time believing the truth if you heard it from me personally,' Ryan said. 'I was waiting for you to wake up when your uncle's guys tried to kidnap you, but they knocked out the dude who was supposed to be guarding you.'

Ethan sounded anxious as his brain suddenly filled with images from a dozen prison movies. 'Am I in trouble with the CIA? All my hacking into accounts and stuff must have been illegal.'

'They told me they'll look after you provided you cooperate,' Ryan said.

'Cooperate how?'

As Ryan said this, a petite American lady dressed in a tartan cape and thigh-high boots stepped into the room. It was obvious that she'd been listening from the adjoining dining-room.

'Dr Denise Huggan,' the woman said, as she reached out towards Ethan. 'But you've gotta call me Dr D. I'm the head of the CIA's Transnational Facilitator Unit.'

'Trans-what?' Ethan asked, as he shook hands warily.

'Trans means across,' Ryan explained. 'National means nations. To facilitate is to help. So TFU targets criminal organisations that help move illegal shit between countries.'

Ethan snorted. 'Why not just call it the Anti-Smuggling Unit?'

Ryan laughed and pointed at Dr D. 'Ask her!'

Dr D explained. 'Most intelligence organisations have slightly cryptic names. It throws people off the scent if there's ever a security breach.'

This had never occurred to Ryan before, but now he knew why he worked for CHERUB, rather than the Kid Spy Agency.

'Without cash flow, your grandmother's organisation will disintegrate quickly,' Dr D explained. 'Now you're awake I'd like you to call her and explain what has happened.'

Ethan buried his head in his hands. 'She'll gut me like a fish,' he blurted. 'Yesterday I was a hero, today it turns out I've allowed the CIA to rip off every penny my family has.'

'You'll be looked after,' Ryan said soothingly.

Ethan shot forward in his chair. 'What, like when they shoved a tracking device up my arse and let my grandma's people abduct me?'

'It didn't go *up* your arse,' Ryan pointed out. 'It's embedded in the fatty part of your buttock.'

'And what bloody difference does that make?' Ethan shouted. 'You were my only friend in the world, Ryan. I thought you really cared about me.'

'I do care,' Ryan said, as Ethan started to sob. 'I didn't have a choice.'

'My whole life . . .' Ethan sobbed. 'Why did my mom have to die? I just want to be a normal kid, with a normal shitty life.'

'If you don't want to stay with your relatives when this is all over, we'll find you a family to live with in the United States,' Dr D said. 'Your identity will be changed, and you inherited a significant amount of money when your mother died, so you'll be wealthy too.'

Ethan found the thought of a new life in some anonymous California suburb soothing, but he still resented being manipulated and the fact that he'd almost died in Botswana as a result.

'All I'm asking is for you to call the Kremlin and introduce me to your grandmother,' Dr D said. 'It'll take ten minutes.'

'I wouldn't piss on *you* if you were on fire,' Ethan shouted, as he grabbed a cushion off the chair and clutched it to his chest.

Dr D's tone firmed up. 'Ethan, I will help you if you cooperate, but you *must* have seen what the Aramov Clan does while you were at the Kremlin. Did you ever stop and think about those poor Chinese girls, shipped off, drugged up and forced to have sex with strange men?

Or the heroin they take out of Afghanistan? Or the weapons dropped into war zones?'

Ethan clutched his cushion tighter. He opened his mouth, but nothing came out.

'I'm in the intelligence game,' Dr D said. 'Sometimes we can only beat the bad guys by stooping to their level. Ethan, I didn't want to hurt you, but I did it because taking down the Aramov Clan might save thousands of lives in the longer term.'

Tears streaked down Ethan's face as he stared silently into his lap.

'I've offered the carrot,' Dr D said, as she moved closer to Ethan. 'But there's a stick as well. If you don't cooperate, I'll have you flown back to the USA and placed in a federal young offenders' institution, awaiting trial for laundering millions of dollars of drug money. I doubt we'll have enough evidence to prosecute you, but it'll take two or three years to bring your case to trial.'

Dr D pointed at Ning. 'Go get the telephone.'

Ryan had always felt shitty about what had happened to Ethan and it was worse than ever as Ning rested the telephone on the arm of Ethan's chair.

'You'll be OK,' Ryan said, as he pulled a couple of tissues out of a box and threw them in Ethan's lap.

'Stop crying,' Dr D ordered.

Ryan spoke softly, playing Mr Nice to Dr D's Miss Nasty. 'Come on, Ethan, mate. Call your grandma. Then you can get on with your life.'

Ethan looked up thoughtfully. 'Are you still living in the beach house with Ted and Amy?'

'Of course,' Ryan lied, as Ethan rubbed his eyes. 'They've finished the repair work after the explosions. We moved back in a couple of months ago.'

'Do you think I could live with you?'

'I'd have to ask my dad,' Ryan said. 'He always liked you.'

'My mom wouldn't be there, but I could go to my old school. And I'd be living in the same place.'

Ryan ached with guilt as he elaborated on his lie. 'Amy and my dad were both really fond of you. Pick up the phone.'

'OK,' Ethan said, taking a deep breath and dabbing his eyes with a tissue before picking up the receiver.

It took a while to dial the Kremlin number and type in his grandmother's extension.

'It's ringing,' Ethan said.

Dr D took the phone after Ethan had nervously told Irena where he was and what had happened with the money.

'Irena Aramov,' Dr D said. 'Nice to talk to you again.'

'Do we know each other?' Irena asked.

Considering what her grandson had just told her, Dr D thought Irena sounded remarkably calm.

'We met sixteen years ago in Moscow,' Dr D explained. 'You tried to smuggle a batch of stolen nuclear triggers from Israel to North Korea. I negotiated a price with you. The triggers were fake, of course. You lost three aircraft and nine of your flight crew got long prison sentences.'

Irena sounded irritated. 'Then you're a clever girl, Dr

D. I'm sure you're very proud of yourself.'

'We've got your money,' Dr D said. 'The collapse of the clan is inevitable. It's a question of whether it's a delicate wind-down, or a destructive orgy.'

'I'm not a fool,' Irena snapped. 'I'm old and sick, but I don't need you to join up dots for me.'

'Your family can be protected,' Dr D said. 'Any members of your immediate family who fully cooperate while the Aramov Clan is dismantled will be given safe passage to the United States and immunity from criminal prosecution.'

Dr D heard two laboured breaths before Irena responded.

'There's an oncologist in Philadelphia,' Irena said. 'Someone showed me a magazine article that said she's getting excellent recovery rates for my type of lung cancer using an experimental drug therapy.'

'You're not in a strong negotiating position,' Dr D pointed out. 'Chaos within the clan will begin as soon as bills stop getting paid.'

Irena laughed. 'You don't want chaos any more than I do.'

'True enough,' Dr D said. 'I'm prepared to make that concession. TFU gets to run the Aramov Clan while it winds down. If you're medically suitable you'll get your drug treatment and immunity for all family members who cooperate with us. If we have a deal, I need your answer right now.'

There was another long pause before Irena spoke. 'I suppose we have a deal,' she said sadly.

38. CHOCOLATES

It was 2 p.m. on Friday when Ryan, Ning and a bruised-and-stitched Kazakov arrived back on campus. Kazakov said goodbye as he stepped out of the lift at the second-floor staff quarters, while Ryan and Ning rode on up to their rooms on seven.

There was nobody around because it was the middle of afternoon lessons. Ning was at her door as she got a text message.

'Mission debriefing in Zara's office at five,' she told Ryan. 'Mystic Ning the Fortune Teller sees a navy T-shirt in your very near future.'

Ryan tried to act modest, but couldn't completely hide a smile at the thought of getting promoted. 'I'd swap a navy shirt for not having messed Ethan's life up.'

'He'll be OK,' Ning said. 'Ethan's got a few days to decide what he wants to do with himself.'

'He hardly spoke to me after I said he couldn't come and live with us,' Ryan said. 'He's got no other mates, so I'm gonna try and keep in touch.'

'They won't let you,' Ning pointed out. 'In training they told us about this girl Bethany. She got kicked out of CHERUB for keeping in touch with a boy she'd met on a mission.'

By this time Ning had her door open and she was erupting into a yawn. 'Hot shower, big bag of Munchies, then a quick power nap,' she announced. 'See you down at the debriefing.'

Ryan unlocked his room a few doors along the hallway. He ditched his bags and crashed on his bed. He'd slept for most of the flight and wasn't tired, so he grabbed his phone to push it into a speaker dock and play some tunes, but the connectors on the bottom were all mangled and it wouldn't plug in.

Ryan smiled at the thought of getting a new phone. He'd had the BlackBerry since he'd first joined CHERUB and he hoped his upgrade would be one of the latest Android phones, or an iPhone like Ning's. He kicked off his trainers and stared at the ceiling, but his ribs were aching so he decided to chill in the bath instead.

He stayed in long enough to get wrinkly and by the time Ryan had towelled off, kids were finishing lessons and there was loads of noise out in the hallway. He put on some running shorts and wondered if this would be the last time he ever had to pull a grey CHERUB T-shirt over his head.

There was a box of fancy Swiss chocolates poking out

of Ryan's flight bag and he slid them out before walking to Grace's room and knocking on the door.

'Come in,' she said.

Ryan was nervous. Even after tangling with Boris Aramov, getting bog washed by a giant and slugging it out with Kuban, Grace remained a scary proposition.

'Well look what the cat dragged in,' Grace said sourly, as she sat on her bed pulling a shin pad over her foot.

'I got you these,' Ryan said, as he reached out with the chocolates. 'Breaking up with you by text message was mean. I should have manned up and done it to your face.'

Ryan placed the chocolates on the end of Grace's bed as she dug striped hockey socks out of a kit bag.

'So are we OK or what?' Ryan asked. 'I'm not asking you to forgive me. I just want you to be OK.'

Silence hung in the air and Grace made no eye contact as she crossed the room to grab hockey boots from her wardrobe.

'I'm around if you want to talk,' Ryan said, as he backed up to the door. 'I hope we can still be friends.'

Ryan wished Grace had been more communicative, but at least she hadn't gone mental like the first time he'd broken up with her. He quickly forgot about the whole thing because his littlest brother was in his room when he got back.

'Hey, Theo!' Ryan said cheerfully. 'How'd you find out I was back?'

'I could smell your stink,' Theo said, grinning mischievously. 'I made you this.'

Theo held out a bunch of bog roll holders, stuck together with PVA glue and sploshed with orange and black paint.

'It was a machine gun, but the shooting bit broke off,' Theo explained.

'I'll put it on my shelf,' Ryan said, as he admired the model.

'I showed it to Daniel and Leon last night. They said it was pants.'

Ryan hid a smirk as he placed the junk model on his bedside shelf, in between framed photos of their dead mum and dad.

'The twins are trying to wind you up,' Ryan said. 'How many times have I told you to ignore them?'

'How was your mission?' Theo asked.

'Yeah, good,' Ryan said.

'I didn't lock the hamster cage and they all got out,' Theo said. 'I got two punishment laps. My first *ever*.'

Theo sounded quite proud of his punishment laps, but before Ryan could answer his door burst open.

'Here's what I think of your bloody chocolates,' Grace shouted.

She'd taken the cellophane off and the box turned into a chocolate cluster bomb as it spiralled across Ryan's room sending brown balls in all directions.

'Possessive,' Grace screamed, as she whacked the back of Ryan's legs with her hockey stick.

'Oww!' Ryan yelled. 'I didn't say you were possessive.'

'I overheard Max and Aaron,' Grace said. 'So don't lie to me, dirt bag!'

Theo looked startled, but recovered quickly enough to scoop two rolling chocolates off Ryan's bed and cram them into his mouth.

Ryan jumped out of the way as Grace swung the hockey stick again, but the return swing painfully cracked his kneecap.

'Put that down,' Ryan shouted. 'Are you a mental case, or what?'

'You're a piece of shit.'

'It didn't work out so I broke up with you,' Ryan said. 'It happens all the time. I apologised for the way I did it, now get the hell over it.'

'I hate you,' Grace shouted.

She swung the hockey stick again, but this time Ryan grabbed hold and ripped it out of Grace's hands. Ryan shoved her back against the wall and pinned her chest behind the stick.

'You've whacked me twice now. Next time I'm not holding off.'

Ryan let the hockey stick drop and backed away from Grace.

'I'm not scared of you,' Grace spat. 'Try hitting me. See what you get.'

'I'm taller and stronger, just cut it out,' Ryan said, then he caught sight of Theo cramming more chocolates into his mouth. 'Theo, stop that! They've been all over my floor and let's face it, I'm not big on vacuuming.'

'Pig,' Grace shouted, as she whacked Ryan with the hockey stick again.

This time Ryan lost it and slapped Grace's face.

'Go play your stupid hockey match,' Ryan shouted, as he bundled her towards his door.

Grace looked shocked and Ryan felt bad for hitting her. Everyone would slag him off for slapping a girl if news got around campus. And news about stuff like that *always* got around campus.

'Right,' Grace roared.

Ryan thought she was going to charge him, but instead Grace snatched a handful of Ryan's school exercise books from a pile near the door and made a run for it.

Ryan shouted after Grace as her hockey boots clattered down the corridor. 'Give 'em back, you stupid cow.'

Grace lobbed her hockey stick on her bed, then rushed into her bathroom and bolted the door.

'You psycho,' Ryan shouted, banging on the door as she turned on her shower. 'What are you doing?'

'I'm giving your books a little wash,' Grace shouted. 'Humanities is starting to look soggy. Maths is getting wet and your French vocabulary book is floating across my bathtub.'

'Open that door,' Ryan roared, as he shoulder-charged.

But the door didn't budge.

'Right,' Ryan shouted, as he grabbed a whole bunch of stuff off Grace's desk. 'You're not the only one who can trash stuff.'

He opened Grace's window and lobbed the whole lot over her balcony.

'What was that?' Grace shouted.

'That was books,' Ryan yelled. 'And this lot's clothes and shoes.'

The bathroom door shot open as Ryan dumped an armful of clothes out the window. The books had plummeted into bushes seven floors below, but wind caught some of the lighter clothes and sent them billowing towards distant treetops.

'AAARGH!' Grace screamed, as she reached for the hockey stick.

But Ryan shoved his hand in her face and grabbed it himself. Grace landed on her bum but before Ryan could move any further she locked her legs around the back of his knees and jerked forward, pulling him down on top of her.

A wave of pain shot up from Ryan's bruised ribs as he found himself lying across Grace.

'Now you've got me,' Grace said, letting her body relax.

Ryan looked into her eyes. Grace either wanted to kiss, or she was making it look like she wanted to kiss as part of some evil plan to knee him in the balls or gouge out an eyeball. But although Ryan was angry, Grace had the cutest expression and her body looked really fit.

Theo stood in the open doorway watching the action and covered his eyes as Ryan kissed Grace on the lips.

'Sicko,' he yelled.

Ryan felt like he'd been lured into a trap and as Grace's hand grabbed his bum, he sprang up like he'd been zapped with ten thousand volts.

'You're cute, but you're insane,' Ryan said, as he

stumbled back towards the door. 'I don't want *anything* to do with you.'

Grace's eyes narrowed and it looked like she was going to go for the hockey stick again, but the carer Beatha was storming down the hallway.

'What idiot threw stuff out of the window?' Beatha shouted, knocking Ryan into the wall as she stormed Grace's room. 'Someone could have been hurt down there.'

Neither Ryan nor Grace answered, so Beatha pointed at the floor.

'OK then,' she said. 'If I'm getting the silent treatment, you two can go down to the Chairwoman's office and discuss it with her.'

'It was only a few clothes,' Ryan said defensively. 'It's not like anyone's gonna get knocked out by a flying bra, is it?'

Beatha inhaled deeply. 'Both of you go down and pick it *all* up. If one of the senior staff sees that lot you'll be in *serious* trouble.'

Grace pointed at Ryan. 'He threw it out, *he* should pick it up.'

'Grace, we've discussed your anger issues and you are on thin ice already. Now if I hear *one* more word it'll be fifty punishment laps each.'

Ryan looked pissed off as he headed out of Grace's room, staring at the hallway floor, with Grace a couple of steps behind.

'Cock,' Grace whispered, as they waited for the lift.

'Loony,' Ryan replied.

'This isn't over.'

Ryan looked at the numbers over the lift doors and saw that the right-hand car was heading their way.

'You come near me with your hockey stick again and I'll break it over your head,' he said.

Grace snorted. 'You'll have a hard time breaking it over *my* head when I've already rammed it up *your* big fat arse.'

'You're so immature.'

'You're the immature one,' Grace replied.

'I bloody hate you,' Ryan said as the lift doors came open.

'And I hope *you* drop dead,' Grace snapped back, as she followed him in. 'I'm gonna miss hockey practice because of you.'

'It's a bloody stupid sport anyway,' Ryan said.

The two thirteen-year-olds glowered at each other as the doors rolled shut, but their expressions had softened by the time a couple of other kids got in on the fifth floor. As Ryan backed up to give the new arrivals space, he couldn't decide whether he wanted to kiss Grace or punch her lights out.

The only thing he knew for sure was that she *completely* did his head in.

The adventure concludes in CHERUB: Black Friday

US Intelligence has taken control of the Aramov Clan, but can they shut down the sprawling criminal network before it splinters into dozens of smaller, more dangerous groups?

Ryan is heading for the USA, trying to stop terrorists who want to blow up malls on the busiest shopping day of the year, while Ning and Ethan must help track down Leonid Aramov – before he can revive the family business . . .

Read on for an exclusive first chapter of
the next CHERUB book, *Black Friday*.

1. THANKSGIVING

November 22nd 2012, Manta, Ecuador
Manta Airport's only terminal felt like its best days were behind it. Built to serve a United States Air Force squadron running anti-drug operations, the Yanks didn't like it when the Ecuadorian government kicked them out and before leaving they'd stripped everything from the main radar in the control tower to the benches at the departure gates.

Fourteen-year-old CHERUB agent Ryan Sharma squatted on a canvas backpack in the airport's sparsely populated passenger lounge, hearing cheesy piped music compete with rain pelting the metal roof.

Ryan had barely slept during a twenty-hour journey from Kyrgyzstan. The long flight had given him a sore throat and bloodshot eyes. A hot shower and soft bed would have been perfection, but it would be a long time before he got near either.

For the past seven months, Ryan had been based at Aramov Clan headquarters in Kyrgyzstan – known as the Kremlin. Ryan's job was to scrape gossip out of the smuggling operation's employees and family members.

The Kremlin didn't offer much in the way of entertainment and the main hangout for teens was an outdoor yard full of weightlifting equipment. Ryan had pumped enough metal to put ten centimetres on his chest. He liked the way he looked with his shirt off now, and so did the girl he'd fallen in love with.

Three aircraft could be seen through plate glass windows across the shabby lounge. It was early morning, but clouds blotted the sun and it felt more like twilight. The smallest plane was a turboprop flown by the Ecuadorian Post Office; next door was a Boeing 737 cargo jet with custard-yellow hull and the logo of *Globespan Delivery*. The company's slogan was painted beneath it: *Anywhere, Anytime, On Time*.

The third much larger aircraft loomed behind these two, standing on eighteen threadbare tyres, with flaking paint and patched-up bullet wounds. It looked badass, like it might roll up to the two smaller planes and make them hand over their lunch money.

It was an Ilyushin-76. The four-engined Uzbek-built freighter had rolled off the production line in 1975 and could swallow a truck through its gaping rear cargo door. This old bird first saw action when the Soviet Union invaded Afghanistan. Records showed the Soviet Air Force selling her for scrap in 1992, but in reality the old freighter had spent twenty years flying the world, carting everything from stolen Mercedes coupés, to Class A drugs.

Anyone could hire her if the money was right, and besides the naughty stuff the Ilyushin had dropped bags of food in earthquake zones, and made deliveries for the US military in Iraq. Over the years, the plane had worn the insignia of twenty different airlines, two national governments and the UN, but anyone smart enough to follow a paper trail of forged maintenance logs and dodgy holding companies would always have found that the real owners were the Aramov Clan.

Ryan had to block out the cheesy airport music as a low voice sounded through the invisible communication unit buried inside his left ear. 'Has she moved?'

The voice belonged to CHERUB instructor Yosyp Kazakov, currently playing the role of Ryan's dad.

Ryan looked up slightly, catching a woman in the corner of his eye. She was touching thirty, sat in a battered armchair, wearing a pilot's uniform. A cap with the *Globespan Delivery* logo on a yellow band rested on the next seat.

'Not yet,' Ryan said, putting a hand across his mouth so that he didn't look like a some loony talking to himself. 'Size of that latte she bought, she's gotta need a piss soon.'

'What's she doing?' Kazakov asked.

The pilot was reading a copy of *USA Today*. She'd made it through the paper itself and now studied a wodge of advertising pull-outs. Home Depot, Wal Mart,

Target, Staples. *Black Friday Special – 40 Inch Sony $399, Two Part Air Con $800, Complete Harry Potter Blu-Ray $29.99.*

'She looks depressed,' Ryan said.

Kazakov snorted with contempt. 'It's Thanksgiving. She wants to be home in Atlanta, watching NFL with hubby and the rug rats.'

Ryan felt a stab of guilt. What he was about to do was hopefully for the greater good. It might save thousands of lives, but this pilot was about to go through the most horrifying experience of hers.

'You really have it in for the Americans,' Ryan noted.

The voice that came back in Ryan's ear was grudging. 'You've got three brothers, Ryan. How would you feel if the Americans had sold a missile to a bunch of terrorists that killed one of them?'

Before Ryan could answer, he saw the pilot fold the crumpled newspaper and post it beneath her seat. As the woman stood, she tucked her cap under her armpit and grabbed the briefcase standing between her legs.

'Showtime,' Ryan mumbled.

He let the woman take a couple of steps before standing up himself. As he swung his pack over one shoulder, Ryan realised the woman was hurrying. Either late for something, or desperate to use the bathroom.

'Shit,' Ryan mumbled, knowing it's much harder to follow someone in a rush.

'Problem?' Kazakov asked.

'I can handle it,' Ryan said quietly, as he tried to catch up without making it too obvious.

'Try getting her in the corridor.'

'I know,' Ryan whispered irritably. 'I can't *think* with you babbling in my earhole.'

Although Manta wouldn't handle a passenger flight for another six hours, there was still a newsagent and café open and a few other people in the lounge. There was a chance the pilot might freak out, so Ryan didn't make his move until she'd walked into a deserted corridor, passed a speak-your-weight machine and was turning into the ladies' toilet.

'Excuse me,' Ryan said loudly.

The pilot assumed Ryan was speaking to someone else, until he repeated the call and tapped the back of her blazer. She looked startled as she turned, then a little irritated.

'Can I help you, son?' she asked, sounding cocky.

'I need you to listen carefully,' Ryan said, keeping his voice flat as he pulled a large touchscreen phone out of his pocket. 'I've got something to show you.'

The woman raised both hands and took a step back. Ryan's olive complexion meant he could just about pass for a local.

'*No* money,' she said frostily as she swiped a finger across her throat. 'It's bad enough kids begging on the street. Clear off before I report you to security.'

Ryan switched on the phone and turned the screen to face the pilot.

'Stay calm, don't make a sound,' Ryan said.

The pilot dropped the cap under her arm as she saw the picture on screen. It was her living room. Her husband knelt in front of the couch, dressed only in pyjama bottoms. A hooded man stood behind, holding a large knife at his throat. On his left stood two small boys, dressed for bed. They looked scared and the older one had wet pyjama legs from pissing himself.

'What is this?' the pilot asked, trembling. 'Is this a joke?'

Ryan kept his voice firm, but felt terrible inside. 'Tracy, you *need* to keep your voice down. You *need* to listen carefully and do everything I tell you to. If you do *exactly* what I say, your husband and sons will be released unharmed.'

The pilot trembled as her eyes fixed on the photograph. 'What do you want?'

'Speak quietly,' Ryan ordered. 'Take deep breaths. Walk with me.'

Ryan pocketed the phone and began a slow walk, leading Tracy back towards the passenger lounge.

'Me and my people came on that big Ilyushin parked out on the tarmac,' Ryan explained. 'But we need a plane with flight clearance to get cargo into the USA.'

'What kind of cargo?' Tracy asked.

Ryan ignored the question. 'We've got friends behind the scenes at this airport. Right now they're loading your 737 with our stuff. You're scheduled to fly to Atlanta in four hours. You're going to take off on schedule, but once you're in US airspace, you'll put out a mayday and do an emergency landing at a small airfield in central Alabama. By the time the authorities realise what's happened, we'll have emptied our cargo and vanished.

You and your family will be released unharmed.'

'I want to talk to my husband,' Tracy said.

'You can want whatever you like, you're getting Jack shit.'

'How do I know that picture isn't Photoshopped?'

Ryan hated what he was doing, but faked a mean smile as he looked back. 'You want your boy Christian to lose a thumb?'

'You're just a kid yourself,' Tracy stuttered, as she touched a wet eye. 'Who are you working for?'

'They like to call themselves the Islamic Department of Justice,' Ryan said. 'But I don't work for them. Me and my dad are just in this for the money.'

CHERUB

THE RECRUIT

Robert Muchamore

A terrorist doesn't let strangers in her flat because they might be undercover police or intelligence agents, but her children bring their mates home and they run all over the place. The terrorist doesn't know that one of these kids has bugged every room in her house, made copies of all her computer files and stolen her address book. The kid works for CHERUB.

CHERUB agents are aged between ten and seventeen. They live in the real world, slipping under adult radar and getting information that sends criminals and terrorists to jail.

CLASS A

Robert Muchamore

Keith Moore is Europe's biggest cocaine dealer.

The police have been trying to get enough evidence to nail him for more than twenty years.

Four CHERUB agents are joining the hunt. Can a group of kids successfully infiltrate Keith Moore's organisation, when dozens of attempts by undercover police officers have failed?

CHERUB

MAXIMUM SECURITY

Robert Muchamore

Under American law, kids convicted of serious crimes can be sentenced as adults. Two hundred and eighty of these child criminals live in the sunbaked desert prison of Arizona Max.

In one of the most daring CHERUB missions ever, James Adams has to go undercover inside Arizona Max and bust out a fellow inmate!

DIVINE MADNESS

Robert Muchamore

When CHERUB uncovers a link between eco-terrorist group Help Earth and a wealthy religious cult known as The Survivors, James Adams is sent to Australia on an infiltration mission.

It's his toughest job so far. The Survivors' outback headquarters are completely isolated and the cult's brainwashing techniques put James under massive pressure to conform.

WWW.CHERUBCAMPUS.COM

Hodder Children's Books

THE RECRUIT
THE GRAPHIC NOVEL
Robert Muchamore

The first ever CHERUB story, now as a graphic novel!
Dark and highly evocative artwork from award-winning illustrator John Aggs

Also available as an ebook

WWW.CHERUBCAMPUS.COM

Hodder
Children's
Books

EAGLE DAY

Robert Muchamore

Charles Henderson is the last British spy left in occupied France in 1940. He and his four young agents are playing a dangerous game: translating for the German high command and sending information back to Britain about Nazi plans to invade England.

Their lives are on the line, but the stakes couldn't possibly be higher.

Book 2 – OUT NOW